THE HERO'S TOMB

www.davidficklingbooks.com

Also by Conrad Mason

Tales of Fayt: Book 1 – The Demon's Watch
Tales of Fayt: Book 2 – The Goblin's Gift
Tales of Fayt: The Mystery of the Crooked Imp
(with David Wyatt)

THE
HERO'S
TOMB

Conrad Mason

David Fickling Books

31 Beaumont Street
Oxford OX1 2NP, UK

The Hero's Tomb
is a
DAVID FICKLING BOOK

First published in Great Britain by
David Fickling Books,
31 Beaumont Street,
Oxford, OX1 2NP

www.davidficklingbooks.com

Hardback edition published 2015
This edition published 2016

978-1-910989-13-5

1 3 5 7 9 10 8 6 4 2

Papers used by David Fickling Books are from well-managed
forests and other responsible sources.

DAVID FICKLING BOOKS Reg. No. 8340307

A CIP catalogue record for this book is available from the British Library.

Printed and bound in Great Britain by Clays Ltd, St Ives plc.

For Katrina, always

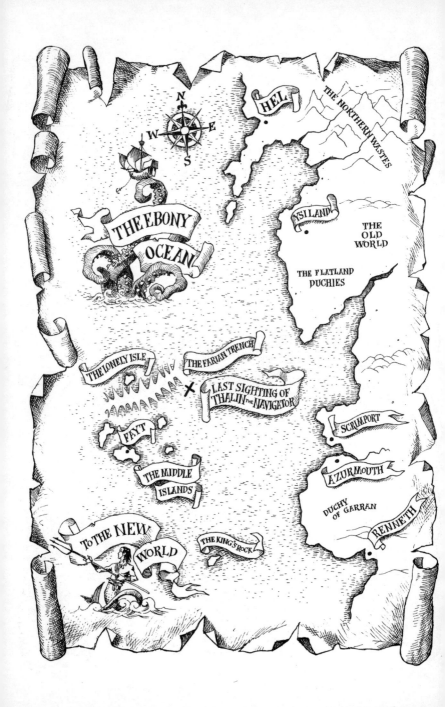

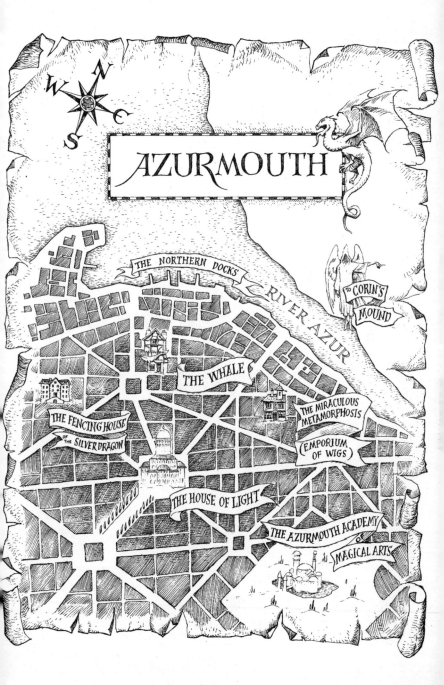

*F*rom the Flatland Duchies, from the Northern Wastes and the Southern Hills, from every corner of the Old World, they have come. They have travelled for weeks, braving bandits, mountain trolls and worse. Now they are here. All of them.

The League of the Light.

The Duke of Garran watches, his fingers resting lightly on the stone balustrade, as the courtyard fills with mounted men dressed in white. Noises float up to his balcony, mingling with the joyful peal of the bells – the jangle of reins, the clopping of hooves and the shouts of greeting.

Some of his guests glance upwards, shielding their

eyes against the late afternoon sun as they admire the façade of the House of Light. There are three hundred windows set into its shining white walls, so that on a bright day it lives up to its name, shimmering with golden radiance.

Let them enjoy it while they can.

The Duke smiles as the lords make their way into the House of Light. He knows what they think of him. He has heard their whispers, cut short as he approaches. They fear him. They are afraid because they do not understand. They do not know what he truly is. They will, soon enough. They will see what he has been planning.

And by then, it will be too late.

His eyes flick to the Golden Sun, the League's banner, flying from the roof of the gatehouse. Fitting – for that is what he shall become. The sun in splendour. The death of darkness. The bringer of the light.

'Your grace.'

Major Turnbull hovers at the balcony doors, her long blonde hair tied back, her uniform dazzling white. In the afternoon sunshine she is even more beautiful than usual. 'They will soon be ready for you.'

He nods.

Their footsteps echo on the marble floor as they pass through mirrored corridors, Major Turnbull keeping pace at the Duke's shoulder.

He has chosen the largest state room in the House of Light to receive his guests. As he enters he enjoys the shifting of position, the widening of eyes. He is dressed in his famous red coat. Dyed with the blood of trolls – that is the rumour, and he has never denied it. After all, it is true.

The Duke surveys his fellow lords, sitting in the comfortable chairs around the fireplace. The men who have held him back for so long. The Marquis of Renneth – a tall, handsome man, his pale blond hair swept back. The masters of the Flatland Duchies – Ysiland, Juddmouth and Henge – tanned and rugged, still wearing their mud-spattered riding boots. Beside them are Storth, Garvill and Tallis – a collection of effete southerners, whose interests extend little beyond fine wines, loose women and fast horses. He can barely keep his lip from curling in disdain.

Last, but not least, the Earl of Brindenheim. A bloated walrus of a man with bristling grey mutton chops, sitting with a soldier's posture in the largest and most comfortable chair of all. Like a king holding court. He has brought his wretched son Leopold with him. The idiot stands at his father's side, a pink, puffy-faced boy with greasy black hair plastered across his forehead. A joke.

The Duke's gaze lingers on the Earl of Brindenheim.

3

The old fool has come dressed in the white coat and breeches of the League's army – the butchers, as their enemies call them. Dressed for battle.

His presence makes things . . . interesting. The earldom is nothing in itself, but Brindenheim is the eldest of the lords, and the most experienced. He commands the respect of every man in the room, and it has made him arrogant. If there is to be trouble, Brindenheim will undoubtedly be at the centre of it.

The Duke would enjoy that.

He clears his throat.

'My lords. Five hundred years ago, a warrior faced down the greatest horde of demonspawn ever to plague the Old World. Trolls, goblins, imps and elves felt the bite of his blade. All in the name of humanity. That warrior's name was Corin the Bold.

'We have all sworn to carry on the work of our great ancestor. To bring a new dawn into every corner of the Old World, stamping out the taint of demon-spawn wherever it is to be found. We are the League of the Light. That is why we gather here each year, in the greatest city in the Old World, to celebrate Corin's Day tomorrow. The date which marks his final victory at the Battle of the Three Forests. To honour his memory. Our first and greatest champion.'

He pauses. The Earl of Brindenheim is watching him

with a peculiar expression. Wary. Like a lone traveller who has sensed a wolf prowling in the bushes. Perhaps even now he can tell that something is afoot.

He is right to be afraid. Nothing can prepare him for what is coming.

Nothing can prepare him for the triumph of the light.

The Duke spreads his arms wide.

'My lords . . . welcome to Azurmouth!'

PART ONE
Azurmouth

Chapter One

'Land ho!'

Joseph jumped up and hurried to the prow. He was supposed to be swabbing the deck, but what did he care? Once he got his feet on dry land, he'd never see the crew of the *Dread Unicorn* ever again.

He strained his eyes, peering across the sparkling water to the horizon. Without a spyglass he could see nothing but the gulls, wheeling and screeching in the blue skies above, as the ship cut through the waves towards the great city of Azurmouth.

Azurmouth. The thought of it gave him a shiver of excitement. *You should be frightened*, he told himself. Every night the crew had delighted in telling him tales of what might happen to a half-goblin boy in Azurmouth. Tales of elves snatched from their beds in the dark of night. Tales of imps dragged from dockside taverns and never seen again. Tales of drunken white-coated butchers who prowled the streets, looking for any excuse to stop you, if you weren't a human . . .

Joseph swallowed hard. Maybe he *was* a little frightened. But it didn't matter. He had crossed the Ebony Ocean for a reason. He had to know the truth. And the truth was here, somewhere in Azurmouth.

There's no turning back now.

The breeze whipped him, and he narrowed his eyes to stop them from streaming. Soon it would all be spread out before him: marble statues and colonnades; wide avenues lined with tall trees, their green-laden branches swaying softly in the breeze; elegant spires that pierced the sky, serene and quiet but for the silver bells that pealed sweet music to mark a wedding, or a triumph, or Corin's Day. *The greatest city ever founded. A beacon of hope for all the people of the Old World.* Or at least, for all the humans of the Old World.

He shivered again.

The sky began to fill up with gulls, and the sea

with ships. First a distant sail, stark against the horizon, then vessels dotting the ocean. There was a red-sailed caravel from the Flatland Duchies. A fat black cog from the north. League galleons, tall and proud, white flags fluttering.

Joseph drank it all in, his fingers drumming on the gunwale with impatience.

At last, the city itself came into view, looming larger as they approached. It took his breath away. A hazy sprawl across the coastline; countless ramshackle buildings, even more motley and crammed in than those of Port Fayt. Thousands of coloured banners flew from the ships in the harbour, and still more from the grubby warehouses that lined the docks.

No trees, after all. No statues. No elegant spires.

Azurmouth.

The last thing to hit him was the smell. A powerful aroma that mingled grog, smoke, sweat and blood – but at the same time was utterly itself, like nothing Joseph had ever smelled before. It smelled of terror. Of desperation. Of hope. He breathed in deep.

The truth, he reminded himself. *I'm going to find out the truth.*

A hand fell on his shoulder, and he looked up to see Captain Phineus Clagg grinning at him with yellowed teeth, his long dirty hair tossed by the breeze and his lazy eye fixed on Joseph, for once. The smuggler's smile said one thing: *I told you so.*

'Azurmouth, eh, matey?' said Clagg. 'I reckon yer goin' to regret this.'

The docks smelled even worse.

Joseph wrinkled his nose, and one of the smugglers, a broad-shouldered dwarf with silver hair in a ponytail, cackled at the sight.

'Get used to it,' he said cheerily. 'And gimme a hand with this barrel. Last one.'

They rolled it down the gangplank whilst Captain Clagg had words with a wiry officer in white – a revenue man, Joseph guessed. Fortunately the hold was empty of contraband for once, and the barrels were filled with nothing more than watered-down grog.

Joseph had thought the docks back in Port Fayt were busy, but he'd never seen anything like this before. Even in the late afternoon sailors and dockhands thronged the cobblestones as far as the eye could see, their chatter assaulting his ears. To his surprise, they weren't all humans: there were a few elves, dwarves, even trolls and the odd ogre too. Most of them looked shifty though, as if they weren't supposed to be here and knew it. The warehouses loomed above, filthy red-brick buildings so big they looked like they'd been built by giants, and threw the whole harbour into shadow.

There was a commotion, sailors scrambling to get out of the way as a column of white-coated soldiers came marching from a side street.

Joseph ducked down into the shadow behind a barrel. *Butchers.* The last time he'd seen men in League uniforms, they'd been spattered with the blood of Fayters. He took a deep breath to calm himself.

Come on, Joseph. It's too late to have second thoughts.

'They've gone now, matey,' said Phineus Clagg, taking Joseph's hand and hauling him to his feet. The smuggler knocked back a swig from a small metal flask of firewater. 'Well, I reckon this is it. Last chance. Yer can come with me, roam the seas and live like a prince of the waves. Or yer can stay here and get yerself killed, most likely. What'll it be?'

'I'm staying here. In Azurmouth.'

Clagg sighed. 'An' here was me thinkin' you were a smart one. This city's crawlin' with butchers, lad. Why in Thalin's name would yer come here?'

It wasn't the first time the smuggler had asked, but the fewer people who knew, the better. Joseph shook his head.

'Well, don't say I didn't warn yer,' said Clagg. 'Just mind yer stay near the docks. The League put up with demonspawn here, see, so's they can trade an' grow rich off the profits. Can't be hurting their customers now, can they? Watch out for the Duke o' Garran's men, though. That cove ain't like the other lords. Reckon he'd stamp out every last trace of demonspawn in the city if he could, traders an' all.'

'Don't worry about me,' Joseph told him.

'Cap'n!' called the silver-haired dwarf. 'Comin' for a grog?'

'Aye, soon enough.'

Clagg knelt. Up close, Joseph noticed that the smuggler smelled even worse than Azurmouth itself. But it was a comforting, familiar smell.

'Here, take this.' He passed Joseph a small leather purse full of coins. 'Ain't much, but it's all the help I can give yer.' He hesitated a moment, then whipped off his coat. 'Come to think of it, best take this too. Turn the collar up. Don't let folk see yer face if yer can help it.'

'Are you sure?'

'Aye, yer'll need it more than me, lad. Trust me.' He helped Joseph into it, the long sleeves engulfing the half-goblin boy's arms, the tails trailing on the cobble-stones. It was heavy and weather-beaten, stained with grog and worse, but with the collar pulled up it hid Joseph's mongrel skin well enough.

As Clagg stood, Joseph thought he saw something in the smuggler's eyes – a glint of moisture. 'Well, this is it. Fair winds and calm seas, eh, lad?'

Joseph shook Clagg's hand, his long grey-pink fingers engulfed in a calloused palm. 'Fair winds and calm seas. And thank you for . . . well, for everything.'

Clagg smiled. 'I'll be thinkin' o' you, matey. Maybe we'll meet again someday. I have to tell yer, though – knowin' Azurmouth, I ain't holdin' out much hope.' He turned and strode away with the dwarf, their boots thudding on the cobblestones.

Joseph watched them disappear into a tavern. Then he set out along the quayside, sticking to the water's edge, with one hand resting on the hilt of his cutlass. His skin tingled with fear, and with excitement. It was time to put his plan into action.

I'm going to find out the truth.

Either that, or he'd die trying.

He pulled Clagg's coat tight around him, keeping his head down and hiding his grey-pink face from any passing whitecoats. The noise of the docks filled his ears: the *thunk* of barrels dumped on cobblestones; the clatter of carriages that moved among the throng; and the coarse insults their drivers hurled at each other.

Street vendors hovered here and there, shouting at the tops of their voices.

'Dragons' teeth! Twelve ducats a molar! Incisors fourteen apiece!'

'Fairy wings! Make a fine pair o' earrings for the missus!'

'Tired o' your hook? See my fine brass hands! You'll look ever so *hand*some and no mistake!'

There was something rotten in the air, and it wasn't just the smell. The people of Azurmouth were louder, busier and angrier than Fayters back home. They seemed tense, like they might snap at any moment.

Joseph reached inside the smuggler's coat and thrust a hand into his own left pocket, his fingers closing tightly round the silver pocket watch that lay inside. It was crudely made and poorly inscribed, and it was the most precious thing he'd ever owned.

His other hand patted his right pocket, checking that the second object he'd brought with him was safe inside. It had stayed there all the time they'd been on the sea – he couldn't afford to take the risk of a smuggler seeing it. Besides, he still hardly dared touch it.

He'd have to soon, though. The plan depended on it.

Joseph strode on, faster now. There were countless

ships bobbing in the harbour, a forest of masts rising high against the darkening sky. But at last he spotted a cluster of hobgoblin vessels in the distance. They were sticking together, as though their captains were nervous of mingling with the human ships that surrounded them.

With any luck it would be there – the ship he had followed here to Azurmouth. A hobgoblin junk, with battered sails and a hull coated in shiny black lacquer. A ship he had sailed on once before.

Finding it was the first part of the plan.

The crowds swelled and Joseph stumbled along, carried by the tide of people on the harbour front. Someone stood on his coat tails. He caught a knee in his ribs, and his foot sank into something soft, wet and smelly. He winced and smeared it off on the cobblestones, trying not to see it as a bad omen. *Marble statues, green trees, silver bells* . . . The stories of Azurmouth had never said anything about horse dung.

A couple of burly humans stopped to stare at him – the funny-looking child in a coat that was far too big for him. Joseph tugged the collar higher to hide his blotchy skin and his pointed ears, and hurried onwards.

Gradually the wavecutters and galleons in the harbour gave way to vessels from further a-seas.

Sampans, barques and, at last, the hobgoblin junks that Joseph had seen from further off.

His fingers found the bulge of the object in his right-hand pocket. He'd never used it before, and the mere thought of doing so gave him a thrill of fear. Hal had told him how to use it, though the magician probably wouldn't have been so obliging if he'd known that Joseph was going to steal it – *no, borrow it* – from under his pillow while he slept, just before running off with Captain Clagg.

By now, the magician must have told the other watchmen what Joseph had done. *The tavern boy's taken it. He's taken the wooden spoon.*

The wooden spoon that was so much more than just a wooden spoon.

What would Captain Newton say when he found out? Joseph didn't like to think.

There! At the end of a jetty a black junk was riding the waves, its sails furled. The lacquered hull had scrapes along its side, the marks of a battle. No doubt about it – this was the ship he was looking for. Two bored-looking sailors sat on the gunwale beside the gangplank, swinging their legs above the water and chewing tobacco. They'd probably been left to guard the vessel while the rest of the crew went ashore.

Joseph hovered, trying to look inconspicuous.

So far so good. But what next? It was all very well finding the ship, but now he had to get on board without being caught.

Before he could figure out how, a terrible sound split the air.

'*Yeeeeeeeeargghhh!*'

Joseph almost jumped out of his skin. The howl seemed to have come from the cabin at the ship's stern. He felt his goblin ears prick up as he heard a calm, murmuring voice follow it, speaking in a reassuring tone.

'I don't give a stuffed lobster!' came the screeched reply. 'You ain't cutting my bleedin' foot off!'

Come on, Joseph. Now or never. He strode forward, stepping onto the gangplank before fear made him question whether it was going to get him killed or not.

'Oi!' said one of the sailors. 'What are you—?'

'Surgeon's boy,' mumbled Joseph. 'Supplies.' He dug in his pocket and brought out the silver pocket watch to show them. It didn't look much like a medical instrument, but then, the sailors didn't look like geniuses either.

'Oh, right,' said the other sailor doubtfully, as Joseph boarded the junk and strode across the deck, coat tails trailing behind him.

The last time he'd been on this ship . . . well, the

memory was a painful one, and he didn't have time to dwell on it. He made for the cabin.

'Wait! You can't go in there without—'

Too late. Joseph hesitated for just a moment.

I'm going to find out the truth.

The truth about my father.

Then he drew his cutlass and barged through the door.

Chapter Two

Tabitha Mandeville already hated Azurmouth, and she hadn't even seen it yet.

She squirmed, trying to get comfortable, but it wasn't easy with her knees squashed up against her chin, sitting inside a barrel with several kilograms of salted herring for company.

The cart rattled over cobblestones, jostling Tabitha and the herring along with it. Surely they should have arrived by now? The sea voyage had been bad enough. She'd spent half of it leaning over the side, emptying her guts into the waves. *Everything will be fine once we're on dry land*, she'd told herself, as the ship had weighed anchor in a hidden cove just west of Azurmouth.

No such luck. If anything, the darkness inside the barrel, combined with the powerful stench of fish and the feel of their slippery, slimy scales against her skin, were making things worse.

Just don't be sick again, she told herself. *Not in here.*

The cart bounced up and down once more, and finally jolted to a halt. Footsteps sounded outside, then *thunks* of metal on wood. Tabitha had a sudden rush of panic. What if they'd been stopped by whitecoats? What if the driver had betrayed them? What if he'd tipped off the butchers that the cart contained more than just salted fish . . . ?

Something hit the top of Tabitha's barrel, and a crescent of dark blue sky appeared as the lid came loose, then was tugged away entirely. She tensed, her hands closing on the hilts of her knives. But the face that appeared above was no human's. It was big, ugly and grinning.

'All right, Tabs?' said Frank. 'You look almost as green as me and Paddy here.'

Paddy's identical face appeared next to Frank's, and the troll twins chuckled.

Tabitha scowled as she rose, sending the herring cascading from her like a waterfall.

They'd stopped in a small cobbled courtyard,

surrounded on all sides by high white walls topped with battlements. Dusk was falling. The driver, a sullen youth with big ears and hair like straw, clambered over the cart with a crowbar, levering open the barrels and freeing the rest of the watchmen.

Tabitha took a big gulp of fresh air. They'd made it. She just hoped their host would be as friendly as Hal had promised.

Captain Newton rose from one of the larger barrels, his blue watchman's coat glistening with fish scales. Tabitha felt instantly calmer at the sight of his shaven head and the shark tattoo on his cheek – the mark of the Demon's Watch. Above, Ty flitted in the darkening sky, giggling at the state of them all. Newton's fairy hadn't needed to hide in a barrel, of course – he'd ridden all the way in the driver's pocket.

'Thank Thalin that's over,' said Frank, brushing herring from his tricorne hat.

Hal emerged from the final barrel, looking even paler than usual as he unwrapped his spectacles from his handkerchief. The magician had been unusually silent ever since they left Illon, as though he were worried about something.

For once Tabitha couldn't blame him. *Thalin knows, we're all worried.*

Someone cleared their throat on the far side of the

courtyard, and Tabitha spun round to see a human, tall, thin and gangly, watching them from the shadow of an archway. A thick black gown hung from his shoulders, and long, lank white hair fell onto it. His chin sprouted a wispy, uneven white beard, and his bulging eyes peered from behind thick eyeglasses. He looked even more anxious than Hal.

Tabitha couldn't blame him either. The two hulking green trolls, the glowing fairy who had settled on Newton's shoulder, the blue shark tattoos they all bore, and most of all the weapons: her knives, the cutlasses dangling from Frank and Paddy's belts and Newton's wooden staff – the Banshee – folded into three sections and poking out of his pocket; none of it looked very reassuring.

'Welcome,' said the man in the gown, 'to the Azurmouth Academy.'

'Master Gurney,' said Hal, stepping down from the cart.

'Ah, Hal! Splendid to see you again. One of my brighter students, yes.'

Hal blushed. 'Well, I don't know about—'

'Now,' said Master Gurney, already turning away. 'If you'd all be so good as to follow me . . .'

As they set out across the cobblestones Tabitha reached under her coat, just to check her trusty bandolier of throwing knives was still in place. It never hurt to be prepared.

The magician led them through a narrow wooden door and up a well-worn spiral staircase. 'I trust you'll forgive the herring cart,' he said, as they climbed. 'Most uncomfortable, I should imagine, but sadly necessary. If the Demon's Watch were to be seen in Azurmouth – and moreover, if a magician from the Academy were seen to be *helping* the Demon's Watch . . . Well, the Duke of Garran would hardly be delighted.'

'We understand,' said Newton. 'Thank you for taking us in.'

The Captain of the Watch seemed a little uncomfortable, but Tabitha knew that they couldn't very well stay in a boarding house. *The Academy is the safest place in Azurmouth. Master Gurney will shelter us for as long as we need, just so long as we don't get him in trouble with the League.* That's what Hal had told them. He'd been a little reluctant to ask the favour, but they'd persuaded him in the end. After all, what choice did they have?

Through a window Tabitha caught sight of a twilit courtyard enclosed by the white stone walls, a gravel pathway cutting through the middle between two rectangles of immaculately kept grass. In the centre of each lawn stood a white statue; on one side a demon, horned and snarling, and on the other a seraph, its face smiling and serene, wings curving round its body. Her father had been the governor of Port Fayt, and she'd still never seen anything so fancy in all her life.

They came to another narrow wooden door at the top of the staircase. The air was cool and still, as though undisturbed since the Dark Age. Master Gurney unlocked the door and pushed it open in a swirl of dust. 'Home, sweet home,' he murmured.

The watchmen followed the shuffling magician, crowding into the room. It was tiny, made even more cramped by the landscape of books heaped on the floor and stuffed into the bookcases that covered every inch of wall. Several lanterns flickered, giving the place a cosy orange glow, and illuminating an egg that floated in the air above Master Gurney's desk, gently rotating.

'An experiment,' the magician explained. 'I'm trying to change it into a chicken, you see? Transformation is one of the most profoundly complex fields of magic, as I'm sure Hal will have explained to you.'

'I'm sure he's told us,' said Paddy.

'Not so sure we listened,' muttered Frank.

'Why?' asked Tabitha.

Master Gurney blinked at her. 'Why what?'

'Why turn the egg into a chicken?' She'd never

really understood magic, and the more she saw of it, the less she liked it.

Master Gurney considered for a moment, before wagging his finger at her. 'Well, young lady, perhaps a better question might be . . . *why not?*' He beamed and flicked his wrist, sending the egg drifting to rest on a small cushion. 'Now, to business. Have a seat, all of you.' He gestured vaguely around the room.

Tabitha perched awkwardly on a heap of books with some of the most peculiar titles she had ever seen: *The Cockatrice: Magical Minion or Foolish Fowl?*; *Fifty Most Useful Applications of Dragon's Breath in the Medical Magics*; *Demons and Doorknobs: a Surprising Correlation* . . .

'You know why we're here?' said Newton.

'Indeed, young Hal explained it all in his letter,' said Master Gurney. 'Your poor young friend . . . Of course you must find him, and quickly.'

'That's right,' said Hal. 'The sooner we can track down Joseph, the better.'

'Then we'll be out of your hair, and back to Port Fayt,' added Frank.

'So what are we waiting for?' said Tabitha. 'We can start on the docks, see if the *Dread Unicorn* has put in and—'

'Good gracious, no!' interrupted Master Gurney.

'That is to say . . . I only wish it were so simple. But you can hardly walk the streets of Azurmouth dressed in those uniforms. You'll need disguises at the very least. And I fear no amount of disguise will conceal the fact that these good gentlemen are trolls.' He smiled at the blue-coated twins.

'No offence taken,' muttered Paddy.

'Besides, night is falling.' The magician gestured to a small window set in the wall above his desk. Through it, the gleaming white towers of the House of Light could just be seen rising above the ramshackle rooftops of Azurmouth.

'We're not afraid of the dark,' said Newton.

'You should be,' said Master Gurney sharply. He frowned for a moment, before spreading his hands and smiling again. 'You are strangers in this city. But I can assure you, it is no place for Fayters to go wandering after the sun has set. Much less trolls. The Duke's men will be out on the streets.'

'Butchers, you mean?' said Frank.

'Indeed. The Duke is extremely committed to the Way of the Light. In theory, of course, the League is a partnership, and its decisions are made jointly. But in Azurmouth, the Duke holds sway. When the sun goes down, his whitecoats do as they please.'

The magician hesitated, and Tabitha saw that he

was frowning again. When he spoke, it was in a small voice. 'If the Duke had his way, of course, he would declare war on Port Fayt at once, and rid the Old World of demonspawn. Starting with Azurmouth. He would send out his butchers and . . .' He shook his head and smiled again. 'Well, it doesn't bear thinking about, does it?'

'Yes, but what are we supposed to do about Joseph?' said Tabitha briskly. She could still picture the tavern boy the way she'd last seen him, sitting cross-legged on a sandy beach, his face glowing from the firelight, his jaw set with determination. She should have seen it then. Should have guessed what he was planning.

I could have stopped him.

It wasn't a pleasant thought. If things got ugly, Joseph wouldn't even be able to protect himself. Tabitha had seen how handy he was with a cutlass. About as handy as a walrus with a knitting needle.

'What about using magic?' suggested Frank. 'Can't we do a spot of hocus pocus and track him down that way?'

'Sadly not,' murmured Hal. 'I'm afraid such a spell simply doesn't exist.'

'What about that wooden spoon of yours?' said Paddy. 'Surely we can use that to—'

'No, that wouldn't work at all,' interrupted Hal. For some reason he had gone red in the face.

Why's he so touchy about the spoon? Tabitha wondered. *It's like he doesn't want to talk about it.*

'Wooden spoon?' said Master Gurney, confused.

'Forgive them, Master. It's not— They don't really understand what—'

'So what *do* we do?' Tabitha demanded, before the conversation could stray off topic.

'Well, my dear,' said Master Gurney. 'If I were you, I should stay here tonight. There's plenty of space in the attic. Then tomorrow morning I can find you some suitable disguises and show you the safest routes through the city.'

'What do you think, Newt?' asked Frank.

'The harbourmasters will have gone home by now,' said Paddy.

'I reckon so.' Newton nodded thoughtfully. 'We'll go into the city at the crack of dawn tomorrow, and we'll find him. Meantime, we should get as much rest as we can.'

'But Joseph is—' began Tabitha.

'Not now, Tabs,' said Newton sternly.

'But he's on his own, and—'

'And he can look after himself,' said Newton.

'Newt's right, Tabs,' said Frank gently. 'He's a bright

lad. He'll be smart enough to keep his head down till we get there.'

'I certainly hope so,' muttered Hal. The blood had drained from his face, and he was looking anxious again.

Tabitha opened her mouth to argue, but thought better of it. She could tell from Newton's knitted brow that his mind was made up. *He never listens.* And she just had to put up with it. Newton was all she'd had, ever since she was little. Ever since her parents had died.

As the others climbed the ladder to Master Gurney's attic, Tabitha hung back, peering out of the window at the ghostly spires of the House of Light. The thought of Joseph wandering the streets of Azurmouth, where the Duke's butchers prowled . . . It made her blood run cold.

If only he had told her where he was going. She could have come too. Looked after him. Helped him. If only she hadn't been so horrible.

I told him I'd be better off without him.

She winced at the memory. And what she'd said about his father . . . Well, she should have known better. She was an orphan too, after all.

Maybe it was her fault he'd snuck away.

Her fault he'd told no one.

She thought about what Frank had said, trying to make herself believe it. *He'll be smart enough to keep his head down.* It *had* to be true, didn't it? After all, he was a mongrel boy, and he was all on his own. He wouldn't just go charging straight into danger.

Would he?

Chapter Three

Joseph leaped into the cabin, brandishing his cutlass.

Inside it was dark and cramped, with only a small window and candles for light. A hobgoblin lay strapped to a table in the centre of the cabin, at the mercy of a surgeon – a human whose apron was smeared with a disturbing variety of colours. One leg of the hobgoblin's breeches had been peeled back and his shoe removed to reveal a nasty wound in his grey foot.

'A mongrel boy,' said the surgeon, lowering his hacksaw. 'How extraordinary.'

At the sound of the door banging open, the patient

had propped himself up on his elbows, and was now glaring at Joseph as though a bad day had just got even worse.

'What in all the stinkin' blue sea are *you* doin' here?' snarled Captain Lortt.

Joseph slammed the cabin door shut and turned the key. His cutlass hilt slipped in his sweating palm, and he gripped it tighter, setting his jaw and trying to look as menacing as he could. *Not easy when your coat is twice as big as you are.*

'Where is he?'

'Where's— What are you talking about?' spluttered Lortt. 'Can't you see we're a bit bleedin' busy?'

'Indeed, young man,' said the surgeon. 'I am about to remove this gentleman's foot, and the least you could do is—'

'For the last time,' roared Lortt, so loudly the surgeon flinched. 'You ain't cutting off my foot! Just make the pain go away. An' do it quick.'

'You know who I mean,' said Joseph. 'I'm looking for Jeb the Snitch. You brought him here to Azurmouth, didn't you? After the battle.'

'What d'yer want with that lousy weevil?'

'Never you mind. Just tell me where he is, and no one'll get hurt.'

'I'm already hurt, mongrel, can't yer see?' snarled Lortt, pointing at his foot. 'That filthy blue-haired friend o' yours done this.'

Tabitha. Joseph's stomach twisted at the thought of his friend. He hadn't told her where he was going. Hadn't even said goodbye. Would she have come after him, when she found him gone? Would she have brought Newton and the Demon's Watch?

He hoped not.

The surgeon rattled a bag hopefully. 'Yes, now, about that foot . . . Perhaps my fine range of whale-bone replacements might change your mind?'

A sudden battering on the cabin door made Joseph's ears twitch. 'Want us to kill 'im, Captain?' came a shout from outside.

Joseph darted around the table, putting the injured hobgoblin between him and the door.

'Where d'you think you're going?' said Lortt.

'Perhaps,' said the surgeon, 'if you would just allow me to—'

'PUT. THAT. SAW. DOWN!'

The surgeon looked pale as he tucked it away in his bag. 'Well, I can't say I'm not disappointed.'

Joseph puffed out his chest, trying to imagine he was big and tough like Captain Newton. 'If you don't tell me, I'll have to, er . . .'

What would he do? The thought of actually *using* the cutlass was too horrifying. Still, he had to pretend at least. What would Tabitha say?

'I'll . . . I'll cut your foot off!'

'That would certainly save me the trouble,' muttered the surgeon.

'And the other one too!'

Lortt smirked. 'Hope you ain't plannin' to charge as much as this quack.'

Joseph felt his face getting hot. The hobgoblin didn't think he had it in him. *Just tell me. Tell me now.* All of a sudden he found that he'd taken a step forward, his cutlass raised. He could just imagine it – bringing the blade down with all his strength . . .

It scared him.

Lortt's eyes grew wide, as though he could sense what was going on in Joseph's head. Obviously it scared him too.

'All right, keep yer breeches on. Me and Jeb, we ain't friends. Matter o' fact, the bilge crawler cheated me out o' half my pay for bringing him across the ocean. So I'll help you out, and in return you can get off my ship. That clear?'

Joseph nodded, lowering the cutlass with shaking hands. 'Tell me where he is.'

'He said he had business here with the Grey

Brotherhood. They got a place called the Whale, on Seagull Alley off Butcher's Cross.' He hesitated. 'Just don't tell 'im I sent yer, understand? The Snitch don't like being crossed.'

'Thank you,' said Joseph. 'And, er . . . I'm sorry about your foot. I hope you—'

'Just *get off my ship.*'

Two minutes later, Joseph was dripping and shivering as he hurried over the cobblestones. Lortt had promised not to hurt him, but he didn't exactly trust the hobgoblin, and he trusted his sailors even less – which meant he'd had no choice but to wriggle out of the cabin window and go plunging into the sea. It had been freezing cold and brimming with slimy seaweed, but that didn't matter.

He had a lead. A real, solid lead.

Joseph had heard tales of the Grey Brothers, back in the Legless Mermaid. They were goblins – underground fighters who hit back at the League, ripping down their banners, rescuing prisoners from their gaols and robbing rich League merchants to buy bread for families who hadn't any of their own. They were heroes.

It was hard to imagine good folk like that doing business with Jeb the Snitch. But then, Jeb had a knack for making people trust him, only to betray them later. Joseph knew that all too well.

The most vicious, treacherous crook in all the Old World. And he's the one person who can help me find the truth.

But first he had to find Butcher's Cross, and that turned out to be trickier than he'd thought. He asked directions from a dockhand who sent him one way, then a revenue man who sent him the other. A gang of kids threw stones at him, and one managed to grab hold of Clagg's waterlogged coat, forcing him to shrug it off and dart down a side street.

After that people wouldn't stop giving him funny looks. Some shouted *mongrel*, and worse. He began hurrying through the shadows, avoiding eye contact with anyone.

It wasn't long before his feet were sore and his belly was rumbling. He used some of Clagg's coins to buy a greasy fish pie, then ducked into a dark alleyway to wolf it down, keeping a lookout for butchers as he ate.

Whatever happened, he wasn't going to give up. He was going to find Jeb the Snitch. The goblin's face had haunted Joseph's dreams every night since the Battle of Illon. Those cold, pale eyes. That smirking mouth and sharp goblin teeth. The ludicrous outfits, so brightly coloured it almost hurt to look at them.

The last time Joseph had seen Jeb, the goblin had been levelling a pistol at him, howling threats of death – and worse.

He brushed the last of the pastry from his face, trying not to imagine what Tabitha would say if she were here. *You're crazy. That goblin would slit your throat for half a ducat. He cheats and lies for a living.* It was all true. But still, Joseph had to find him.

He set out again, striding faster this time and tipping his hat down low, now that he had no outsized coat to disguise what he was.

At last, as the sun had set and his clothes had dried stiff with salt, Joseph found Butcher's Cross. It was a narrow avenue running into the heart of Azurmouth, lined with stalls and shop fronts that stank of meat on the verge of going bad.

Joseph hurried along it, dodging the occasional passing carriage, weaving in and out of the crowds. A group of whitecoats were playing dice on upturned crates by the side of the road, and Joseph hurried past, head down. He couldn't bear the thought of being picked up by the League's soldiers when he was so close.

At least it's dark now. So long as I stick to the shadows, I—

He froze, sensing that someone was watching

him. But when he looked up he saw that it was only a horse, loitering under a shop's awning in the glow of a lantern, as though waiting for its owner to come out. A dappled beast, with a silvery mane that flopped over its eyes and gave it a faintly comical look. It blinked at him.

Definitely not a whitecoat. For the first time that day, Joseph allowed himself a smile.

He turned into a smaller, darker street where the buildings overhung most of the cobblestones. *Seagull Alley* proclaimed a rotten board propped on the street corner. Halfway down was a building with a black studded door, in the shadow of a whale.

Joseph hesitated. It really was a whale – a small one, but big enough to cause some serious discomfort to anyone who might be underneath if it fell. It was suspended like a tavern sign by a pair of chains wrapped around each end, and the carcass was half rotten and turned some indeterminate colour by weather and age and Thalin knew what else. A gull perched on the whale's head, glaring at Joseph.

His pockets were still full – the pocket watch in one, and the wooden spoon in the other. If Jeb the Snitch was in there, he'd have to use the spoon.

If I can even make it work. Hal said you don't have to be a magician, but he didn't say it would be easy.

He ran through the magician's explanation one last time, his stomach twisting with nerves. Then he took a deep breath, strode up to the door and knocked.

It swung open at once, and a pair of dark goblin eyes blinked out at him. 'Come for the fight?'

'Er . . .'

'Well, don't just stand there.'

Bony fingers clamped down on his shoulders and pulled him inside.

'S oon you will be dead. You and all your kind.'
      *Morgan makes no reply. He sits, still and silent
in the corner of the study, dressed in League livery, as a
draughtsman sketches him in charcoal at an easel. The
artist is capturing every detail of the ogre's anatomy.
The jutting jaw. Piggy eyes and tapered ears. A twisted
parody of a human.*

*A burst of laughter sounds from the floor below,
voices raised in drunken song. The lords of the League
have been feasting for hours now, ever since they arrived
at the House of Light. The Duke had almost forgotten
how much he despises them.*

He leans forward from his own seat at the

draughtsman's side. In this room there is no sound but the scratch of the draughtsman's charcoal, the crackle of the fire and the ticking of the clock. 'Are you afraid?' he asks the ogre softly. 'I am only curious.'

Morgan's brow creases, as though he has been asked to perform some complicated arithmetic. He seems troubled, but does not speak.

Does the creature feel anything at all? Did he ever? Perhaps the years of servitude have worn him down. Or perhaps he has always been this way, his thoughts no more complex than a dog's.

The Duke cannot tear his eyes from the misshapen monster in white. It has always been like this for him, with demonspawn. They revolt him even as they draw him in.

He knows he is not alone. Morgan has been in his service for years now, and still the other footmen spurn him, talk of him behind his back and play tricks on him. They are fascinated. They cannot understand why the Duke has brought him here among them.

Another clamour from downstairs, as the lords hoot and stamp their feet. Soft, rich and well-fed, they have forgotten what demonspawn really are. How base. How foul.

The Duke knows how easy it is to forget. To stray from the Way of the Light. He knows it all too well. Every day, Morgan's silent presence reminds him. Morgan is the curse he must endure until his work is finally done.

'Finished, your grace.' The draughtsman hands him the sketch.

'Very good.' The Duke has already chosen a spot for it on the wall of the study, along with the other drawings. Diagrams of goblin skulls. Dissections of impish ears. Comparisons of the elf's anatomy at different ages. They will make a valuable historical record once the Old World is free from the blight of demonspawn.

He smooths out the sketch, admiring the draughtsman's accuracy. To get inside the mind of such a creature . . . What must it feel like? To be so corrupted by evil? If only he could experience it for himself – just once.

Perhaps it is better that he does not.

The artist hurries out with his easel, almost colliding with Major Turnbull as she enters. She comes to attention smartly.

'Your task is accomplished?' asks the Duke.

'Yes, your grace. I have set men to guard it night and day. It will not be found.'

'Very good.'

'Your grace, I wished to ask you. I—' She shoots a glance at Morgan, still sitting like a stone statue in his chair.

'Whatever you have to say, you may say it in front of Morgan.'

'The other lords – have you informed them of your plans? They will not like it if you act without their blessing.'

The Duke smiles. 'Tomorrow is Corin's Day, Major Turnbull, yet my fellow lords can talk of nothing but the Contest of Blades. Whether Lucky Leo will triumph again. The proper technique for a lunge. They are not worthy to know.'

'But surely—'

'It is time to open their eyes, Major. Our great ancestor showed us the Way of the Light, and I intend to follow in his footsteps. Corin the Bold shall walk again.'

She frowns at that. 'Those words . . . I've heard them before, somewhere.'

'A figure of speech. You heard it when you were a child, no doubt. You may leave.'

After she is gone, the Duke lays a hand on Morgan's shoulder. Even to touch such a creature sends a jolt of horror through his body.

'You have been my burden for many a year, Morgan,' he says softly. 'Like a whetstone to a blade you have kept me determined. Do not think you will go unrewarded.' He bends down to whisper in the ogre's ear.

'When the Light comes . . . when it shines into every dark corner of the Old World, burning away every last trace of evil . . . you shall be the first to die.'

Chapter Four

Captain Newton crept through the darkened corridors of the Academy, rubbing at the red marks on his wrists. He'd sworn he'd never return to the Old World. Sworn it on the lives of his mother, his father and his grandfather. Sworn it on the scars that marked his wrists and had never healed. Yet here he was, back in the Old World.

Worse still – in Azurmouth.

'Where are we going, mister?' asked Ty sleepily. The fairy was riding on his shoulder, and had barely woken up.

'Keep it down,' Newton murmured.

There was something sinister about the Academy

at night. The way the shadows gathered in crevices and stretched across the flagstones, and the deathly silence – no sound but his own footsteps, and not a soul to see him pass by. So much the better. He had work to do.

Ever since the Battle of Illon, a terrible weight had settled in the pit of Newton's gut. It wasn't just Joseph that bothered him. That was a worry, of course. No – there was something more. Something that had taken his appetite away and brought him from his bed tonight. If he could just lay it to rest, then he could concentrate on finding Joseph before—

A shadow stirred, and a figure stepped into a pool of moonlight ahead, blocking his path.

'Found you,' said Tabitha.

Newton cursed under his breath. *Should have been more careful.* 'Go back to bed.'

'Not until you tell me where you're going.' She was scowling, hands on hips. 'I couldn't sleep, then I heard you sneaking out with Ty. Do you have any idea what time it is?'

He had spoken those same words to her when she was a little girl, and had crept downstairs to raid the larder of fresh pies at Bootles' Pie Shop. He gave the same answer she had given him then. 'Time for you to be asleep.'

Tabitha shook her head. 'Why can't you tell me what's going on? You're not the only one in the Watch, you know.'

'I'm going to the Academy library.'

'I don't think we're going to find Joseph in a library.'

'I said *I'm* going. And this isn't about Joseph.'

'Then what *is* it about?'

'And what's a library?' added Ty.

'Never you mind,' said Newton. 'Just go back to bed, right now.' Tabs didn't need to know about this. None of the watchmen did.

But instead of leaving, Tabitha crossed her arms and glared at him. 'We should be out there looking for Joseph.'

'First thing tomorrow, Tabs – that's what we agreed. Right now the city will be crawling with whitecoats.'

'That's exactly why we should start looking!'

Her voice was rising in anger, and Newton laid a finger on her lips. 'That's not what I meant,' he said, as gently as he could. 'Joseph's not reckless. He's quick on his feet, and he's a sight less conspicuous than us. Besides, he chose to come here. So we have to trust that he knows what he's doing. We'll start looking for him at the crack of dawn – I promise.'

Tabitha didn't breathe a word, but the fierce set of her jaw made it clear what she thought of his plan.

Maybe she's right. Maybe we should be scouring the streets of Azurmouth right now . . . Lately it seemed like Newton was always questioning his own decisions. It never used to be that way. But then, Tabitha didn't know what he knew. She didn't know about the other reason they'd come to Azurmouth.

'Bed. I won't ask you again.'

'Good, because I'm not going.' She tensed, as though he might try to drag her back to Master Gurney's rooms.

Which is tempting . . . except she'd wake up the whole Watch, not to mention half the Academy.

It wasn't much of a choice.

'Keep quiet, then. And stick with me.'

She nodded, still scowling. Only the glint in her eye betrayed her excitement, as she followed him to the end of the corridor.

Above the entrance to the library was a wooden plaque inscribed with the Academy motto in gold: *To LEARN is to DO.* The words didn't make much sense to Newton, but that was magicians for you. He pushed open the doors.

The sight beyond took even Tabitha's breath away.

'Blimey,' said Ty. 'I think I like libraries.'

The Library of Magical Arts was one of Hal's favourite subjects of conversation – and Newton could see why. The shelves reached up like cliffs, hundreds of feet high, extending so far into the distance that the library seemed to go on for ever, like some vast, shadowy maze of books. Craning his neck, Newton could make out the ceiling – a glass dome through which the dark sky could just be seen.

The only sounds were the scratching of quills and the gentle buzzing of fairies' wings as they flitted around the shelves, retrieving books for the few black-robed magicians studying late into the night at heavy wooden desks. The only light came from the soft glow of the fairies, and the iron lanterns of the magicians.

'Can I help you?' It was a slight woman in a magician's robes, with long, straggly grey hair and a kindly face. She was carrying a pile of books, which must have been almost as heavy as she was.

Newton cast a glance at Tabitha. She was busy watching a pair of fairies struggle with a hefty volume of an encyclopaedia, before dumping it in a shower of dust onto the desk of a surprised elderly magician.

'Aye,' he said, in a low voice. 'I'm looking for books about Corin the Bold.'

The librarian raised an eyebrow. 'I see.' She nodded

at a sweep of shelves disappearing into the distance. 'That section is for books about Corin's battle strategies. Over there' – she indicated another set of shelves – 'you will find a selection of studies on the nutrition of Corin's army.' She smiled. 'Perhaps you could be a little more specific?'

Tabitha was chatting to the fairies now, completely oblivious to Newton's conversation.

'I want to know about the Sword of Corin.'

The librarian's eyes widened. Then she set down her load of books and led Newton and Ty across the floor of the library. It was carpeted so thickly that their feet barely made a sound. All the same, Newton caught more than one magician shoot them an irritated glance.

'Reckon we're breathing too loud,' whispered Ty.

'*Shhh!*' said a nearby magician.

Ty waited till they were round a corner, then made a face. 'Why are you so bothered about this sword, anyway?' he asked.

'I'm just interested.'

It wasn't a lie. He *was* interested. *Very interested.* But he wasn't about to explain why, even to his own fairy.

'Here,' said the librarian. She handed Newton a pair of black velvet gloves with a golden sun stitched onto them. 'Wear these at all times when handling the books. I'll send you a lantern and a fairy to fetch them down. You'll find a private reading room through that doorway, where no one will disturb you.'

Newton looked up at the wall of leather-bound tomes: *The Sword of Corin – A History*; *A Hero's Sword*; *The Metallurgy of Corin's Blade*. He felt suddenly weary.

This was going to take a while.

Half an hour later, he'd flicked through every single one, his head hurt and he was none the wiser.

'What are you looking for?' asked Tabitha. Newton glanced up from his desk to see her leaning against the doorway to the reading room, arms folded, frowning.

'I don't know,' he said.

She rolled her eyes. 'You must have *some* idea. What are these books about?'

Reluctantly he held up the final tome: *Blades of the Dark Age: The Sword of Corin*. They'd all started to blur into one. Endless speculation about how the blade was forged, the details of its engravings and the battles it was used in – and none of it was remotely helpful.

Before he could stop her, Tabitha stepped outside, cupped her hands and shouted down the length of the library, 'Hey!'

There was a distant chorus of tutting and shushing, then the slim grey-haired woman came hurrying towards them, one finger against her lips. 'Please,' she said. 'The magicians are studying!'

Tabitha shrugged, unbothered. 'We want to know about Corin's sword, *for some reason*,' she said pointedly. 'Is this all you have?' She flung out an arm at the piles of books that had built up on and around Newton's desk. Ty was sitting on the highest pile, happily gnawing on a sugar lump.

'I'm afraid so,' said the librarian. She hesitated, as though about to say something.

'Yes?' said Newton. 'There are other books?'

'Well . . . I believe we do have one or two in the children's section. But I can't imagine—'

'Bring them out.'

Tabitha perched on the edge of his desk as the librarian quietly closed the door to the reading room and bustled off. 'So why do you care about Corin's sword?' she asked. 'It's just an old relic.'

'Maybe.'

'And it's safe in ol' Governor Wyrmwood's place in Fayt, isn't it?'

Newton bit his lip. *I should tell her. Shouldn't I?* So many questions and so few answers. Lately he was feeling overburdened, like a ship so full of zephyrum it could barely keep afloat. It didn't feel good. And keeping secrets from Tabitha made it feel even worse.

He opened his mouth, just as the door swung wide again.

'Here,' said the librarian triumphantly, setting a small, battered book on the desk in front of him. '*The Tale of Corin's Sword.* A century old at least, so do please be careful.' She cast Ty a nervous glance, as the fairy licked sugar-sticky fingers and belched happily. Then she disappeared back into the library.

Newton leaned forward, lifted the cloth-bound cover and began to flick through the pages. They were thin and yellowed, covered in swirling letters and illustrated with colourful figures acting out the story.

'What's "the Scouring"?' asked Tabitha, reading over his shoulder. She pointed to a picture that took up an entire page. It showed winged figures swooping from a black sky, carrying golden weapons – spears, bows and swords. On a green field below, more figures were fleeing the attack – misshapen creatures with long noses, sharp teeth and pointed ears. At the head of the flying army was a man all in white, his surcoat emblazoned with a winged sword. He was galloping on a charger and wielded a shining blade, the hilt studded with white star-stones. Above his head three words were written in tiny gold letters: CORIN THE BOLD.

'It's an old legend,' said Newton. 'Just a story.'

'Well, get on with it then,' said Tabitha impatiently.

'Some folks say that seraphs will return one day to scour the Old World. That is, to kill the trolls, the goblins, the dwarves . . . anyone who isn't human. Like I say, it's just a story. Something for men full of hatred to cling onto. Folk like the League, with all their talk of demonspawn.' He laid a finger on the picture. 'I don't know what it has to do with Corin, though.'

Tabitha reached over his shoulder and turned the page. The reverse was blank except for four lines, written by hand.

At the call of the sword, twelve stones shall sing,
Twelve seraphs rise, in a golden ring.
At the river's birth where the hero was lain,
Corin the Bold shall walk again.

'What does *that* mean?' asked Ty. Newton had been so engrossed in the book that he hadn't noticed the fairy alight on his shoulder.

'Beats me,' he said.

'It's just nonsense,' said Tabitha briskly. *A little too briskly.*

'Aye,' said Newton. 'This is a children's book, remember?'

Even so, he had a funny feeling it was this that he'd been looking for. He was no poet, and he didn't understand it all. Just enough to raise the hairs on the back of his neck.

Corin the Bold shall walk again.

Chapter Five

Joseph stumbled into a gloomy, cavernous stone hall. Pigeons warbled up in the exposed rafters above, which explained the spatterings of bird mess on the flagstones below, where a group of goblins were clustered around something, yelping and squawking with excitement. Joseph craned his neck, and what he saw there turned his stomach.

His first glimpse was of a blur of bright colours, scrabbling across the floor, before the shapes resolved themselves into creatures – two of them – screeching and pecking at each other.

Joseph had seen the long, shimmering tail feathers of a cockatrice before, laid out on market stalls in Port

Fayt. But he'd never seen the magnificent beasts they came from. Talons extended, bright and sharp. Proud yellow beaks, curved and coloured as though dipped in egg yolk. Beady black eyes shining like those of the goblins surrounding them. The cockatrices were beautiful. Their bodies shimmered, now gold and red, now blue and green as they moved in the light.

One of the birds spread its wings and hissed like a snake, forcing the other away. The flagstones were streaked with blood as well as pigeon droppings. Some old, dark and encrusted. Some fresh, bright and red.

The Grey Brotherhood were supposed to be heroes. But instead they looked like cruel children, drinking up the bloodshed, cackling at each other, whooping and hurling insults at one bird or the other. It made Joseph feel sick.

All of a sudden he realized he was being watched by someone at the rear of the crowd. It was a big goblin, dressed in torn, filthy clothes and worn-out shoes. He scowled, and Joseph suddenly felt awkward, like he had no place being here.

'You're new,' said the goblin suspiciously.

Joseph nodded, unable to say anything. He had just noticed that the goblin's nose was missing, and that instead he had a fake nose carved out of wood and held onto his face with a length of twine.

A strangled squawk of pain came from the centre of the circle, and the Grey Brothers' voices rose in excitement.

The goblin stepped in, clamped his fingers round Joseph's face, tugging him closer. 'Whath wrong with your fathe? Ith all blotchy.'

Joseph spoke as best he could. 'My mother was a human.'

'A mongrel!' said another goblin, who'd started to take an interest. 'Well, strike me colours and call me Nancy! Don't see too many o' them in Azurmouth.'

'I'm from Port Fayt.'

The goblin with the wooden nose tightened his grip. Joseph felt sharp nails pressing into his skin, felt the pressure build on his teeth. He let out a gasp of pain.

'Don't tell lieth, mongrel,' said the goblin.

'I promise. From the Marlinspike Quarter.' Joseph pulled up the sleeve on his right arm. 'Look, I'm a watchman. We're like you. We fought against the League at the Battle of Illon.'

The goblin peered at the blue shark tattoo scored into Joseph's skin. Behind them, the Grey Brothers let out an almighty roar, a mingled sound of triumph and disappointment. Joseph caught a glimpse of a small, broken body stretched on the flagstones, a pool of blood steadily growing all around it. The one surviving cockatrice was scooped up in someone's arms and held aloft like a trophy, squawking with confusion.

More goblins crowded around, peering at Joseph.

'Who's that?'

'Look at his funny skin.'

'Ugly little cockroach.'

Joseph swallowed. Things weren't going the way he'd hoped, but it was too late to back out now. 'I'm looking for someone. I think he's a friend of yours. Do you know a goblin called Jeb the Snitch?'

He felt the atmosphere shift instantly. The Grey Brotherhood weren't suspicious any more. Now they were downright hostile. Shoulders hunched; eyes narrowed.

Wooden-nose smiled and ran a pale tongue across his teeth. 'Almotht had me fooled with that fake tattoo, mongrel,' he snarled. 'Got your number now. You're no wathman. You're working for the League of the Light, ain't you? You're a *thpy*.'

Several hands seized hold of Joseph, jostling him towards a door at the rear of the Whale. A grimy, half-rotten door hanging off its hinges. Not a reassuring door.

'No, please,' said Joseph. 'You've got it wrong, I'm—'

But no one was listening.

His heart hammering, Joseph scrabbled in his pocket for the wooden spoon. The thought of using it flooded his body with fear. He'd never tried it for real, and if it went wrong – well, who knew what would happen? Would he black out? Lose his mind?

Another shove sent him crashing through the door. He tripped on a cobblestone and went sprawling, one hand splashing into a puddle of murky brown water, the other holding on tight to the wooden spoon. He rolled over, scrambled to his feet.

He was in a narrow, darkened alleyway, a sliver of night sky overhead. At one end was an unforgiving bare-brick wall where a couple of tired-looking horses were tied up. The other end led out to the street, but immediately several goblins crowded in, blocking his one possible escape route.

Wooden-nose cracked his knuckles, an ugly grin painted on his face.

A bully. He's just a bully.

'Don't touch me!' yelled Joseph.

He didn't know where the anger had come from. All he knew was that he'd come all the way across the Ebony Ocean, and this wasn't fair. *I'm not going to be beaten up by Jeb's horrible friends.*

'Look at you! The Grey Brotherhood are supposed

to be heroes. That's what all the stories say. You're supposed to be freedom fighters! But instead you sit around watching chickens fight to the death and . . . and threatening children!'

The smile had frozen on Wooden-nose's face.

'Hit him,' said a reedy-voiced goblin. 'Why ain't you hit him yet?'

'Heroeth?' said Wooden-nose. 'The League run thith thity, mongrel. Athurmouth ain't no plathe for heroeth.' He drew back his fist.

Almost without thinking, Joseph tugged the wooden spoon from his pocket. He held it out at arm's length, quivering inches from Wooden-nose's face. The goblin jerked away.

A cold wave of fear swept through Joseph's body, but he did his best to ignore it. *It's a question of mental focus*, Hal had told him. So he screwed his eyes shut, concentrating harder than he'd ever done before, trying to think the right thoughts.

The spoon trembled in his hand.

It felt ridiculous, but he pushed on. *Please let it work. Please* . . . He tried to feel something. Anything. Was that a tingle of magic running up his arm? Or was he just gripping too tightly?

'Oi,' said Wooden-nose. 'That'th a thtinking *thpoon*. What are you gonna do, *thpoon* me to death?'

The other goblins began to cackle, a raucous, horrible sound that reminded Joseph of seagulls fighting over a fish carcass. His confidence drained away in an instant. *Idiot!* What in all the Ebony Ocean had made him think he could make it work? He wasn't special. He was just a stupid tavern boy.

Wooden-nose slapped the spoon aside and grabbed him by the collar. Joseph tensed his jaw, trying to prepare for the inevitable pain. He'd been hit before, back in the Legless Mermaid, by his uncle Mr Lightly. This goblin was half the size. How bad could it be? Through a half-closed eye Joseph glimpsed his attacker's bony fist, the fingers festooned with spiked iron rings.

Pretty bad, then.

But the punch never came.

Opening his eyes, Joseph saw that the goblin had been distracted by something at the end of the alley. A horse, ambling out of the shadows, hooves clip clopping on cobbles. A grey dappled horse with a mane that flopped down over its eyes. It looked like the one that had given Joseph a fright in Butcher's Cross. Quite a lot like it.

Exactly like it.

'Oi,' snarled Wooden-nose. 'Whith o' you idioth forgot to tie up the hortheth?'

Before any of them could reply, the horse reared up, let out a fearsome neigh and kicked the two nearest Grey Brothers hard in the chest. The goblins went flying, smacking into their friends like stray cannonballs.

'For the Corin'th thake, thomebody get that horth under contr—'

Wooden-nose never finished his sentence. The horse kicked out again, and his words turned into a pitiful screech as he stumbled backwards, clutching at his face, trying to keep it all in one piece.

It was now or never. Joseph bolted past the startled goblins, running for the end of the alleyway, clenching the wooden spoon.

With a clatter of hooves the horse was in front of him, blocking his path. It stood, waiting, as though it wanted him to climb on.

The Grey Brothers were already picking themselves up. One was loading a blunderbuss. Wooden-nose had found a broken bottle, and was brandishing it like a cutlass.

Joseph thrust the spoon back into his pocket and threw himself at the horse. It had never occurred to him before that it might be difficult to mount a horse. It looked so easy when he'd seen merchants and militiamen do it. But the best he could manage was a kind of belly flop, landing like a sack of hay, half on and half off.

The horse took off down the alleyway and out into the street, rapidly reaching a gallop. Joseph let out a long, inconsistent wail as he bumped up and down on its back. His stomach was pummelled again and again, until he was sure he was going to spew fish pie over his rescuer's flanks. His fingers dug into the dappled hair, desperate for purchase.

Where in Thalin's name are we going?

Not to Jeb the Snitch, that was for sure.

He caught an occasional glimpse of the streets around him: the glow of light from a tavern doorway; a startled seagull rising into the black sky; a pair of beggars sitting in the shadows and laughing at him. But he couldn't keep track of which direction they were heading in.

At last the gallop slowed to a canter, then a trot, until finally the horse was walking. Joseph heard the creak of a door opening up ahead, felt a lintel graze his back as the horse carried him into a gloomy interior. They came to a halt, the hooves thudding on wood.

Joseph let out a low moan. He tried to move, but that sent a jolt of pain through his belly. He was dizzy, disoriented and hurting all over.

'Off you get,' said the horse briskly.

Wait – what? There was no way the horse had just spoken. Somewhere along the line Joseph must have taken a knock to the head and—

'Come on. Haven't got all day.'

Joseph slid to his feet, then slumped to his knees. He knelt, panting, fixing the floorboards with an intense stare as he tried to make sense of what was happening.

I've been rescued by a horse. A horse that talks. A talking horse.

He was dimly aware of someone else in the room, a conversation, movement, but right now it meant nothing to him. He just needed to keep staring, and maybe if he stared hard enough he wouldn't be sick.

'Don't try to stand,' said the horse. Except when Joseph looked up the horse wasn't a horse any more. Instead he was a broad-shouldered man in a silk dressing gown, smoothing back his long grey-and-white streaked hair and watching Joseph curiously. There was something peculiar about the man's eyes. So big, so dark, and not human at all. A horse's eyes.

The horse had turned into a man. And there could only be one explanation for that.

A shapeshifter.

'It's him, isn't it?' said the horse-man to his companion. 'The mongrel boy.'

'Yes. It's him.'

Shapeshifters were as rare as cockatrice teeth. In fact, Joseph had only ever met one other shapeshifter before, and that was . . .

'You've done well,' said the horse's companion. 'I can't tell you how much I've been looking forward to seeing him again.'

This time, Joseph recognized the voice. The voice of a shapeshifter he knew well . . .

No, it can't be. Please, no. His hand went to the wooden spoon, but he knew now there was no point trying to use it. He should never have got on the horse. He should have stayed and taken his chances with the Grey Brothers.

He tried to stand but was pushed down again. He looked up into the face of the man who'd just spoken, and he knew it was all over. *I'll never learn the truth about my father. I'm going to die, here in this room.*

'Hello, mongrel.' The man was young and slim and dressed in a smart velvet jacket. He had neat ginger hair, and the glittering yellow eyes of a cat. 'Last time we met you humiliated me, locked me in a cage and shipped me across the ocean.' The man licked his lips, like a kitten with a bowl of cream. 'Rather cruel of you, I must say. But don't worry. I'm sure I can think of something worse to do in return.'

INTERLUDE

*T*he wyvern comes from the sky, wings beating the air in slow, powerful strokes. At a distance it could be a bird – an eagle or a hawk. But as it flies closer its distinctive lizard's tail can be seen, streaming behind it. Then the shimmering green of its scales and the translucent red of its bat-like wings. It swoops down in a rush of air, landing on the Duke's hunting glove with a soft thud.

It is barely two years old, this one, and still a long way from fully grown. He offers it a lump of raw meat which it snatches gratefully. Small, but deadly. It has already felled two hinds this morning.

'Nothing this time, eh?' says the Earl of Brindenheim.

He is riding a huge, heavy carthorse, all the better to support the man's vast weight. As podgy as he is, he still sits ramrod straight, the breeze gently ruffling his whiskers and the long coloured plumes that sprout from his tricorne hat. He is still dressed in white, spattered with mud now from the morning's hunting.

The other lords are mounted further away, prattling about the previous night's debauchery. Brindenheim's son, Lucky Leo, cannot hold his wine, and has already stopped twice to be sick in the bushes. Even Tallis, famous for once drinking an entire keg of blackwine in one go, looks a little pale and sweaty.

Brindenheim's wyvern rises up above the wood, flapping hard, something caught in its grasp.

'Ah ha!' chortles the Earl. 'What have we here?'

The wyvern swoops down beyond the fringe of trees, dropping its cargo on the grass. Huntsmen rush forward armed with knives, to finish off the kicking deer.

'Two apiece,' says Brindenheim, his eyes flashing. 'Two apiece.'

Brindenheim flicks his reins, coaxing his massive carthorse over. Leans in, checking that no one is listening. Of course, the others are too busy talking of cards and serving girls to pay attention.

'Did you have to bring that . . . creature?'

There, among the huntsmen, Morgan is lumbering

forward, still limping a little from when a citizen threw a stone at him last week. Space clears around him wherever he goes, and the lords cast him nervous glances. Some have never seen an ogre before.

'You are referring to Morgan, I take it. Are you frightened of him?'

Brindenheim's bushy eyebrows knit together in displeasure. 'Don't be absurd.'

'The others are. As they should be.'

The Earl's wyvern returns, landing softly on his hunting glove and folding its wings, meek and obedient.

'On the contrary. The last army of demonspawn in all the Old World was crushed months ago, at the Crying Mountains. Victory is ours. Those few that still resist us are wretched creatures, scattered, pitiful and—'

'I have no pity for demons.'

They watch in silence as Morgan lumbers back towards them, bearing the deer on his shoulders. One of the braver huntsmen swipes a branch at the ogre's feet, making him skip out of the way and stumble. The others snigger.

'They say you have hunted demonspawn before, with your wyverns,' says the Earl of Brindenheim, without looking at the Duke. 'They say you round them up, set them loose in the forest and send the wyverns after them, as though they were animals.' His eyes flicker towards the Duke, a moment of weakness. 'Is it true?'

'And what if it is?'

Brindenheim shakes his head but says nothing. 'In a few hours the Contest of Blades will begin,' he says at last. 'My son has been training hard.'

'That is well.'

Brindenheim's whiskers tremble, as he finally loses his temper. 'I know what you are implying, and I will not stand for it. You believe you are better than all of us, but—' He checks himself and draws a deep breath. 'We are here to celebrate Corin's Day, and we are your guests. But remember, we are all equals in the League. My fellow lords are tired of war. Tired of your restlessness. We command all the wealth of the Old World – so why do you waste your time gazing across the ocean, seeking to capture Port Fayt?'

'You are referring to the Battle of Illon.'

'Indeed. You sailed without even discussing it with us, and see what happened: ships sunk and men lost in their hundreds in a petty squabble with the Fayters and the merfolk. All for the Middle Islands. A handful of rocks in the middle of the sea. Let them keep their little islets.'

The Duke makes no reply. The Battle of Illon was never about the Middle Islands. There was a far greater *prize at stake. A prize won in secret, and brought back to Azurmouth. But, of course, Brindenheim knows nothing of that.*

The wyvern on his hunting glove screeches, impatient, and he feeds it another scrap of torn meat. Blood stains the creature's snout, and he smears it away with a gloved finger.

'Silence – very well then,' says Brindenheim. 'But be assured, I am not alone in these thoughts.'

The Duke does not doubt it. Only the support of the other lords would give Brindenheim the courage to speak to him like this.

The old walrus hesitates. 'You're planning something, aren't you?' he says finally. 'I swear to you, whatever it is, I will find out.'

Chapter Six

At first glance, the Azurmouth docks didn't seem so different from the ones back home. Tabitha could see stalls flogging steamed lobsters, battered fish and pastries. She spotted beggars and pickpockets. Then she began to notice the dirty looks that dwarves, imps and ogres drew as they passed by.

She tried to imagine Joseph stepping off the gang-plank here, and it made her feel queasy.

'What are we waiting for then?' she said.

'You're right,' said Hal. 'Let's find a harbourmaster, and fast.'

The docks were bustling, but even so Tabitha felt exposed as the watchmen strode in among the crowds.

The bundled-up trolls weren't helping, of course. They were wrapped up in long cloaks, with scarves wound around their faces, despite the bright morning sunshine. Even Tabitha had hidden her blue hair with a bandana, swapped her watchman's coat for a fisherman's jerkin and covered up her shark tattoo.

Not that it made much difference. Master Gurney had been right – no amount of clothing could hide how big and bulky the Bootle twins were. *At least you can't see their green skin*. The thought made Tabitha feel ashamed, but it was the city's fault. The longer she stayed in Azurmouth, the less she liked it.

She quickened her pace, scouting out for the blue sash of a harbourmaster. The sooner they found one, the sooner they'd find Joseph.

Stay out in the open, Newton had told them. *The whitecoats will take any excuse to arrest you, so don't make a scene*. That was all very well for him to say. He'd disappeared not long after dawn, saying there was something important he needed to do. It made Tabitha angry just thinking of it. Why did he have to be so mysterious? And what could possibly be more important than looking for Joseph?

The crowds pressed closer all around them. Tabitha had to dodge as a chamber pot was emptied from a first-floor window, then again as a procession of carts came trundling over the cobblestones. She gasped as she saw that the last of them was a wooden cage on wheels, and inside it was a beast as big as a horse, with a curved beak, furred hindquarters, a feathered breast and wings. *A griffin!* It lay at the bottom of the cage, watching the world outside without interest.

Tabitha was about to turn away when her gaze snagged on something beyond the cage. No – someone. A pale face that seemed familiar. A pair of watching eyes. But when she looked properly, whoever it was had gone.

A little shiver ran down her spine.

She hurried after her fellow watchmen, rounding a stack of crates to see that Hal and the twins had already accosted a large man wearing a blue sash and sweating heavily.

''scuse me, mate,' said Paddy. 'We're trying to find a ship called the *Dread Unicorn.*'

The harbourmaster drew a small leather-bound book from his pocket, casting a curious glance at the trolls as he did so.

'It would have arrived yesterday,' said Tabitha, as he flicked through his book. 'Or maybe the day before. It had a friend of ours on board – a mongrel boy, half human and half goblin.'

'Can't promise nothing,' said the harbourmaster.

'This is Azurmouth, sweetheart, not some little fishing village. Hundreds o' ships dock here every day. Besides, we're busier than usual right now, on account o' the Contest of Blades.' He jerked a thumb at a peeling poster attached to the side of a nearby cart. It showed a crude drawing of two men in the middle of a sword fight, and above them the words:

The Azurmouth Contest of Blades!
A Corin's Day tradition
By order of The League of the Light

Do YOU have what it takes to best the finest
swordsmen in all the Old World? If so, enter
the Contest of Blades! Enrol at your nearest
fencing house, and perhaps YOU will lift the
much-coveted zephyrum Dagger of Victory!

Also needed: SURGEONS, to assist on the day
of the contest.

'Contest of Blades?' said Paddy, his voice muffled by the scarf.

'Aye, the opening ceremony's at noon, over in the House of Light. Then there are bouts in the fencing houses for the rest o' the day, and the finals tonight, back at the House of Light. Not that it'll be much of a show. Lucky Leo barely even knows which end of the sword to hold, but the other fighters are all frightened to death of his pa, so they let him win.'

'This ship we're looking for—' Tabitha began impatiently.

But the harbourmaster was well into his stride now. He leaned in close, with a gust of fishy breath. 'One year there was this fella from the countryside who didn't know that, and beat Leo black and blue. The old Earl of Brindenheim had the fella strung upside down and left for dead. Wanna guess how long he lasted?'

Tabitha wrinkled her nose. 'We'd rather you told us about the *Dread Unicorn*. We need to find our friend, remember?'

The harbourmaster tutted and went back to his book, running a finger down a page. 'Here it is! Aye, the *Dread Unicorn* was here.'

'Was?' said Hal.

'It's gone now. Set sail before dawn.'

Tabitha wanted to scream. Hadn't she told Newton they should have been out looking for Joseph as soon as they arrived in Azurmouth?

'What now?' said Hal, scrubbing at his spectacles with a handkerchief, as the harbourmaster strode off.

Tabitha noticed dark bags under his eyes, as though he'd barely slept a wink.

'We could ask around,' said Frank. 'See if anyone spotted a mongrel boy here yesterday.'

'That could take weeks,' replied Hal. 'Besides, we mustn't stay here too long.' His gaze flicked nervously to a pair of off-duty whitecoats moving through the crowds. People skipped out of their way as they passed.

A tiny glowing figure dropped out of the sky, landing lightly on Tabitha's shoulder.

'Any luck?' asked Paddy.

Ty shuddered. 'I don't like this place, mister. They got fairy-catchers all over. Ones with bad breath and big nets. Lucky I'm so fast.'

'What about Joseph?' said Frank.

'The docks go on for ever, mister. It's like looking for a splinter in a galleon.'

'So far so bad,' said Paddy, as Ty darted down to hide in Tabitha's coat pocket.

'Then we'll think of something else,' snapped Tabitha. 'There must be some other way to find Joseph. Imagine you were him. Where would you have gone?' She concentrated, trying to put herself in the shoes of the tavern boy. She was fairly sure who he had been looking for, at least. *Jeb the Snitch*. Joseph was convinced that lying goblin knew something about his father.

So where would you find the Snitch in a city like Azurmouth?

It hit her like a lightning bolt.

An abandoned stall stood nearby, its blackboard advertising cockles at a half-ducat a pound. Tabitha leaped up onto the counter and stood on tiptoes, peering over the heads of the crowd.

'Whoa, miss!' yelped Ty, poking his head out from her coat.

'What are you doing?' hissed Hal. 'You know there are butchers everywhere, don't you?'

Tabitha ignored him. She saw a pair of children fighting with wooden swords, whilst a group of drunk men cheered them on, laughing, slamming tankards together and singing rude songs. One carried a placard with *Lucky Leo for champion* painted on it. She saw a group of fishermen arguing over a game of dice. An old woman bartering for a tin pot. A gaggle of children hovering suspiciously close to a fat fairy-catcher's money bag. None of it helpful.

And then, finally, she saw what she was looking for.

She leaped to the cobblestones and set off, heading for a side street.

'Wait for us, Tabs,' came Paddy's voice from behind. But Tabitha didn't slow her pace. She weaved through traders, sailors and stevedores, catching up as fast as she could.

It was the wooden cage on wheels. The horse that pulled it was straining every muscle in its body to keep the load trundling over the cobblestones. A thin man in a robe and a turban walked alongside, leading the horse by a halter.

Up close, the griffin didn't look much like the ones Newton had described in Tabitha's old bedtime stories. The colours of its feathers were muted, and she could see its ribs, as though it hadn't been fed properly. Its eyes were dull and rheumy, its beak blunted and battered. And those great wings were tied to its body, far too tight. There was a small wooden board attached to the cage with a name painted on it: NELL.

It seemed like Nell wasn't enjoying Azurmouth any more than Tabitha was.

'I don't like this, miss,' murmured Ty, from inside Tabitha's pocket.

'Just keep your head down.' She outpaced the man in the turban, planting herself firmly in the way. 'Excuse me.'

The man scowled and brought the horse to a halt.

Inside the cage, Nell the griffin turned to look at Tabitha, and blinked.

'What do you want?' barked the man. He had an accent Tabitha couldn't place. 'I am in a hurry.'

Tabitha swallowed. 'I was just wondering . . . You have a griffin there, so I thought maybe you might know something about the griffin bile trade?'

'Why do you ask?'

Hal and the Bootle twins had caught up now, but they were hanging back, waiting to see what would happen. Frank raised an eyebrow at Tabitha, and she put up a hand to tell him she knew what she was doing.

Griffin bile. Back in Fayt, she and Joseph had hidden out in one of Jeb's warehouses, and the stench of the bile wasn't something she could forget in a hurry.

'I'm looking for a bile trader. A goblin called Jeb the Snitch. Do you know where I could find him?'

The man's eyes narrowed, and in that moment Tabitha knew that he did. Her heart quickened. 'Maybe,' said the man. 'If I tell you, what will you give me in return?'

'Tabs!' yelled Frank.

Tabitha whirled round.

Hal was on his knees, spluttering, held tightly in the grip of a tall, thin figure. A slender rapier was drawn, the edge pressed in close against his neck.

'Uh-oh,' said Ty.

The trolls had edged away, and a space was forming, as people saw the figure with the drawn blade and hustled to get away from him. He was dressed in black, and his face was pale.

The face Tabitha had seen earlier, watching them.

Except now, up close, she knew at once who it was.

Chapter Seven

'Colonel Cyrus Derringer,' said Paddy. 'What a delightful surprise.'

Tabitha went for a throwing knife, but the elf saw and pushed the edge of his blade closer into Hal's neck. 'Touch that, and your friend dies.'

Reluctantly Tabitha slid the knife back in its sheath, weighing up her options. Derringer didn't look much like the elf that she remembered. Back in Port Fayt where he commanded the Dockside Militia, he was fresh-faced and clean shaven, dressed in a uniform so smart he looked like a child's tin soldier. Today he was wild-eyed and scowling, his ears hidden underneath an oversized, wide-brimmed hat. There was something on his face too – some kind of make-up that made his skin look darker than normal. More human, in fact.

Disguise, she realized. *He's in disguise, just like us. As a human.*

It would have been laughable, except that Tabitha didn't really feel like laughing, considering that Hal was about to get his throat cut.

'Help,' gurgled the magician.

'I spotted you on the docks,' sneered Derringer. 'You think those disguises fool anyone?'

'Look who's talking,' muttered Frank. 'Anyhow, aren't you supposed to be back in Port Fayt with the militia? What are you doing here?'

'We'll discuss that after you've dropped your weapons, nice and slow.'

'I don't think so,' scoffed Tabitha.

'Do it, Tabs,' said Paddy, reaching to unbuckle his cutlass belt.

'But—'

'Look around.' Paddy indicated behind her. A circle of citizens had formed around them, and it was getting bigger by the second. *They just want to see some bloodshed.* For a moment Tabitha hated them even more than Cyrus.

'We'd best get this over with,' said Frank. 'Won't

be long before the whitecoats show up, and then we'll all be in serious trouble.'

Reluctantly, Tabitha reached for the buckle of her knife belt.

'You too,' Derringer snapped at the man in the turban. 'Hands in the air.'

'Kill him, I don't care,' said Nell's owner. 'I want nothing to do with—'

It happened so fast Tabitha barely registered it. Frank lunged into the crowd, snatched something and hurled it at Cyrus. The elf lashed out instinctively, fending off the missile. At the same instant Paddy dived forward and tugged Hal from Derringer's grasp.

It was only when Hal was stumbling free, and the trolls were drawing their cutlasses, that Tabitha saw the weapon lying on the ground and realized what it was.

A wet, gleaming halibut.

Derringer took less than a second to recover himself. 'Very funny,' he snarled. 'But I suspect you won't be laughing with a sword in your guts.' His blade cut the air in a complex pattern that gave Tabitha a sick feeling. She'd almost forgotten – this elf was the best swordsman in Port Fayt.

Derringer swung at Paddy first, driving the troll

backwards. Paddy was strong, and his cutlass was bigger, but he was no match for the elf's speed. Derringer danced around him, blade flashing, toying with his victim. Frank tried to come to his rescue, but the elf's leg swept round, knocking him off balance and sending him crashing to his knees.

A murmur swelled among the crowd, and a few shouts broke out.

'Go on, mate!'

'Kill 'em! Kill the trolls!'

If the butchers weren't coming already, they will be now. Tabitha snatched up a throwing knife again, but as she drew it back she felt a hand on her arm.

'No, Tabs,' said Hal. 'You might hit one of the twins.'

He was right. Derringer was a fast-moving target, and he was far smaller than the Bootles. His rapier flashed again and Frank let out a soft grunt as the point nicked his arm, and troll blood stained his sleeve. Derringer twirled his blade, a mad grin painted on his face.

'We've got to do something!' Tabitha yelled. 'Hal, can't you use the wooden spoon on him?'

'I don't, er . . .' stuttered the magician. His face was white as a sail. 'I don't have it with me.'

Typical. He must have got worried that it would fall

into the wrong hands and left it at the Academy. The one time they actually needed Hal's magic, he was as useful as a rubber cutlass.

'Is it over yet?' came a tiny voice. Ty was cowering deep inside Tabitha's pocket. It didn't look like he was going to save them either.

Tabitha licked her lips. *So it's up to me.* But what could she do? She couldn't take on Cyrus Derringer herself. She needed something else. Some kind of distraction.

She turned to see that the griffin owner was crouched down, hiding behind his horse. Nell the griffin was on her feet, watching the fight intently. Tabitha raced to the cage, saw that the side swung open and was lashed in place with a couple of strips of leather. She got to work, sawing at it with her knife.

Behind her, she heard the clash of steel, and a gasp from the crowd. She didn't turn to find out what had happened. She didn't have time.

The first strip came apart, and she moved to the second. Nell let out a soft squawk and cocked her head to one side, watching Tabitha with curiosity.

'Don't worry, girl, I'm not going to hurt you.'

'Are you sure this is a good idea, miss?' asked Ty. His head was poking out of her pocket, and he looked sceptical.

Tabitha ignored him. The second strip came loose, and she pulled the door open with a creak. Hands trembling, she reached for the ropes that tied Nell's wings to her side, undoing them as fast as she could.

The griffin owner finally noticed what was happening. 'What are you doing? Leave her alone this—'

Too late. Nell took a step forward, pushed her beak out into the air beyond the cage. She made a low, warbling sound.

'Go on!' Tabitha told her. 'Fly!'

Nell flew. She burst out of the cage, letting out an almighty squawk and spreading her wings like ragged banners.

The crowd's reaction was even better than Tabitha could have hoped for. At once cheers turned to squeals of fear. The next moment there was chaos, people stumbling over each other in their efforts to escape. Tabitha saw Derringer turn, eyes widening as he saw what she had unleashed.

It was all the Bootle brothers needed. Paddy dived at the elf, barrelling into him and sending him crashing to the floor, his sword skittering across the cobblestones. 'Got him!' called the troll.

The griffin strutted on the cobblestones, flapping her wings, sending scraps of greased paper gusting across the street with the force of her downbeats. Her owner scurried towards her, drawing out a whip and shouting obscenities at Tabitha.

I hope he doesn't catch you, Nell.

Hal laid a hand on her shoulder. 'We have to go,' he hissed. 'Look!'

Tabitha followed his pointing finger, and saw men approaching through the chaos, from the end of the street. Men in white, with hard, lean faces. They dealt out savage blows with their muskets. They elbowed people out of the way, kicked aside fallen citizens. And they were heading towards the watchmen.

Don't make a scene – that's what Newt had said.

Apparently it was too late for that.

Frank grabbed Tabitha by the arm, dragging her in the opposite direction, away from the butchers. Paddy was following, bundling Derringer along with him, snatching up the elf's fallen sword in one hand.

'Wait!' Tabitha yelped. 'The griffin owner – he knows where Jeb is! We can find Joseph, we need to—'

'He's not going to help us now, Tabs,' said Frank firmly.

'Yes, but—'

There was a thundering of boots on cobblestones and a clattering of cutlasses as the whitecoats broke into a run, and suddenly Tabitha wasn't arguing any more. The sight of those charging butchers brought back memories of the ones at the Battle of Illon, of their sabres rising and falling as they attacked the Fayters, their white coats spattered with red . . .

And then she was running along with the crowd, along with Hal, along with Frank and Paddy, her heart thumping with terror.

Somewhere at the back of her mind guilt nagged at her, not quite strong enough to overcome her fear.

I'm sorry, Joseph. We failed you.

Chapter Eight

J oseph was safe.

Safe in Port Fayt, in the house with the green front door. Safe at home.

He lay in his cot, a baby all over again, nestled in blankets. A fire crackled in the hearth and his father's face hovered above him, shining with love.

'Sleep tight, young 'un.'

Joseph could hardly believe it. After so many years they were really together again – his family. The only thing he'd ever wanted. He looked up into the face of his father, Elijah Grubb, marvelling at the magic of that smile. The sparkle of those eyes.

'Again!' he begged.

His father wiggled his ears up and down, and Joseph chuckled.

'Again!'

His father crossed his eyes and stuck out his tongue. 'It's time to sleep now, Joseph,' he said gently, when Joseph's laughter had died down.

'No! Story. Please!'

'You've already had a story. But I'll sit beside you while you fall asleep. How's that?' He held out his silver pocket watch, and Joseph lost himself in the *tick tock, tick tock* of the second hand. 'I'll keep watch, Joseph. I'll make sure the mice don't nibble your toes. I love you, Joseph. Don't ever forget that.'

Joseph's lips curled into a smile to match his father's. He closed his eyes.

'What are you doing?' said a new voice.

He opened them again and saw that another face had appeared.

'Mother?'

No, it was someone else. A girl with blue hair.

'Why are you being a baby?' said Tabitha.

Joseph tried to answer, but he couldn't.

'Come on! You've got to get out. You've got to keep going. You can't just give up . . .'

*

When Joseph woke, the wigs were still there.

Wigs in all shapes and sizes. Some were draped over wooden heads on shelves, covered in silky cobwebs. Others exploded out of old, half-rotten boxes. Still more lay limp and trampled on the floorboards like dead rats. Enormous, white-powdered monstrosities for flashy merchants; subtle wigs that looked like natural heads of hair; even bizarre multi-coloured creations decked out with ribbons. In the glow of a lantern that hung from the rafters they seemed to watch Joseph, like an audience of malicious animals, waiting to see what he would do next.

Nothing, apparently.

He'd already examined every inch of the attic, and found no hope of escape. No windows – just the solid oak beams of the rafters. The only light came from the lantern and what little filtered around the trap door. It was thick, heavy and bolted shut. Maybe if he was an ogre he could have jumped on it and broken it from its hinges. *Maybe.* But he was just a weedy mongrel boy.

In the end he'd given up and done his best to sleep, but he hadn't managed more than a few hours of fitful slumber all night long.

Perhaps this was part of the cat's revenge – making

him wait in horrible uncertainty. The ginger-haired shapeshifter clearly hadn't forgotten what had happened back in Fayt when Joseph had first met him. How Joseph had turned him over to the Demon's Watch. How the watchmen had sent the shapeshifter back to the Old World, soaking wet and trapped in a cage.

He slumped in his corner, one hand clenched tight around the silver pocket watch. A gift from his mother to his father, and now it was his. The only thing he had left in all the world. The shapeshifters had taken his cutlass and his money pouch, and worst of all, the wooden spoon.

They know exactly what it is.

Without it, his plan was hopeless. He had no hope of getting out of here. No hope of getting Jeb the Snitch to talk.

The metal of the watch glowed orange in the light of the lantern, and Joseph's fingers ran over the inscription once again, as they had every day he'd been on the sea, travelling to Azurmouth. *To my dearest Elijah, with all my love, Eleanor.* He'd dwelt on those words more than he'd admit to anyone. They fired his heart, driving him to keep going.

For six years, he'd been on his own. *Elijah Grubb was murdered by dockhands.* That was what the blackcoats had said. *They killed him for marrying a human.* Joseph's mother had died soon afterwards, and he'd been all alone.

Until the day Jeb told him that his father was alive and well, somewhere in Azurmouth.

The truth. I have to find the truth. His father had always told him not to give up. That he was as good as any of the boys in the street who called him mongrel, or blotch-face, or half-and-half. Better, because he was special. *Half goblin and half human. There aren't many who can say that, eh, Joseph?*

Whatever it took, he was going to hear that voice again. See that smile. He was going to get the wooden spoon back. Escape the wig shop and the shape-shifters. Find Jeb the Snitch and make that slimy bilge bag talk.

Joseph leaped up and paced the floorboards, searching for anything he might use to get out. But this time he did more than look. He walked slowly and deliberately, feeling the plaster of the walls, listening to the creaks of the boards beneath his feet.

He could hear voices coming from below, and he knelt, pushing his ear to the floor. The sound was too muffled to make out any words, but he could distinguish the deep, rumbling voice of the horse, and the playful, rapid patter of the cat.

There was a third voice too, though he didn't recognize it.

A door creaked as it opened, and the mystery voice rose in farewell. The door closed, and the cat and the horse held a brief, murmured conversation.

And then Joseph heard the thud of feet on steps, as they began to climb the stairs.

They're coming. Coming to take revenge on me.

He didn't have time to be frightened. He cast around again, looking for something – anything – to use against them. Some kind of weapon. But there was nothing except the lantern, and the wigs.

Wait . . .

Joseph surged to his feet and seized an armful of wigs from the nearest shelf. He dumped them on top of the trap door. He grabbed another load and piled them on top. Then another, and another, until there was a heap of hair covering the door, like a mound of dead rats.

Like a bonfire, waiting to be lit.

Hands shaking, Joseph unhooked the lantern from its chain, placed it on the floor and carefully took out the stub of candle inside. Slowly, cautiously, he brought it to his heap of hair. If the flame went out, he'd be left in darkness, with no hope of escape. If it didn't, he'd soon have a raging fire on his hands.

He hesitated. *Is this crazy?* If it worked, the fire might burn right through the trap door. The flames and the smoke might distract his captors enough for him to make a break for it.

Or I'll be trapped in a burning attic with no escape.

'Yes, I see the problem.'

Joseph jerked backwards, setting the candle flame guttering. The voice had come from right beside his ear – but the attic was empty.

'I'm here.' It was a soft, hissing voice, no more than a whisper. 'Look a little closer.'

Movement blurred at the edge of Joseph's vision. Yes – there *was* something there. Something dangling from the rafters, on a glistening thread of silk.

'I've been watching you,' said the spider, and it made a strange little clicking sound that could only be laughter.

At any other time, in any other place, Joseph would have thought he was going mad. But he knew at once what this was.

A shapeshifter. Another one.

He felt a sudden rush of anger. 'Spying on me, you mean.'

'If you like.'

'How long have you been there?' The spider's limbs curled. A shrug, Joseph realized. 'Who are you?'

'They call us the Quiet Three. The cat, the horse and the spider.' The spider revolved slowly on its thread. 'Now it's my turn. You are an enigma, little boy. You have come across the ocean, bringing that wooden spoon with you. You know what it is, don't you? What it can do?'

'Of course.'

'Which only deepens the mystery. Think of the danger you have brought upon yourself. In this city even a pure goblin is in danger. A mongrel . . . it is an abomination. A foul union of seraph-born and demonspawn. So why are you here?'

'You tell me,' snapped Joseph. 'You're the ones who kidnapped me.' It wasn't so hard, standing up to a spider. 'The cat and the horse – who were they talking to just now?'

The spider laughed. 'If you hold your silence, I'm afraid I must hold mine.' And without another word it began to ascend the thread of silk, disappearing into the shadows of the rafters.

For a moment Joseph thought of lunging forward, trying to catch the shapeshifter in his cupped hands. Too late, he remembered the footsteps on the staircase. *Idiot! If I hadn't let the spider distract me . . .*

He reached forward again with the candle, but the

trap door opened and wigs scattered in all directions. Yellow eyes gleamed in the darkness, watching him, rooting him to the spot.

'Come along now, mongrel,' said the cat. 'It's time.'

Chapter Nine

It's time, thought Newton. *Time to find out if I'm right.*

Corin's Street was a little less filthy than the surrounding city, but no less packed with citizens. Salesmen had set up in the shadow of the trees that lined the road, flogging toy swords and colourful flags with the names of contestants emblazoned on them. Grifters moved among the throng, taking bets on the fighting. Newton heard the name 'Lucky Leo' mentioned more than once.

He was beginning to regret the hooded cloak he'd borrowed from Master Gurney. It was supposed to make him inconspicuous, but from the awed looks

100

people were giving him he reckoned he was wearing some kind of official magician's gown. He kept his head down and pushed on uphill, craning his neck to get a glimpse of the building they were all heading towards.

It wasn't hard to spot. The House of Light shone gleaming white at the end of the road, reflecting the noon sunshine so brightly that he had to shield his eyes.

Newton felt a flicker of doubt. *Am I doing the right thing?* The other watchmen didn't know where he was going. But if he'd told them, they would have tried to stop him. They wouldn't have understood – *this isn't a choice.* He'd made a mistake, and it was up to him to put it right.

No matter what it cost.

If you believed the stories, Corin the Bold had built the House of Light after the Battle of the Three Forests, and laid some of the foundation stones himself. Since then the dukes of Garran had passed it down, one to another, maintaining it at the heart of Azurmouth. 'Let the sky have its sun,' went the saying. 'Azurmouth has the House of Light.'

As he got closer, Newton could make out black shapes on the outer battlements – figures fixed on long metal spikes, high above those white, pristine walls. They were goblins, most of them, with the odd imp and a dwarf or two. A troll or an ogre would probably have been too heavy. He realized he was rubbing at the marks on his wrists again, and forced himself to stop. His heart felt heavy. His legs too, as though they were unwilling to carry him any further.

He strode on through the gate.

A cobbled courtyard lay beyond, crammed with excitable citizens. In the centre was a wooden platform, raised up above the heads of the crowd so that everyone could see it. Beyond, the façade of the House of Light extended upwards, so high that the top of it could barely be seen. A balcony two floors up had been hung with an enormous banner – the Golden Sun, embroidered in thick gold thread.

Newton found a spot in the shadow of the outer walls and drew his hood up around his head, counting whitecoats. There were at least a hundred posted around the battlements of the outer walls, he reckoned, and a good fifty or so stationed around the courtyard. Thalin knew how many more would be inside.

Breaking into the House of Light wouldn't exactly be a stroll along the pier, but if his hunch was right, he would have to do it all the same. He had to make up for what he'd done.

The face of an ancient elf flashed in his memory, just as it had every day – every hour – they'd been on the sea. The face of a blue-coated watchman. The face of a friend he'd let down.

You didn't die for nothing, Jon. I'll make sure of it.

A trumpet sounded, and was joined by many more, a triumphant fanfare that rose to one long, swelling note before dying away. Immediately the sound was replaced by whoops and cheers and applause as figures appeared on the balcony up above. The marks on Newton's wrists began to prickle again at the sight of them.

They were all dressed in white, festooned with sashes, medals and plumed hats. First came a bevy of young men, their faces soft and fat with privilege. Then older statesmen, grey-haired and worn. The lords of the League. These men were responsible for everything. For the zephyrum mines. For the Crying Mountains. *For the Battle of Illon.*

An enormous, walrus-like man with bristling grey mutton chops took his place near the centre of the balcony. His chest was a sea of gold and silver medals, and his sash was bright red in contrast with the pure white of his companions' uniforms.

'Hail the Earl of Brindenheim!' shouted someone nearby, and others took up the shout. The walrus man smiled and raised a hand to acknowledge the greeting.

Next came a white-coated woman, long blonde hair tied back, icy blue eyes as calm as ever. Major Turnbull, whose father had run the zephyrum mines at Wyborough, and who had fought Newton on board the League's flagship at the Battle of Illon. A deadly swordswoman, and a magician to boot.

Looming beyond her, in the shadowy interior, Newton saw something he would never have expected. An ogre, dressed in footman's livery. He was staring blankly into space, as though he had seen enough of the world and decided it wasn't for him. *Probably from the mines*, thought Newton. *And now kept in the House of Light as some kind of servant.*

A spark of anger flickered in his belly.

The crowd stirred as a small figure appeared from inside and began to make his way to the very front and centre of the balcony. *There he is. The man who killed Old Jon.* The spark flared into a bonfire, and Newton felt his hands clench into fists.

The Duke of Garran was baby-faced, pink-skinned and clad in white just like the others. But at the same time there was something different about him. Something in the easy way he greeted the other lords, and the way he brushed off his coat as he took his place in the centre of the group, his pale eyes sweeping the crowd.

Then Newton realized it wasn't something in the Duke himself. It was the way the others looked at him. Their nervous glances. Their shuffling feet.

They're afraid of him.

'Citizens of Azurmouth,' said the Duke. He spoke softly, but it carried out across the courtyard, silencing every conversation at once. 'Today is Corin's Day. Welcome, all of you, to the House of Light!'

Applause broke like a wave through the courtyard.

'Long live the Duke of Garran!'

'Here's to the Duke!'

'Corin save him!'

The cheering swelled again as the League's swordsmen began to climb onto the wooden platform, tall and strong and handsome in white. Trumpets sounded as the champions strutted, smiled and waved.

Newton spared them no more than a glance. They all looked the same, anyway: athletic and smug. Instead his gaze was fixed on the balcony, where the Duke of Garran stood, his white plume quivering in the breeze. The Duke, who'd shot Newton's oldest friend in front of him, left him bleeding on the deck, and smiled as he did it.

The anger burned hotter, fiercer in the pit of his stomach.

No. Not now. It was his anger that had got Old Jon killed in the first place. He couldn't afford to lose his temper. Not now. Not ever again.

Something caught his eye in the courtyard below. A plump, dark-haired youth had taken to the platform, and the cheers from the crowd had grown even louder with his appearance.

'Lucky Leo!' someone called out. 'Let's make it six times, eh?'

Leopold smirked as he acknowledged his admirers, tossing his dark fringe from his face, drawing his sword with a flourish and posing as if he were some mighty warrior from the Dark Age.

That sword . . .

The hilt – shining silver and studded with milk-white star-stones. The blade – long and slender, carved with swirling patterns from an ancient time.

It was the sword that had lain for centuries at Wyrmwood Manor, until Newton had brought it to Illon, to use in battle against the Duke of Garran.

The sword the Duke had snatched from him and brought back to Azurmouth.

The sword that Newton had crossed the Ebony Ocean to retrieve. *The Sword of Corin.*

*

Something is wrong.

The Duke feels it as soon as Lucky Leo takes the stage. Turning, he sees that the Earl of Brindenheim is watching him.

He stiffens. There is a look on the old fool's face that makes him wary. Brindenheim is smiling, but even more smugly than usual. There is energy in that smile and – yes – triumph.

For once, Brindenheim knows something he doesn't.

'Leopold of Brindenheim!' calls a herald from below.

'Bravo,' calls the fat old Earl, clapping his podgy hands together and spraying spittle into the air. 'Bravo, Leo.'

Lucky Leo is preening and posing, basking in the applause. His black hair is oiled and combed back for the occasion, and he is dressed in dazzling fencing whites, yet still he manages to give the impression of a plucked chicken ready for the pot. He takes up position in the centre of the platform, legs wide apart, and places his hand on the hilt of his sword.

The Duke peers closer. That sword . . .

Leo grins inanely and draws, the blade flashing in the sun as he holds it aloft.

Yes – the Sword of Corin.

'I know what you think of my son's fighting skills,' says the Earl of Brindenheim. He is leaning in close, lowering

his voice so the other lords cannot hear him. 'So I'm sure you will agree – if he is to win the contest, he must have a fine blade.'

The Duke thinks of the secret room where Major Turnbull left it. The iron door that held it, and the four whitecoats charged with its protection. It cannot have been easy for Brindenheim's men to find where the sword was hidden, and the whitecoats would not have given it up without surrendering their own lives first.

He smiles icily. 'I wonder where you found such a thing?'

'I think you know where,' replies Brindenheim. 'I heard a rumour that you had recovered it at the Battle of Illon, and I hoped you would have no objection if I . . . borrowed it. After all, the spoils of war should be shared openly amongst the lords of the League. We are all equals, are we not?'

'But of course.'

'Then naturally, I see no need to tell our fellow lords that the blade my son is wielding is the legendary Sword of Corin.'

Blackmail – who would have guessed the old walrus could be so bold?

So bold, and so foolish.

Brindenheim did not take the sword because he has guessed what the Duke is planning. He did not even *take it so that his prancing fop of a son has something pretty to fight with. He took it to prove that the Duke is no more powerful than him.*

That they are equals.

They are not.

'Your son is most welcome to it,' the Duke says softly. 'I am only sorry he will not be borrowing it for very long.'

Brindenheim's grin falters, as though he has an inkling of the mistake he has made. Yes – soon enough, he will be sorrier than he can imagine. No man stands against the Way of the Light.

The words of the rhyme run through the Duke's head, as they have so often since his return to Azurmouth.

At the call of the sword, twelve stones shall sing,
Twelve seraphs rise, in a golden ring . . .

He turns back to the courtyard, where Lucky Leo has lowered the blade above the heads of the crowd nearest the platform. They reach up like lambs begging to be fed, desperate to lay their fingers on it.

They have no idea what it is they are touching.

PART TWO
The Contest of Blades

Chapter Ten

Tabitha flung open the door to Master Gurney's rooms, panting heavily. The magician was bent over his desk, peering at a chicken, which sat on a pile of books, ruffling its feathers as though it didn't have a clue what it was doing there.

'You managed it, then?' asked Frank. 'Bravo.'

Master Gurney looked up sharply. 'Managed what? Oh yes, I see. No, my good fellow, turning an egg into a chicken turned out to be rather troublesome. So what I am now attempting to do is to turn this chicken into . . . er . . .'

'An egg?' said Tabitha. She pulled off her bandana and dropped it on a pile of books. They'd run almost the whole way back from the docks, and her clothes were sticky with sweat.

'Quite right! Yes, you'll go far, young lady.'

The door swung open again and Paddy wrestled Derringer into the room. The elf had been stubbornly silent since the fight on the docks. His make-up was peeling off, and his hat was lopsided, but he still glared at them as disdainfully as he had when he wore his official Dockside Militia uniform. Ty took off from Tabitha's pocket to settle on top of a bookcase, watching the elf suspiciously as Paddy settled him in a chair.

'And who, pray, is this gentleman?' asked Master Gurney, examining Derringer over the top of his spectacles.

'We're so sorry for the interruption, Master,' said Hal, mopping his brow. 'This is Colonel Cyrus Derringer, of the Dockside Militia.'

'I see. And what is he doing here?'

'Good question,' said Frank. 'How about it Cyrus? What *are* you doing here?'

For a moment Derringer looked like he was going to keep playing dumb. Then his lip curled. 'You're all under arrest.'

Ty giggled from his bookcase. 'Maybe I heard that wrong.'

'*You're* not supposed to be here,' snapped the elf. 'None of you! Governor Skelmerdale has ordered me to take you back to Fayt at once. Did you really think that after the Battle of Illon, you could simply sail straight into the League's greatest port? If the Duke of Garran caught you he'd execute you as spies and send another fleet over the ocean.'

'Well, personally, I'm flattered,' said Frank. 'Never knew old Skelmerdale cared about us so.'

'What about Joseph?' Tabitha cut in. 'Do you know where he is? Did you see him anywhere on the docks?'

'Who in Thalin's name is Joseph?'

Tabitha slumped onto a pile of spell books, sending up a cloud of dust. So far so bad. They'd barely escaped the whitecoats with their lives. Their only lead had been the griffin owner, and he was long gone by now. And where was Newton? He was supposed to be leading them, not sneaking off on mysterious missions all by himself.

We'll find you, Joseph. I promise. He had to be here, somewhere in the city.

'If you'll allow me to interject,' said Master Gurney, 'I should really prefer it if—'

The door swung open once again, and a large figure in a hooded gown ducked under the lintel.

Tabitha shot up from her seat. 'Newt!'

'Nice outfit,' said Frank. 'Very . . . magic-y.'

'Don't tell us you've been transmogrifying chickens too?' said Paddy.

Newton drew back his hood and gave Master Gurney a nod. Tabitha saw at once that he was sweating, as though he'd been moving fast, but his eyes were gleaming. 'Had one or two things to take care of,' he said.

'Yes, but what does that have to do with Joseph?' Tabitha demanded. 'We're supposed to be rescuing him, remember? That's why we came here in the first place!'

They were running out of time – she just knew it. Any moment Joseph could be caught and strung up by butchers. Or stabbed in an alley. Or sent to the zephyrum mines. The tavern boy was a total, utter bilge brain for coming to Azurmouth on his own, chasing some crazy lies about his father. What was he thinking?

She tried to imagine what she would do, if someone told her that her own father was alive. She'd only been a baby when her parents died, but somehow she knew exactly what they were like. Alfred Mandeville, governor of Port Fayt – tall, gentle and kind. And Jessica Mandeville, young and beautiful, with a smile for everyone she met . . .

I'd want to know the truth. Whatever it cost.

Her face felt hot and uncomfortable, and she dabbed angrily at her eyes.

I will not cry. Whatever happens, I will not cry.

'Don't worry, Tabs,' said Paddy gently. 'We'll find him. Besides, Joseph can handle himself. He's got his cutlass, hasn't he?'

Newton cleared his throat. 'Aye, we'll find him. But first things first. Will someone explain to me what Cyrus Derringer is doing here?'

The elf glared at Newton, but held his tongue.

'Ran into him on the docks,' said Frank. 'He says he's here to arrest us. Caused a right scene with all his fancy sword-swishing. We had to run from the butchers.'

'Pardon me,' said Master Gurney, who seemed to have totally lost interest in his chicken. 'But did you say the *butchers*?'

'They followed you?' asked Newton.

''Fraid so,' said Paddy. 'Reckon we lost them, though.'

'But they saw you?'

Frank nodded.

'That's bad. They'll be looking for us. And you got no leads on Joseph?'

117

Paddy shook his head and jerked a thumb at Derringer. 'Not before we ran into this cheery cove.'

'Dear, oh dear,' muttered Master Gurney.

Newton sank into an old rocking chair in the corner and pulled out his pipe. For half a second Tabitha could have sworn he looked weary, as though it was all too much for him. She couldn't remember ever seeing him like that before. There was a long silence as he stuffed his pipe with tobacco, his brow creased in thought. Then at last he spoke.

'My apologies, Master Gurney. Seems things aren't working out as quick as we'd hoped.'

Derringer sneered. 'Typical incompetence.'

'Shut it,' said Frank.

'Please,' said Master Gurney, waving a hand dismissively. 'Your business is your own. Just so long as you refrain from bringing the League to my door, I shall be content. Now, it seems you gentlemen have things to discuss. I'll give you a little space, shall I? As it happens I need to pay a visit to the henhouse. I fear this chicken may be defective.' He gazed sadly at the bird on his desk, which was still undeniably a chicken, and not an egg, before sweeping it up in his arms and bustling out of the room.

As soon as they were alone, Newton let out a sigh. 'Nothing else for it. We'll have to lie low until the end of the day. First thing tomorrow we'll figure out a better way to find Joseph.'

Tabitha could hardly believe what she was hearing. 'But he could be anywhere by then!'

'He could be anywhere now,' said Newton firmly. 'I'm sorry, Tabs, but we can't allow the League to find out that the Demon's Watch is here in Azurmouth. It could put everyone in danger – not just us and Master Gurney, but the whole Academy, and Port Fayt too. They'll think we're spies, or worse. Can you imagine what would happen if the League sends another fleet to attack Fayt? We beat them once, but we couldn't do it again.'

'So what do we do, Newt?' asked Frank.

'I'd say Ty's our best bet for now. He can head out and scour the city. He doesn't have a shark tattoo, and he can escape quickly. Back by dusk though, understand?'

'I'll do my best, mister,' said Ty, saluting. 'Not promising nothing, though.' He leaped off the bookcase and darted out of the window.

'And what do you intend to do with me?' Derringer demanded.

Newton ignored him. 'The rest of you – sit tight at the Academy till I get back.'

'What do you mean, *till I get back*?' snapped

Tabitha. She felt the tears welling again, and fought them down fiercely. 'You can't tell us to wait here, then head out into the city all on your own.' He was up to something. Something to do with that night in the library. Something to do with the Sword of Corin. *But what?*

Newton lit his pipe, avoiding Tabitha's glare. 'I won't be on my own,' he said. 'I'm taking our friend Cyrus here with me.'

Chapter Eleven

Joseph was bundled down the steps into a big room directly below the attic. Sunlight filtered through a small, grubby window, leaving most of the room in shadow. The walls were shelved and cluttered with busts and wigs, just like in the attic, and in the middle of the room sat a plain wooden table and chairs. A selection of tools was spread out on the table. Tinderboxes. Wooden clothes pegs. Crowbars. Keys. Knives.

His heart jumped at the sight. *They're going to torture me!* No, that was ridiculous. You couldn't torture someone with clothes pegs. Could you?

The horse thrust Joseph into a chair, pinning him

down with hands that felt large, strong and entirely immoveable. The cat came behind, closing the door quietly. He moved so much like the animal that Joseph half expected him to curl up in a patch of sunshine and start licking his paws.

No such luck.

A third figure materialized out of the darkness from a corner of the room. A pale, cadaverous woman, dressed entirely in black. Her eyes were tiny, solid black and glistening, and she was completely bald – without even any eyebrows. She looked like a walking skeleton.

The spider, Joseph realized with a jolt.

The three shapeshifters loomed over him, watching, appraising. They made an odd trio, but no less menacing for that. The cat leaned suddenly across the table, peering curiously at Joseph's face. For a second Joseph could have sworn his nostrils flared, as though he were snuffling at a mouse hole.

Joseph changed his mind again. *They're definitely going to torture me. Or kill me. Or both. They're dangerous criminals, and I got one of them arrested.*

He didn't stand a chance.

'I—' he began, but the spider laid a long, bony finger over her lips.

'You took this from me once,' said the cat. He

drew the wooden spoon from his pocket. 'Back in Port Fayt. I stole it, and you stole it back from me. Do you recall?'

Joseph was gripped by sudden desperation. Somehow, the thought of his own death seemed less terrible than the loss of the spoon. 'Please,' he said. 'I need it. Just for a day. You can have it afterwards, I swear, then you can do what you like to me.'

Maybe they'd take pity on him? His father had always told him, *There's a little bit of demon and a little bit of seraph in everyone, Joseph. Don't let anyone tell you different.*

'We don't want it,' said the spider. Even in human form her voice was barely a whisper, and her strange black eyes gave nothing away.

'Don't need it,' said the horse.

'You underestimate us, mongrel,' said the cat. He leaned forward and tucked the spoon into Joseph's pocket. 'We are no greedy, grasping goblins. We care nothing for the value of what we steal. What we care for is the game. And we have found a new game to play.'

'A bigger game,' said the horse.

'A better game,' said the spider.

Joseph clamped his hand firmly over his pocket. What kind of cruel trick was this? Surely, any moment now, the cat would laugh and snatch his prize back.

'You're going to let me keep it?' he said cautiously.

'Indeed,' said the cat, his yellow eyes twinkling. 'Though if I were you, I should leave it well alone. Such a powerful wand in the hands of a mongrel boy. You really have no idea what it could do to you, if you were to misuse it.' The spider chuckled.

Joseph thought fast, trying to ignore the thumping of his heart. After all the shapeshifter had gone through to steal it, he was content to pass up the spoon. *So what does he want from me?*

'Can I go then?' he asked.

'How precious,' said the cat. 'But I'm afraid not. My lady, if you'd be so good?'

The spider produced a large scroll of paper and unfurled it on the table. It looked like one of the maps Joseph had seen captains poring over in the Legless Mermaid. Except instead of islands and currents, the map showed a building. A vast, sprawling building, seen from above, with windows, doors and walls marked on in thin, delicate lines of ink.

'What is this?'

'Why, this is our game, of course,' said the cat. 'A game for which we require your assistance. A mongrel boy with a certain wit. It is the least you owe me, after your troublesome interference when I visited

Port Fayt. And who knows?' He smiled, stirring up Joseph's unease all over again. 'Perhaps your little spoon will prove useful too.'

If Azurmouth smelled bad, its sewers were a thousand times worse. Even the wooden clothes peg clamped over Joseph's nose could barely protect him from the stench of the dark sludge that flowed around their ankles, carrying with it the occasional lobster shell, broken tankard or shattered pair of eyeglasses. They said that goblins had a better nose than most, but Joseph would have traded his for anything at that moment.

That reminded him of the wooden-nosed goblin who'd tried to kill him at the Grey Brotherhood, which didn't make him feel any better.

Instead, he concentrated on the vaulted brick tunnel extending into blackness ahead, and forced himself not to look at the sewage below. He could still feel it of course, now liquid, now uncomfortably solid . . . The shapeshifters were wearing long, heavy wading boots, but there hadn't been a spare pair for Joseph. The next chance he got, he was going to scrub his feet like he'd never scrubbed them before.

Where are we going? They hadn't killed him – not yet. They'd even given him a bowl of stew to eat, and let him have his cutlass back. When he'd asked why, the spider had laughed and replied, 'Why not?' *It's an insult*, Joseph had realized. *They know I couldn't hurt them, however much I wanted to.*

He felt the reassuring weight of the wooden spoon in his pocket. But even that gave him a twinge of unease. What was it the cat had said? *You really have no idea what it could do to you* . . . Did the shapeshifter know something he didn't? And anyway, why was he here – what could a mongrel boy like Joseph have to offer the Quiet Three? And what had the cat meant about the spoon being useful?

So many questions. But whatever was happening, he had no choice except to go along with it. The cat and the horse went ahead, still in human form, the horse striding casually through the centre of the sewage, the cat skirting round the edge of it, hopping between bits of dry brickwork like . . . well, like a cat.

Every now and then Joseph heard a rustle of clothing behind him, but nothing more. The spider was disturbingly quiet as she brought up the rear. No danger of Joseph running away, with that dark presence behind him. If he was going to bolt anywhere, it would be forwards, and he didn't fancy his chances with the massive bulk of the horse in the way.

'Nearly there.' The horse's voice echoed off the brickwork.

Nearly where? They'd been going for hours, Joseph reckoned, but it was too dark to check the time on his father's pocket watch. All he knew was that he was tired, and his feet hurt, and still they kept walking.

The sewers were empty and silent but for the distant rumble of cartwheels above and the echoes of dripping in side tunnels. Some time ago, they'd crossed paths with a pair of imps dressed in ragged, filthy clothing. The strangers had watched them with a haunted look, and only moved on when they seemed sure the shapeshifters wouldn't hurt them.

Beggars, or prisoners fleeing from justice. The League's justice.

'Here,' said the spider suddenly. She pulled the clothes peg from her nose, and Joseph and the others followed suit.

Joseph peered all around him, but he couldn't see anything except the tunnel carrying on in both directions. The brickwork was old and ramshackle. Weeds grew through cracks, clinging on to life against the odds. Joseph was glad of the darkness – the smell wasn't so bad here, but the dripping and scuttling noises from the shadows weren't exactly making him curious about their surroundings.

The cat lit a lantern and held it up to a patch of the wall. In the soft glow, Joseph saw that his captor was smiling. Brimming with excitement. *The game has begun.*

'Excellent work, my lady,' the cat said.

'It's just a wall,' said Joseph dumbly.

Ice-cold fingers found the back of his neck, making him gasp and flinch away. The spider chuckled, a sound like ancient, rustling paper.

'*Just* a wall?' she said. 'But to one such as myself, a wall can be many things. A home. A ladder. Or even an *entrance.*'

The spider smiled, a horrible leer that made Joseph's skin crawl. And the next moment her black clothes fell in a heap, empty. She was gone. The horse reached down and plucked something from among them, holding it up against the brickwork – a small black shape which scuttled off his hand, climbing upwards and disappearing suddenly through a crack.

'She glides through gaps,' said the horse.

'Crawls through crevices,' added the cat. 'She will find us a way in.'

'A way in to where?' tried Joseph.

'Patience,' said the cat.

Chapter Twelve

'Whatever you want from me,' said Cyrus Derringer, 'I won't do it.'

Newton gripped the elf's arm tightly as they made their way through the back streets of Azurmouth. Derringer was back in his make-up, and Newton wore a plain cloak with the hood drawn up to conceal his shark tattoo. Even so, they stuck to the shadows.

'You and I haven't always seen eye to eye,' Newton murmured. 'I know that, Cyrus.'

'You betrayed me at Illon. The fleet was mine to command, but you took charge of it yourself.'

'Aye, someone had to. And before that, you stabbed me in the leg with that fancy rapier of yours. But let's let bygones be bygones. Trust me, I'm doing this for Port Fayt.'

'Trust you? You won't even tell me where we're going.'

They turned into a narrow alleyway, where a back door was set into the rear of a large townhouse. The door was guarded by two men in silver coats, their hair tied back with silver ribbons, their cutlass hilts moulded into the shapes of roaring dragons. Probably the classiest bully boys Newton had ever seen. Above the doorway words were etched into the stone lintel – *The Fencing House of the Silver Dragon.*

Derringer's eyes widened, and he stopped dead. 'Wait . . . you want me to enter the Contest of Blades?'

'I'll be straight with you, Cyrus. The Duke of Garran took something from me, at the Battle of Illon. A sword. I need it back, and I reckon this contest is the best way to get it.'

Derringer scowled. 'That's ridiculous. Why go to so much trouble for a sword?'

'I don't know. Not exactly. I just . . . I have a hunch that it's important.' He paused. 'For Fayt.'

At the call of the sword, twelve stones shall sing,
Twelve seraphs rise, in a golden ring . . .

Newton licked his lips. 'Admit it, Cyrus. You've always wanted to enter the contest. You're the finest swordsman in Port Fayt. But are you the finest in the Old World?'

'I see what you're trying to do,' said Derringer. 'It's pathetic.'

But Newton could tell by the glint in his eye that he was tempted. Arrogance had always been the elf's weakness. *He thinks he's the best, and I'm giving him a chance to prove it.*

It was all or nothing now. Newton drew the elf's rapier from beneath his cloak and held it out, hilt first.

'Maybe this'll help you trust me. Here, take it.'

Cautiously, Derringer closed his fingers around the hilt.

'I don't buy that story you told us,' said Newton, still holding the blade flat on his palms. 'You didn't come all the way over the Ebony Ocean to arrest us, did you? Not all on your own. Where are your black-coats?' Back in Port Fayt, Derringer had never gone anywhere without an escort of militiamen to back him up.

For a moment, the elf's expression flickered with something unexpected. *Is he . . . embarrassed?*

'They're . . . I mean, they were . . . captured by the butchers.'

'If you say so. I reckon there's some other reason you're here. And I don't know what that is, but I know one thing – you'll never get a chance like this again. A chance to win the contest. *Cyrus Derringer – greatest swordsman in all the Old World*. Imagine it.'

The elf hesitated, and for a moment, Newton half expected him to bury the blade in his guts. His whole plan depended on this. Master Gurney had pulled a lot of strings to get Cyrus entered into the contest – a magician's word counted for a lot in Azurmouth. But if the elf refused to fight, everything would fall apart.

'I'll do it,' said Derringer suddenly.

'Really?'

A smug smile spread over the elf's face. He whipped the blade up and flicked his wrist, cutting the air close to Newton's right ear with a soft hum. Newton managed not to flinch – just.

'But if I win the contest, you and your watchmen will come quietly back to Fayt with me. You'll surrender to the governor, and whatever punishment he deems suitable. Understand?'

Newton's jaw clenched, but he nodded all the same. 'Aye. It's a deal.'

Half an hour later the crowd were chanting Colonel Derringer's name.

'Cyrus! Cyrus! Cyrus!'

Newton had never seen the elf look so happy. Strutting on the fencing floor, he was practically glowing with joy, which would have been easier to stomach if he didn't look quite so pleased with himself. He raised his sword in triumph, and the chanting crashed like a wave in an almighty cheer.

The fencing floor rose like a scaffold, bounded with red velvet ropes – a touch of class that seemed a little wasted on the drunken spectators. Newton's eyes watered from the pipe smoke that hung above them, haunting the dark, cavernous interior of the fencing house like a bad omen. Someone had sloshed a tankard of grog onto his arm, and a child who couldn't see was shoving at him from behind. But he kept his gaze fixed on Cyrus Derringer.

One more. Just one more fight, and then we're through. Through to the final of the contest, in the House of Light itself. Where, according to Master Gurney, Lucky Leo would be waiting for them.

Lucky Leo, and the Sword of Corin.

Newton had to admit it – Cyrus was good. He'd beaten two opponents, each in less than five minutes. The first had been a merchant with an expensive sword and none of the skill to go with it. Derringer had disarmed him on the first stroke and tripped him over.

Some of the crowd had laughed, but others had jeered, angry to be cheated out of a proper fight. Derringer hadn't liked that.

The second was a country boy, strong and quick-witted. This time Derringer had indulged his audience, showing off some fancy footwork and slashing dramatically, unnecessarily. By the end of the bout the boy was collapsed on his knees, a blade at his throat, the crowd whooping with glee.

There was a tense hush as Derringer's final opponent climbed the steps and ducked under the velvet rope.

Just one more.

It was a League fighter, dressed in white. He was sandy-haired, big and flabby – but the easy way he carried himself made Newton nervous. He turned to smile at the crowd, and Newton breathed in sharply.

'Ain't seen one o' them before?' said the child, who'd managed to push in next to him. 'That's the League's brand, that is.' Seared into the fighter's forehead was a symbol – a blazing sun formed of white ridges.

Newton ran his thumb over one of the red marks on his wrists. The League had scarred them both. 'What did he do to deserve that?' he asked.

The child giggled. 'He ain't *do* nothing! He *chose* to get branded. Shows how tough he is, I reckon. Like that funny shark you got on your cheek.'

Newton hastily pulled his hood across to cover the tattoo. *He chose it.* The pity he'd felt had disappeared at once, like a blown-out candle.

Still smiling, the branded man drew a heavy, curved blade, dulled and battered and stained with blood. It sent another chill down Newton's spine.

A silver-coated marshal stepped forward. 'When the handkerchief touches the platform, you may begin.' He tossed the scrap of silver silk in the air, then scrambled into the crowd as it floated gently down.

Here we go.

Derringer struck first, leaping forward into a lunge. The branded man sidestepped and shoulder-barged straight into him, sending the elf stumbling away. Derringer rallied, swinging his blade faster than thought. The branded man deflected it effortlessly and slapped Derringer in the face with an open hand, the meaty smack of it echoing through the fighting hall.

Some of the spectators began to laugh. The man wasn't fast, but he was nimble and strong. Smart too. He was treating this like a wrestling match, and Thalin knew, Derringer couldn't win that kind of contest.

The elf was sweating now, his face twisted with

anger. No doubt that slap had been humiliating as well as painful. He advanced more cautiously this time, his sword darting, looking for an opening. But somehow the League man managed to skip inside his guard, grab hold of Derringer's hat and toss it aside.

There was a collective gasp as the spectators saw for the first time what many of them must have guessed.

'Cyrus is an elf!'

'Oi, Pointy Ears! Get it together!'

Derringer snarled and threw himself at his opponent, and the fight began in earnest.

It wasn't pretty. Newton winced as the elf got kicked, punched and slammed around the fighting floor. All his clever footwork and swordplay was gone, his energy channelled into nothing more than staying on his feet. The League man was enjoying himself, Newton realized. It made him feel sick.

And now, finally, the man began to use his sword, chopping like a butcher with a meat cleaver.

It was only a matter of time.

Newton had seen enough. He began pushing, shoving his way to the edge of the platform. He had to get up there. *Till one fighter gives quarter – or to the death.* That was the rule. And there was no way Derringer would give quarter.

The League fighter began to move harder, faster

and with more determination. Like a shark that had sensed the inevitable kill. He swung, double-handed, sent Derringer's sword skittering away. It clattered across the wooden planks, well out of reach.

Newton reached the front and pushed himself up, one knee on the edge of the platform. He caught Derringer's eye – and he hesitated. The elf was looking at him fiercely, as though in warning. *Stay where you are.*

The curved blade was raised for the killing blow. And all at once, Derringer made his move. Quick as a darting fairy, he rolled to the side and sprang up straight at his opponent, grabbing him by his throat.

The branded man let out a strangled sound. There was a flash of metal, and then both of them were still. It took Newton a moment to realize what had happened. Derringer had a tiny knife pressed at his opponent's cheek. Where it had come from, he had no idea. There was no blood – not yet – but all it would take was one fast movement.

The silence which followed seemed to stretch out for ever. The crowd held its breath. And then the branded man uncurled his fingers. With a dull clank, his sword dropped onto the wooden platform.

Applause erupted on all sides.

Newton sank back, relief flooding his body, as the marshal clambered onto the platform to raise up Derringer's arm. 'Cyrus Derringer is the Champion of the Silver Dragon! He shall now progress to the final . . . at the House of Light!'

The elf was beaming, and for once, Newton couldn't blame him. *He's smarter than I thought.*

Where they were going, he'd need to be.

Chapter Thirteen

'**S**he is coming,' announced the cat.

Finally.

Joseph pushed himself off the sewer wall, blinking in the dark. His legs ached, but there was no way he would have sat down in the filthy sludge swirling at their feet.

The whole time the spider had been away, the other shapeshifters had said nothing. Just waited, still and silent. Every once in a while Joseph had caught the gleam of their eyes watching him, the cat's glowing like two yellow moons.

What are they planning for me? Whatever it was, he was about to find out.

The horse laid a finger on the brickwork, and Joseph watched the spider squeeze out of a narrow crack beside it, onto the horse's hand.

'This way,' said the hissing voice of the spider.

They set off. This time the horse went first, holding the spider in the palm of his hand like a compass. Joseph followed with the cat at his shoulder, so close Joseph could hear him breathing. He felt like a mouse caught in a trap.

Perhaps he was.

'Here,' said the spider suddenly.

'Where are we?' asked Joseph. His voice cracked a little – the first time he'd used it in a while.

'Another wall,' said the cat.

'A wall that is weak,' said the horse.

'And weakened still further by my little expedition,' said the spider.

'But most of all,' said the cat, 'this wall is in a very *particular* place.'

The horse passed the spider to the cat, then reached inside his coat and brought out a metal crowbar, which he wedged into a gap in the brickwork. His muscles bulged. He let out a soft grunt, and then with one powerful movement a whole section of brickwork came free, tumbling into the sewer water in a thunder of crashing, splashing sounds.

Joseph stood back, covering both ears with his hands.

The horse thrust the metal bar in among the bricks again and levered another chunk away. Dust filled the air, forcing Joseph's eyes half-closed. Again and again the horse struck at the wall, smashing and pulling it away.

Joseph could see that this wasn't ordinary strength, even without Hal to explain. It was magical. Maybe Newton and the troll twins together would have been able to do this, but one man on his own, pulling down a wall like it was wet paper . . . Joseph had never seen anything like it. The air filled with brick dust, as debris fell into the waters below.

The horse kicked the last few bricks out, leaving a gaping hole to a darkness beyond, big enough for a human to squeeze through.

'Out. All of you,' said the horse. For an instant Joseph was confused, and then a figure came cautiously through the gap. It was an elf, or had been. She was as pale as a corpse, and so thin it made Joseph wince. Her clothes were rags, her eyes hollow and haunted.

'Be off with you,' said the cat.

'I . . . Th-thank y—'

'Go,' hissed the spider.

The elf turned and ran, scuttling away like a rat, her feet splashing in the sewer water. Joseph noticed that she wasn't wearing any shoes, and that the soles of her feet were torn and bloodied.

More creatures followed. A pair of imps holding hands, a troll and a dwarf. They all looked pale, haggard and lifeless. The dwarf's beard and hair had been shorn off, and the troll was missing its ears. Joseph felt like he might be sick. They peered at the shapeshifters and at Joseph, cautious, fearful, before they took off through the tunnels, splashing away until the darkness swallowed them.

'Do you know where we are, mongrel?' said the cat, unmoved.

Joseph shook his head.

The horse took hold of Joseph and lifted him through the gap. The cat followed, still holding the spider in his hand, picking his way silently through the rubble.

They were in a round room with no ceiling – or none that Joseph could see. The brick walls extended upwards into darkness. In fact, 'room' was pushing it. If Joseph had lain down on the floor and stretched out his arms and legs, he might have been able to touch both sides of it. Of course, lying down on the floor was the last thing he wanted to do. Something scuttled near his foot, making him flinch.

'They call it the End,' said the cat. 'A hole, six feet wide and twenty feet deep, where prisoners can be left and forgotten about. No food but whatever the whitecoats on duty care to throw down. No privy, which accounts for the smell. That and its proximity to the Azurmouth sewers.'

'Why?' was all Joseph could say.

'They say it was the Duke of Garran who devised the End. They say he comes here at night, sometimes, to talk to the prisoners. To ask them questions. What it feels like to be an elf. Whether they can talk to demons. What they think of humans. He has a peculiar . . . *fascination* with demonspawn. Some say he enjoys watching them go mad down here. And they do go mad, mongrel.'

Joseph remembered the frightened looks the prisoners had given him, and shuddered. 'You could have rescued them whenever you wanted,' he murmured. 'Why didn't you?'

The cat shrugged. 'It never suited us until now. You see, mongrel, the End provides us with an ideal opening for our game. My lady, if you'd be so kind . . . ?'

The spider dived from his hand onto the wall, scuttling over the brickwork, climbing upwards.

'Now listen to me, mongrel,' said the cat. He took hold of Joseph's shoulders and brought his face up so close that Joseph could see the black slits of his pupils widen in those yellow eyes. 'You might think we are a threat to you, but I can assure you that if we're caught here, you would be lucky to be thrown into the End. More likely, you'd be sliced apart and fed to a wyvern, bit by bit. I doubt you would enjoy that very much.' He grinned, showing perfect white teeth. 'So I would suggest you keep your mouth shut. Don't breathe a word, and do exactly as we say. Or you *will* regret it.'

There was a scuffling sound from above, and a rope came tumbling down.

'You still have the wooden spoon, don't you?' said the cat.

Joseph nodded.

'Good,' said the cat. 'Now climb.'

Joseph massaged his rope-burned hands as the shape-shifters unpacked the horse's satchel and pulled on white breeches, shirts and coats. The open hole of the End lay in the centre of a small, dank cell, and through the bars on the door Joseph could see a dark corridor stretching out, lined with more heavy prison doors. There was a flash of white as a man marched past the end of the corridor, and Joseph shrank back.

He was starting to think he knew where they were.

'Stick with us, boy,' said the horse. 'You'll come to no harm.'

The cat took Joseph's shoulder and guided him out through the door, sweeping a white tricorne hat onto his head as he did so. In their new outfits the shape-shifters looked just like whitecoats of the League. That was if you ignored their strange, terrifying eyes. The horse went first: the muscle, in case of any trouble, Joseph guessed. The cat and the spider – back in human form – came behind, both almost silent as they glided down the corridor.

Joseph kept looking forward, willing himself not to glance through the bars on either side. This was the second prison he'd been inside. But back in the Brig in Port Fayt the prisoners had been clamouring at him as he passed, desperate for attention. Here they were silent, as though they didn't dare utter a word.

At the end of the corridor they came across a pair of real whitecoats, lounging on barrels, playing dice. One of them did a double take as they passed by, frowning at Joseph, before he shrugged and returned to his game.

A prisoner. They think I'm just a prisoner. Is that why the shapeshifters need me? Joseph let out a breath he didn't know he'd been holding. He couldn't shake the memory of those creatures from the End. Their hollow eyes. Their frail bodies.

They entered a spiral staircase and began to climb upwards, higher and higher. At last they reached a locked door, and the cat drew out a small pouch full of metal instruments which he used to tinker with the lock. After a minute or so there was a soft click, and the door swung open.

Ahead of them was a wide, high corridor, about as different from the prison as it was possible to be. The floor was polished white marble, and the walls were white too, covered with mirrors in all shapes and sizes. Chandeliers hung from the white ceiling, and their candlelight reflected off the countless mirrors, making the corridor dazzlingly bright despite the fact that it was surely night outside.

'Welcome,' said the spider, 'to the House of Light.'

Chapter Fourteen

Three mahogany tables stretched the length of a massive, candle-lit dining hall, towards a raised dais where the oldest, most decrepit and most magical magicians sat in high-backed chairs.

The others crowded onto benches, draped in their oil-black gowns, gossiping, arguing about spells and stuffing their faces. There was an enormous haunch of roast venison in a rich, sticky onion sauce. Octopus fried with garlic. Lampreys in honey.

Tabitha couldn't enjoy any of it.

She sighed and watched morosely as the Bootle brothers demolished plate after plate. Ty perched on the edge of a gravy boat, barely even touching his sugar lump, mesmerized by the spectacle of the trolls gorging themselves. Beyond, Hal was nibbling at a bread roll, most of his food as untouched as Tabitha's. He looked awful – as though he were getting paler and more exhausted every hour they spent in Azurmouth.

The afternoon had dragged on for ever. Tabitha had spent it practising with her throwing knives in an empty courtyard and trying to think up new ways to find Joseph. If she could track down that griffin salesman she'd make him talk, whether he liked it or not . . . But first she would have to leave the Academy, which Newton had strictly forbidden. Right before he had disappeared himself with Cyrus Derringer.

In the end, the only thing to do was wait for Ty to return. When he finally did, it was another disappointment. He'd been pelted with rotten apples, almost been caught in a fairy-catcher's net on several occasions, and had found no trace of Joseph anywhere.

Tabitha pushed the food around her plate one last time, before finally giving up and dropping her fork. She needed to talk to someone, or she'd go mad. Opposite, Master Gurney was staring vacantly as he chewed.

'Thinking about your chicken?' she asked.

'What? Delicious! Yes, indeed,' said the magician, startled out of his trance. 'The mushroom sauce. A sheer delight.'

'No, I mean – the one you were trying to turn into—'

'An egg! Yes indeed, well remembered, young lady. You'll go far. Yes.'

'So did it work?'

The magician frowned. 'Not exactly. Transformation is an extremely slippery area of magic, my dear.'

Tabitha was already starting to regret this conversation. But the magician carried on, oblivious.

'Shapeshifting is my chief interest, you see. An extraordinary natural instance of transformation. And particularly fascinating on account of the frequent size differential involved.'

'Size differ— what?'

'To turn an egg into a chicken is a challenge, you see. But to turn an egg into a man. Or into a castle. That would require a far greater magical effort. Do you see?'

'I s'pose so.'

'A bear shapeshifter ought, in theory, to find the transformation easier than an ant shapeshifter. But we don't know yet whether that is the case. Yes, and there are other peculiar aspects of shapeshifting. Did you know, for example, that a shapeshifter can only ever take human and animal forms? Where are the troll shapeshifters? Or the dwarves, or the imps?'

'I didn't know that.' To her surprise, Tabitha was actually starting to become a little bit interested. She began tucking into her venison again. 'I saw a shape-shifter once. Not long ago, actually, back in Port Fayt. He was a thief. A cat with ginger fur.'

Master Gurney sighed and his eyes glazed over, as though in a happy daydream. 'How I should love to see a real shapeshifter . . .'

Tabitha wrinkled her nose. 'You've not even— But isn't that what you're studying?'

'Well, yes indeed my dear, but shapeshifters don't just grow on trees, you know. Unless, I suppose, they were a *squirrel* shapeshifter!' Master Gurney chuckled at his joke, spraying crumbs across the table. 'They're rather rare in Azurmouth, and they keep themselves to themselves. I do keep records of sightings, however. The Academy pays half a ducat for any decent report of an incident involving a shapeshifter. Sadly, many of them are too absurd to be believed.' He began to chortle again. 'Why, just this afternoon I heard an extraordinary tale of a sighting near Cockle Alley. It was a poor old lady who'd rather lost her mind, I fear. She claimed she'd seen a dappled grey horse trotting down the lane at night with a goblin boy slung over its back. Then it went into a wig shop, bold as brass, and a few moments later a grey-haired man came out to lock the door. She said he had a horse's eyes. A horse's eyes, indeed! I honestly can't—'

'A goblin boy,' said Tabitha. 'Is that what you said?' Her venison-laden fork was frozen halfway to her mouth.

Master Gurney looked disappointed, as though she had missed the point of his story. 'Well, yes,' he said. 'Or was it . . . No, you're quite right, it was a mongrel! Half human, half goblin. Would you believe it?'

Tabitha shot up from her seat, startling several elderly half-asleep magicians into wakefulness.

'Tabs?' said Frank, looking up from the lobster pie he was munching on. 'What's bit you?'

'We need to go. We need to go now.'

'But—' said Paddy, gesturing at the spread of food in front of them.

'We've been over this, Tabs,' said Frank, setting down his pie. 'Newt told us to stay put, remember?'

Tabitha turned to Master Gurney. 'How long ago?'

'How . . . er . . .'

'How long ago was this sighting?'

The master looked utterly confused. 'Well, let me see, it would have been . . . yesterday.'

Tabitha's heart jolted. *Yesterday!* That meant it was a lead. A good, solid lead.

'I know where Joseph is,' she said. 'Well, I know where he *was*. Yesterday.'

'Goodness!' said Master Gurney. 'Do you mean to say your friend is a mongrel boy?'

'I'm still not sure about this,' said Paddy. 'Newton said we—'

'I don't care what he said,' snapped Tabitha. 'He's out there right now, and he won't even tell us where he's gone! It's like he's not thinking straight. Don't you think he's been acting a little funny lately?'

Paddy looked uncomfortable. 'Maybe so, but—'

'Besides, who knows what kind of danger Joseph could have got himself into? So I'm going to find him, whether you like it or not.'

Hal rose. The colour had returned to his cheeks, and behind his spectacles his eyes were shining with determination. 'In that case,' he said, 'you're not going alone.'

Chapter Fifteen

The body left a smear of blood as they dragged it away, a red trail that glistened in the flickering torchlight. Newton shifted uncomfortably on his wooden bench, trying to ignore the savage roar of the spectators that surged up all around him.

The courtyard of the House of Light was even more crowded now than it had been earlier in the day, and in the darkness the sweating, heaving mass of citizens had turned feral, fired up with cheap grog, outrageous bets and the spectacle of violence. A line of whitecoats stood guard around the wooden fighting platform, handing out blows with their muskets when things got too rowdy.

Still, Newton half wished he was down there among the crowd. Up on the tiered wooden seating of the trainers' enclosure he felt horribly exposed, and he was starting to worry that he'd made a mistake. Of course Derringer was an excellent swordsman. He could beat Lucky Leo, then claim his opponent's sword as a prize.

That was the easy part.

Newton's fingers reached under his cloak and curled around the three wooden sections of the Banshee – his weapon. The Duke of Garran wasn't just going to let them walk out of here with the Sword of Corin. So as soon as the fight was won, he would have to wade in, get Derringer off the platform and into the crowd. If they could lose themselves in the throng, maybe they could make it out of here alive.

Maybe.

The crowd was getting louder, impatient for the next fight. Servants were scrubbing at the platform, trying to clean off the blood, whilst the victorious Champion of the Broken Crown strutted for his friends. Behind the warm glow of the torches, the façade of the House of Light seemed to glow, ghostly pale. *Let the sky have its sun. Azurmouth has the House of Light.* But at this hour it seemed more like the moon against the twilight sky.

Newton looked up, drawing his hood further over his face, glad of the chill in the air that gave him an excuse to wear it. There, leaning on the balustrade, surrounded by the other lords of the League was the Duke of Garran. Newton couldn't make out his expression at this distance, but his posture was relaxed.

How can he be so calm? This next fight was the one they had surely both been waiting for. Lucky Leo's first of the evening. *And, hopefully, his last.*

'The next duel!' announced the herald. His voice was already hoarse from shouting over the crowd. 'To my left, the defending Champion of the Contest of Blades, Leopold of Brindenheim . . .'

Lucky Leo stepped from the shadows onto the torchlit platform, arms raised to acknowledge the roar of his admirers. His smug face was lit up with happiness, as though he couldn't wait to get stuck into the fighting. He drew the Sword of Corin with a flourish. The blade glittered, looking every inch the legendary weapon that it was. Newton couldn't imagine how many trolls' heads that blade had severed; how many goblins it had killed; how many widows it had made.

He realized he was rubbing at the marks on his wrists again.

'To my right, the Champion of the Silver Dragon,' barked the herald, 'Cyrus Derringer!'

The elf stepped forward and whisked off his hat to reveal his pointed ears. Newton cursed under his breath, as a murmur ran through the crowd. Derringer had promised to keep his disguise on. After the fight at the Fencing House of the Silver Dragon it was hardly a secret that he was an elf, but if he'd just been discreet, the lords of the League might have overlooked it. Now, if they lost, death was almost a certainty.

Not that Derringer cared. He was grinning at the crowd, looking every bit as smug as his opponent.

Newton rose, taking care to keep his head down so the men on the balcony didn't see his face. The trainers were allowed to have a word with their fighters before the duel, and on the opposite side of the platform the Earl of Brindenheim already had an arm round his son, murmuring in his ear.

Thalin knew why he bothered – from what Newton had heard, Leo couldn't fight his way out of a paper castle. But the threatening presence of his father was probably enough to scare most opponents into throwing the fight.

'I'd like to carve him up,' said Derringer, as Newton reached the platform. The elf's eyes gleamed in the light of the torch fires. Newton had never seen him so alive.

'No. The sword's all we need. We had a deal, remember?'

'He needs to be taught a lesson.'

Newton just stopped himself grinding his teeth. 'Maybe you need to be taught a lesson yourself. If you hurt him there's no way we'll walk out of here alive. His father will murder us on the spot. That's if the Duke of Garran doesn't get us first.'

A scowl passed across Derringer's face for an instant before he shrugged. 'Maybe.'

Newton could hardly believe it. Was Derringer actually agreeing with him?

Better late than never.

'Gentlemen! To your places.'

There was a tense hush as Newton returned to his bench, and the two fighters took up position on opposite sides of the platform. Their blades hovered in the air, twin ribbons of fire in the orange glow of the torches.

Newton leaned forward, holding his breath. He could feel the spectators around him doing the same. In the courtyard. On the benches. At the balcony above.

'Let the fight begin!'

Lucky Leo darted forwards, lunging with all his weight. A ridiculous move. The kind of move that would instantly get you cut down in a real battle. Derringer simply stepped aside, not even bothering to raise his sword. There were titters from the crowd. The Earl of Brindenheim scowled, and for a moment Newton thought he might lurch out of his seat and throttle the elf.

No, Cyrus. Please, no. They couldn't afford to humiliate this idiot, however much he deserved it. Newton risked a glance upwards at the Duke of Garran. The other men on the balcony were still laughing, joking and sipping from wine glasses, while the Duke stood silent and still, watching, giving nothing away.

Down on the platform, Lucky Leo scowled and staggered upright, rearranging his grip on the hilt. *Probably the worst swordsman ever to handle that blade.*

Newton caught Derringer's eye and mouthed at him. *Make it last.* They'd been over this several times. It needed to seem like a real fight, so Lucky Leo could keep as much dignity as possible when he lost. Derringer gritted his teeth, but nodded. His next attack was a wide, slashing move. Nowhere near his best. *Perfect.* The first clatter of steel rang out as Leo deflected it.

That seemed to break the spell of silence on the crowd. They began to cheer, to talk amongst themselves, to shout out warnings and encouragement. The fighters moved around the platform, blades flashing as they fought.

Within less than a minute, Leo was tiring. Newton could see it in his podgy red face, glistening with sweat, and in the way he moved – cautious, plodding steps as he looked in vain for an opening. Derringer's lip curled in a sneer. If he was trying to hide his contempt, he wasn't trying hard enough. He began to bounce on his feet, showing off how much energy he had left.

Newton looked up again, and froze. The lords of the League were still there, drinking and laughing. But the Duke of Garran was gone. His skin prickled, and he glanced around the seating. Where was the Duke? And what in Thalin's name would make him stop watching the fight?

A surge of noise came from the crowd, and Newton's attention was drawn back to the platform. Derringer had made his move. A feint to the right, drawing Leo's eyes away from his own sword. And in the same instant, one, two steps in, close as sweethearts, and a twist of Leo's arm.

Lucky Leo yelped like a child as his blade flashed,

and then the blade was no longer his, and Derringer stepped away, both swords pointed at his opponent's face, his own plastered with a grin that made Newton feel sick.

And suddenly there was a third figure on the fighting platform, streaking like a bolt of lightning from the shadows beside the wooden stands. A figure dressed in white.

The Duke?

No. Someone slimmer, taller, her long blonde hair tied back in a ponytail. Moving so fast it might almost have been magic. *Knowing her, it might well be.*

There was a whistle of sharp metal moving fast, a wet *thunk*, and Derringer howled. Blood spattered the wooden platform as the elf's two swords clattered away. Lucky Leo backed off, face pale, as Derringer staggered, clutching his hand. Standing in between them was the figure in white, poised like a stone seraph. Major Turnbull's own blade dangled at her side, dripping, and her foot was placed firmly on the Sword of Corin.

Newton stood, fingers working fast, slotting together the three lengths of black lacquered wood that formed the Banshee. He twirled it as he stepped forward, sending panicked trainers scurrying away from him.

Come on, then. He'd beaten Turnbull before, and he could beat her again.

A soft click to his left, alarmingly close to his ear.

'You stay where you are,' said a quiet voice.

He turned to see the Duke of Garran right beside him, watching him with those cold, colourless eyes and pointing an ornate silver-and-gold-chased pistol at his head.

Newton knew that pistol. He had seen the Duke use it before, on board the *Justice*.

It was the pistol that had killed Old Jon.

Rage flooded through him, burning him up.

'No,' said the Duke, still icy calm. 'I said, stay where you—'

Too late. Newton had shrugged off his cloak and swung the Banshee with all his strength. It wasn't anything Tori the hobgoblin had taught him. *Control,* the hobgoblin had always said. *Control is everything.* Tori's moves were precise and focused.

This was anything but.

The Banshee cracked into the Duke's face with a sound like a hammer driven hard into a slab of meat.

BANG!

The Duke's pistol flashed as it went off, and the few trainers still on the benches bolted, howling in fright. The baying of the crowd turned frantic, desperate.

It took Newton a few moments to realize that the shot had gone wide, and that he was still alive. The Duke bent over, the pistol dangling limply from one hand, the other held against his face. Time seemed frozen for an instant, until the Duke's pale eyes found Newton once again, peering between his plump fingers. There was no pain in them. No anger.

He was smiling.

'Oh dear,' said the Duke.

Someone barrelled into Newton from behind, two arms like tree trunks grappling him into a crushing embrace. An ogre's arms – they were much too big and powerful to be a human's. Newton squirmed to free himself, but it was hopeless. The ogre's hands found the Banshee, tore it away from him like a mother taking her baby's rattle. The giant thumbs flexed against the middle of the staff.

'No,' growled Newton. 'Do that and I'll—'

There was a sharp snap as the Banshee broke in two, and the hands discarded the weapon like two bits of damp firewood.

Newton clamped his teeth together hard to stifle the cry rising in his throat.

The Duke of Garran straightened, still smiling, still watching Newton. His hand came away from his face, and Newton saw a red mark forming on his cheek. A trickle of blood. The Banshee had glanced off, raking his face but causing no real damage.

'What in all the Old World is going on?' roared a voice from the fighting platform, rising above the panicked wails of the crowd. Newton saw that the Earl of Brindenheim had drawn his sword. His whiskers quivered with fury and confusion, as he stepped in front of his cowering son.

Major Turnbull had sheathed her own blade and retrieved the Sword of Corin.

Derringer hovered, his hand still dripping red splashes onto the platform, his eyes flicking from Turnbull to Newton, unsure what to do next.

The Duke of Garran spat out a gobbet of blood and a broken tooth, and dabbed at his lips with a hand-kerchief. He was examining Newton with amused fascination, like a schoolboy observing an ant through the glass wall of a jar.

An ant he's about to crush.

'So you came.' His voice was thick with blood. 'All the way from Port Fayt, across the Ebony Ocean, to Azurmouth. How brave. How foolish.'

He waved his pistol, and the arms that held Newton tightly in place shoved him down onto his knees. Looking up, Newton saw the ogre he'd seen on the balcony earlier that day. He was still dressed in League livery. His shaven head was sheened with sweat, and his eyes were empty of all emotion.

'I need only give the word, and he will crush your skull,' said the Duke softly. He dropped the blood-stained handkerchief, letting it flutter to rest on the platform. 'I will not do it. But rest assured, by the time I am finished with you, Captain Newton, you will wish I had.'

Chapter Sixteen

The cat led the way, striding much faster now, casting quick glances in every direction. They twisted and turned through the corridors, heading deeper and deeper into the House of Light.

Every inch of it looked the same. White marble floors, white ceilings and white walls covered in mirrors. But still the cat seemed to know exactly where they were going. Joseph realized suddenly that even with the shapeshifters' disguises there would be no excuse for bringing a mongrel boy here, out of the cells. He swallowed hard.

Once or twice he heard the distant noise of a cheering crowd, and the clash of steel. *The Contest of*

Blades, he remembered. *Of course*. The shapeshifters had chosen the perfect night for their game.

The cat stopped at the end of a corridor, in front of white double doors. Above was a moulded wooden shield emblazoned with a winged sword. Two words were carved beneath it: *Corin's Hall*.

'Where is he?' said the horse. 'He should be here by now.'

'He'll be here,' said the cat.

Footsteps came echoing towards them from a nearby corridor, and a figure turned the corner. It was a whitecoat, big and broad-shouldered, moving with an easy grace. He swept off his hat, revealing sandy-coloured hair and some strange mark on his forehead. Joseph winced as he realized what it was – a blazing sun, etched out in white scar lines.

The spider's hand fell on Joseph's shoulder, holding him in place. 'His name is Hoake. He's a friend.'

A friend of whose?

'You took your time,' said the horse.

'My apologies. It was the contest,' said the butcher, in a low voice. 'I had to throw the fight just to be here. Some filthy elf.' He looked around, checking they were alone, and Joseph caught a whiff of something strong and unpleasant on his breath. *Firewater*. Up close he saw that the man's eyes were red-rimmed and glassy.

'Next year, perhaps,' sneered the cat. 'If the drink doesn't get you first.'

Hoake grunted and pulled a ring of keys from his pocket. 'This bit you'll have to do yourselves. I won't risk being found out.'

The spider's voice came suddenly from beside Joseph's ear, making him jump. 'Have you ever seen a man die before?'

'Keep him out of it,' said the cat, waving a hand at Joseph. 'We'll do the rest.'

The whitecoat thrust a key into a lock, turned it with a clunk and stepped back as the horse kicked the doors wide open.

Joseph was thrust through, stumbling, into an enormous hall. The cat and the horse were already ahead of him, moving fast. Joseph saw dark red wallpaper covered with paintings, saw a statue in the middle, spouting water into a stone pool surrounding it. Saw the two whitecoats beside it, whose confusion was turning rapidly into aggression. Sabres flashed from scabbards.

'What in Corin's name are you—?'

And then the shapeshifters were on them. A pair of muskets were propped up against the stone pool, and the cat kicked them over the edge, splashing harm-lessly into the water. The horse launched himself at the nearest whitecoat, smashing his shoulder into the man's belly and falling with him into the pool in a great crash of spray that spattered the marble all around.

Something blurred at the edge of Joseph's vision and he turned to see a third butcher charging at him from the shadows at the corner of the hall. Before he could react, the spider stepped past him, grabbed hold of the whitecoat's sword arm and twisted it in a way arms aren't meant to be twisted. The man yelped and groaned. Blood spurted onto the floor. The spider stood back as her opponent sank to his knees, his sword thrust through his own chest.

Just like that, it was over. The horse was rising, dripping, from the water, his opponent motionless as the fountain continued to play. The cat was dabbing at his jacket where a few spots of blood had appeared. The whitecoat he'd been fighting was flat on his back with no obvious wound, but it was clear that he wasn't getting up again.

The waters of the fountain were clouded with red.

The scarred whitecoat came through the door, closing it quietly behind him. 'All done here?' he asked. The spider nodded.

'I thought there'd be more,' said the horse, cracking his knuckles.

Joseph felt ill, and he tried to distract himself by

looking around the room. Now he had time to take it all in, he saw that the paintings and the statue in the centre were all of one man. Tall and muscular with long, shaggy dark hair, craggy features and piercing blue eyes. In the painting nearest Joseph he was bare-chested, standing on a rock and pointing with a sword as he shouted to the men below – an army of metal-clad humans, cheering and jostling to follow him into battle. In another he was fighting off a horde of trolls, all black-skinned and red-eyed. He gripped one by the throat, while his sword clashed with his opponent's cleaver.

Joseph would have recognized that sword, even if he hadn't already guessed who this figure was: Corin the Bold – the greatest warrior who had ever lived.

Almost every painting showed some battle or another; only in the central statue was Corin at rest, standing with his feet apart, hands placed gently on the pommel of his sword and smiling, as though at a job well done. It took Joseph a moment to notice the stone body of a goblin sprawled at the great hero's feet, its face twisted in a grimace of death. The fountain's streams were gushing from its many wounds.

'So . . .' said the cat. He had just finished cleaning his jacket and turned his yellow eyes on the one living whitecoat. 'Where is our prize, Hoake?'

'It's here, just like you were told it would be.'

'Show us,' said the horse.

'Show us now,' said the spider.

Hoake crossed the marble floor to a painting of Corin receiving the surrender of an elf lord on top of a mountain, their armour battered and blood-stained. The whitecoat reached for the frame, feeling along it until there was a soft click.

From the far corner of the room came a creaking sound, and Joseph turned to see that part of the wall had swung open to reveal a room beyond. A secret room, small and dark.

'You'll find it in there,' said Hoake. 'That's our side of the bargain. Now I'll take what was promised in return. I trust you weren't planning to cheat him again.'

Him . . . Who was 'him'? All of a sudden Joseph remembered being in the attic, hearing the voices in the room below. The cat, the horse . . . and the third voice. Their visitor.

Him. A chill ran down his spine.

Joseph felt the spider's hands on his shoulders again, but this time they dug in hard. He winced and tried to squirm away. It was no good – the spider had him in her grip. They were all looking at him now. Why? He hadn't done anything. He had nothing to do with this.

His eyes met those of the cat, and he saw something there that he hadn't noticed before. Anger. Fury. Triumph.

The horse grabbed hold of Joseph and the world pitched as he was turned upside down and shaken like a salt cellar.

'No! What are you—?'

The wooden spoon fell clattering onto the marble.

'There,' said the horse, as he turned Joseph the right way up. 'All yours.'

Joseph snatched the spoon, but before he could scramble away the whitecoat was there, sword drawn and held up hard against Joseph's throat. He took the spoon and twisted it out of Joseph's grip.

'What do you want with me?' said Joseph desperately. 'Let me go!'

The horse shook his head sadly.

'*Let you go?*' said the cat. His voice was full of venom. 'Have you forgotten what you did to me? How you dumped me in the sea, then locked me in a cage so small I could barely move? And you think we should *let you go?*'

'I . . . I don't . . .'

Too late, Joseph realized what an idiot he'd been. To come here, to the House of Light, trusting a shape-shifter who hated him. He should have fought, kicking and screaming, not to come. He tried now, lashing out at Hoake and kicking blindly, but the butcher was far too strong and just caught him in a grip even tighter than before.

'What are you going to do with me?'

The cat smiled coldly. 'That is for our mutual friend to decide. Now, Hoake. We have delivered you both the boy and the wooden spoon, as promised. We will take what we came for, and be on our way.'

'There's a lantern by the fountain,' said Hoake. He hauled Joseph back to the double doors and swung them open.

'Wait,' hissed the spider.

Lantern light fell on the secret room now. A tiny, cramped cave of bare stonework and cobwebs, and in the centre of it a small podium. Empty. The shape-shifters were glaring at Hoake.

'Where is it?' said the cat. His voice had lost all trace of calm. *Where is the Sword of Corin?*'

Hoake shrugged as he pushed Joseph out of the hall. 'He promised you I'd get you in, and I've done that. It's no business of ours if your prize isn't there any more.' He slammed the double doors and locked them, leaving the shapeshifters trapped inside. Then he cupped his hands and shouted down the corridor. 'Help! *Help!*'

There was a distant answering call, and a thunder of footsteps.

'Who is it?' asked Joseph. 'Who are you working for?'

He knew the answer even before the words left Hoake's lips. Three little words.

All through the House of Light, as he was hustled along mirrored corridors, down winding stairs and out into the darkness, even as he was gagged and bundled into a waiting carriage, Joseph wasn't thinking about the cat, or the wooden spoon, or the Sword of Corin.

Those three words ran through his head, over and over.

Jeb the Snitch.

Chapter Seventeen

'Just a few more minutes,' said Tabs. 'Please. I have a *feeling.*'

'I have a feeling too,' said Paddy, peering into a mirror and adjusting an enormous purple wig. 'I have a feeling I look fantastic.'

Frank snorted. '*Fat*-tastic more like. Come on, Tabs. We don't want Newt to get back to the Academy and find us missing. We can try again tomorrow.'

Tabitha rolled her eyes. It might have earned her a friendly punch under normal circumstances, but fortunately she was crouched behind a mountain of wigs, and it was so dark the trolls probably wouldn't have seen anyway.

They'd been waiting in the wig shop for two hours now. At first they'd barged through the door, pistols and cutlasses at the ready. But there was no shape-shifter and no Joseph. Instead they'd found a set of bare rooms, a few mattresses, a locked strong box that no amount of levering would open and a large wardrobe of different outfits, everything from beggars' rags to merchant finery. That was it.

Apart from the wigs. Hundreds and hundreds of wigs, every colour of the rainbow. There was even a tiny cabinet of fairy wigs, with a set of tweezers for fittings.

Still, they'd waited. Perhaps Joseph and the shape-shifter were out somewhere. Perhaps they would come back. So they'd taken up position, hiding among the wigs and waiting for the door to open.

Waiting . . .

. . . and waiting.

Tabitha shook her head. *Focus. That shapeshifter could be back any minute.* 'You can go if you like,' she said. 'I'm staying.'

'Unfortunately, I think the twins may have a point,' said Hal. The magician was crouched uncomfortably behind the counter. The troll twins had made him accept one of their pistols for protection, and he was holding it between finger and thumb, as though it might go off at any moment. *Which, actually, it might.*

'We're putting ourselves in danger here, with absolutely no guarantee that Joseph and this shape-shifter will return. If indeed they were ever here in the first place.'

'Two minutes,' said Frank. 'Then we're all going back. That means you too, Tabs.'

Paddy swapped his purple wig for a towering, pink-powdered monstrosity festooned with ribbons. 'Now this is more like it . . .'

Tabitha turned her attention back to the door, willing it to open. Any moment, Joseph might come through. She knew she ought to feel angry with him. He'd run off without any explanation and forced them to follow halfway across the Ebony Ocean. He'd let Jeb the Snitch trick him over and over again. He was just a tavern boy with no skills and a head full of bad ideas.

And still, she missed him. She missed him so much it hurt.

Wait.

'Did you hear that?'

Everyone froze. Ty peered out from between the hairs of the long blonde wig he was hiding in.

Yes – footsteps, in the alley outside. Paddy took off

his wig and silently replaced it on the stand, sinking down behind the nearest set of shelves and drawing his cutlass. Frank dropped to the floor behind a mannequin, a set of pistols in his hand. Slowly, cautiously, Tabitha slid her favourite knife out of its sheath. She'd sharpened it that afternoon.

There was a scrabbling at the lock, and the door swung open. Tabitha tensed. In the dim light that filtered from the street she saw three figures in white coats and tricorne hats.

Butchers! What in Thalin's name was the League doing here?

The closest whitecoat began hunting for a lantern. Tabitha caught Hal's eye, but he looked just as clueless as she felt. They hadn't planned on this. Where was the shapeshifter? Where was Joseph? And what were they supposed to do now?

'No-good scum-sucking bilge-bag maggot,' spat the biggest of the whitecoats. Tabitha noticed that the figure was limping. Then she saw that another was clutching its arm, and the third, a woman, had a long tear in her white coat. They'd been in a fight. *Some sort of tavern brawl?*

'We'll find him,' said the whitecoat with the injured arm. His voice was soft, sinister and strangely familiar. 'Tonight. Right now. He won't get away with this.'

'What troubles me most,' hissed the woman, 'is that he thinks he's clever. Ordering that drunkard Hoake to lock us in Corin's Hall . . . Did he really think we would not escape? That a few whitecoats could arrest the Quiet Three? He needs to be taught a lesson.'

'What troubles *me* most is how we nearly got killed. Look at my leg!'

'It will heal. More than I can say for the butcher who—'

'Wait.' It was the familiar voice again. 'Something's wrong.'

A lantern flared suddenly into life, picking out the three figures in its warm glow. The whitecoat with the injured arm was half turned towards Tabitha, and the light glinted in his odd, inhuman eyes.

Yellow eyes.

Cat's eyes.

'You!' gasped Tabitha out loud, before she could stop herself.

If the cat's eyes were strange, the others' were even stranger. The big man's were enormous, like those of some large animal. *Like those of a horse.* The woman's were tiny and black, like glittering shards of coal.

The troll twins rose from their hiding place, weapons ready.

'Stay right where you are,' said Frank. 'In the name of—'

There was an ear-splitting gunshot, and one of the wig shop windows cracked into a web of fractures. Hal dropped his smoking pistol like it was a crab that had pinched his fingers.

'My apologies,' he stammered. 'I didn't mean to—'

Too late. The three whitecoats had turned tail and sped out of the shop, faster than could possibly be natural.

'After them!' yelled Tabitha. She leaped over the mountain of wigs and shot through the door, leaving it to swing shut behind her. There was a soft *thunk* as Ty flew straight into it, then a tiny beating of fists from within.

'Oi!' cried the fairy. 'Wait for me!'

But Tabitha didn't have time to help him out. The cold night air sharpened her senses. There, at the end of the alley – three white figures. As they reached the main road they split up, each heading down a different back street. Tabitha charged after them.

For a moment she considered going after the limping one, but thought better of it. The one with the injured arm – the cat – that was who she wanted. He was the leader. If anyone knew where Joseph was, it would be him.

She followed.

The shapeshifter was fast, but the injury seemed to be slowing him down. He veered left, boots slamming the cobblestones, and Tabitha followed. Then right. Tabitha followed again.

'I've got him!' she yelled. 'I've got him!'

But she was on her own. Hal was no runner. The Bootle brothers were strong, but heavy and slow on their feet. Ty might have made it out of the shop by now, but he hadn't caught up with her yet – assuming he could even find her.

Tabitha was panting now. She pulled a second blade from its sheath, one in each hand, like the professional knife-fighters she sometimes saw back in Port Fayt.

On my own.

She swerved round the corner and found herself facing a brick wall scrawled with obscene messages.

'Come out! In the name of the Watch!'

Silence. Then a movement, somewhere to her left. She spun, but it was only an empty tankard rolling across the cobbles. Rolling – but there was no breeze. She strode towards it, and immediately something *crashed* behind her. She spun again to see the shattered remains of a pottery jug, dropped from somewhere above.

Someone chuckled. A low, threatening sound.

Tabitha's skin began to crawl. 'I said come out!'

Silence. And then a voice. 'You're a long way from home, little girl.'

'A long way from your friends too,' said a second voice.

'A long, long way,' said a third.

Tabitha bolted. Up the alleyway, still clutching her knives. Behind her, footsteps, following. *Idiot!* How could she let this happen? Cornered by all three of them. If those trolls hadn't been so slow . . .

She ran left and came out into a small cobbled square. Black-beamed house fronts loomed on all sides, and a Golden Sun banner hung limp from a flag-pole on a boarded-up tavern. On the far side of the square was a raised platform with three pillories set into it.

Two of them were empty, but the third held a skeletal elf prisoner, his neck and wrists locked in by wood, pale face even paler than it should be, long hair matted with the remains of rotten eggs and fruit. A strip of sackcloth was wrapped around his head like a bandana, equally clotted with food.

He raised his head at Tabitha's arrival. 'Help!' he croaked. 'Help me!'

Heart thudding, Tabitha raced across the square

towards him. Beside the pillories was a sign bearing the words: KNOW YOUR ENEMY. She sheathed one knife and thrust the point of the other into the rusted lock that held the wooden clamp in place, working it as fast as she could. Maybe she could get the elf free. Maybe he'd fight with her.

Two against three . . .

'Thank you! Thank you!' burbled the elf.

But the metal wasn't giving. *Come on!* She'd seen Newton pick locks before. He made it look so easy.

The elf let out a sudden screech. 'Whitecoats!'

Tabitha turned and saw three figures loping into the square. The woman, as gaunt as a walking skeleton. The big, muscular man with the limp. And the cat, smiling as he approached, his wounded arm dangling at his side, his yellow eyes narrowed . . .

Tabitha tried to spring into a fighting stance, but a sharp pain in her scalp told her that someone had got hold of her hair. She twisted, but the fingers held on tight. Half turning, she saw the elf watching her.

'I've got her,' he yelled out. 'I've caught her for you!'

Tabitha tugged desperately at the elf's fingers. 'They're not real whitecoats, you dung head! Can't you tell?' Out of the corner of her eye, she could see the three shapeshifters getting closer . . .

Nothing else for it. She reached up with her knife

and hacked savagely at her hair. Two blows and she was free, leaving the elf with nothing but a handful of blue curls. She dived off the platform and instantly tripped over an outstretched foot, hitting the cobblestones hard.

When she rolled over she saw her three captors looking down at her, silhouetted against a black sky pricked with stars. Behind them the elf was quietly sobbing, his fingers clutching her lock of blue hair. 'Sorry,' he mumbled. 'I'm so sorry. They took my wife. They took my little Caroline. I've got nothing. Nothing . . .'

'How fortunate,' purred the cat. 'I've already dealt with the mongrel boy. And now you come along.' He knelt down next to her, and his yellow eyes glinted in the light of the moon.

'This is a good night for vengeance.'

Chapter Eighteen

The carriage clattered through the darkness. It was a rickety old thing, and Joseph felt as though every muscle in his body would be bruised black and blue by the morning. Not that it mattered. He was sure there would be worse to come, where he was going.

'You're taking me to him, aren't you?' he said. 'To Jeb the Snitch.'

Hoake sat opposite, his face hidden by shadow, one hand gripping the seat against the bouncing of the carriage, the other a flagon that had to be nearly empty by now. Hardly paying Joseph any attention at all.

'But why?'

The whitecoat took another swig, and a dribble of grog spattered his white breeches.

It didn't make sense – Jeb had been after the wooden spoon ever since he'd first heard about it, but he'd never shown any interest in Joseph before. What did the goblin want with him?

Perhaps he should be glad. *This was what you wanted, wasn't it? A chance to get the truth about your father* . . . Except the way he'd imagined it, it was him finding Jeb, not the other way around. And without the wooden spoon, he had no chance of getting the goblin to talk.

He had to get out. He had to be the one in control.

His eyes strayed to his cutlass, propped up beside Hoake, then to the wooden spoon, poking out of his captor's pocket and jolting with the motion of the carriage. Maybe he could seize it, shove the door open and dive through.

And get smashed to pieces on the cobblestones.

Great idea.

But if he could somehow stop the carriage . . .

The whitecoat took another pull at his flagon. Joseph had seen men like Hoake before, back in the Legless Mermaid. Men who came to the tavern every day. Who couldn't help themselves. Who always needed another drop.

Come on, Joseph. You've got nothing to lose.

'What are you drinking?' he asked.

'What?'

Joseph shrugged. 'It's just . . . my uncle's a land-lord, back in Fayt. He brews his own grog.'

The butcher narrowed his eyes, and took another swig.

'Folk come from all over the town to taste it,' said Joseph. 'From all over the Ebony Ocean, in fact. He calls it . . . er . . . Lightly's Golden Elixir.' Actually he called it *Lightly's Finest Bowelbuster*, but Joseph didn't think that would have the same effect.

'That right?' said Hoake. He scowled and knocked back the flagon again. There couldn't be more than a few dregs left by now.

'I've never tried any myself,' Joseph went on. 'But they say it tastes amazing, like, er . . .' What *did* grog taste like? 'Like honey and hazelnuts and, um . . . like . . .' He suddenly remembered the words of an old soak who had propped up the bar every day he'd worked there. 'They say it tastes like the tears of a seraph.'

Hoake emptied his flagon, swore and tossed it through the barred window. 'Curse you, mongrel,' he growled. He reached up and thumped the roof of the carriage three times.

Joseph almost went flying as they lurched to a halt.

'Wait here. I need a drink.' The whitecoat picked up Joseph's cutlass, took a key from his pocket and clambered out of the carriage, shutting and locking the door behind him. A strange scent filled the air. Strange, but familiar. Musty. Sickly. Somewhere between fresh vomit and rotten fish.

From up ahead came the voice of the driver. 'We're nearly there, for Corin's sake.'

'You shut your mouth.'

'Not another flagon, Hoake. Ain't you had enough?'

'I said shut up. And wait here.'

Joseph heard another door open, releasing a burst of music and loud voices, then close. A tavern, he guessed.

No time to lose.

He tried the carriage door, but it wouldn't budge. He pulled at the bars on the window, but they were surprisingly solid, and like Mr Lightly had always told him, he didn't have much strength in his puny mongrel muscles. He reached through them. He could get at the lock with his fingers, but of course Hoake had taken the key with him.

He could feel his ears drooping with disappointment. *We're nearly there*, the driver had said. Nearly at Jeb's hideout, wherever that was. Last time Joseph had seen Jeb, the goblin had tried to shoot him dead.

He had a hunch the Snitch wouldn't have become any more pleasant since then.

There was a creak from outside, as the tavern door opened.

Only one thing left to try. Joseph edged to the opposite side of the carriage, giving himself as much of a run-up as he could.

The key scraped in the lock, the carriage door swung open and Hoake clambered back inside, and at the same instant Joseph launched himself forwards.

'What are you—?' said Hoake, dropping both the cutlass and a fresh flagon of grog, as Joseph slammed into him. The stench of firewater filled his nostrils. He struggled, trying to squirm past to the open door, but Hoake caught hold of him. He flailed, and his fingers closed around something in the whitecoat's pocket. *The wooden spoon.* He tugged hard, and it came free.

Hoake flung him to the floor, and his forehead slammed against the bench. He blinked, his head throbbing with pain as the whitecoat crouched over him, eyes rimmed with red, jaw set with anger.

Maybe he wasn't as drunk as I thought.

Hoake held out his hand. 'Give me the spoon, you little wretch.'

Joseph's fingers tightened on the wood. Maybe it was the knock to his head, but he was sick of being a victim. Sick of being passed from crook to crook, like some sack of dragon scales to be traded at whim. Sick of this city, and the people in it.

What would Thalin do?

What would Newton do?

What would my father do?

Joseph locked eyes with the whitecoat. He gripped harder and harder, until his knuckles went white. *It's a question of mental focus.*

'What in all the bleeding Ebony Ocean are you doing?'

What *was* he doing? He'd already tried and failed back in the alleyway, with the Grey Brothers. And even if it worked . . . *You really have no idea what it could do to you, if you were to misuse it.*

He gritted his teeth. He just had to think the right thoughts.

Wait – *the right thoughts.*

Not *his* thoughts. Not the thoughts of Joseph the mongrel. The thoughts of Hoake. Hoake the butcher. Those were the right thoughts.

What was Hoake seeing? What was Hoake thinking?

'I said, hand it over, before I beat the living daylights out of you.'

Joseph climbed out of himself, worming his way

inside Hoake's mind. *I'm a human. I'm a whitecoat.*

A tingling grew in his head, building, spreading down through his chest and into his arms.

It's happening. It's really happening.

'Last chance, mongrel.'

His whole body began to quiver, buzzing with power, and he closed his fingers around the spoon until he and the wand were one.

I'm tall. I'm strong. I'm angry.

The butcher's face twisted into a snarl and he lunged forward, grabbed hold of the wooden spoon. At the same instant, the power surged out through Joseph's hand and into the wand. The warmth turned ice cold, and Joseph wasn't Joseph any more, he was . . .

. . . Hoake.

Richard Hoake, his head awhirl and his guts roiling from six flagons of grog.

Who had joined the butchers at the age of sixteen.

Who was branded with the Golden Sun two years later, a mark of honour for slaying a troll the size of a bear.

Who liked his wine, then loved it, then couldn't do without it.

Who'd once swapped his boots for half a cup of firewater.

Who needed money for it so badly he'd do anything, anything to scrape together half a ducat for another bottle, just one more and then he'd stop, maybe, but more likely not, who—

The whitecoat tumbled backwards, letting go of the wooden spoon, his eyes mad and staring like those of a bolted horse. He panted, his knees pressed up against his chest.

Joseph flinched. *What in Thalin's name . . . ?* It had worked. For a few moments at least, it had actually worked. His head ached and he felt woozy, as though he'd just woken up from a long sleep.

The driver's voice carried from the front of the carriage. 'What's going on down there?'

The words were like a jab in the ribs. Joseph stuffed the wooden spoon into his pocket. He saw the carriage door still ajar and hurled himself through, snatching up his cutlass as he went, sending the door banging open and hitting the cobblestones hard.

Up on his feet, rounding the back of the carriage and flying down a side street.

The strange, musty smell was stronger here. He skidded through a black puddle and reached instinctively to check that the wooden spoon and his father's silver watch were still safe in his pockets.

Wait. A black puddle . . .

He looked again. It was sludgy as wet mud and glistened like a beetle's shell. He bent down and sniffed. Yes – that smell – that musty, sickly, familiar smell. He knew what it was. *Of course.* Why hadn't he thought of it before?

We're nearly there, for Corin's sake.

'Mongrel? I'm coming for you, mongrel!'

Joseph turned and ran through the streets, his heart leaping. He had done it. He had actually controlled Hoake's mind with the wooden spoon, and he'd got out of it alive.

No more being pushed around. No more being told what to do.

It was time to put his plan into action.

Chapter Nineteen

'That's him,' said the cat.

Tabitha leaned forward, watching the whitecoat stumble out onto the street. It was almost dawn, but the tavern was still lit up and bustling with activity. A second figure, big and burly, appeared in the doorframe.

'And don't come back till you're sober, understand?' The door slammed shut.

The whitecoat paused for a moment, swaying, and threw an obscene gesture back at the tavern.

Tabitha shifted position, uncomfortably aware of the big man with the horse's eyes who gripped her collar, forestalling any attempt to escape. They were

crouched in an alleyway, sticking to the shadows
where they couldn't be seen. Tabitha was exhausted
and her whole body felt bruised and tender. They'd
been walking all night, ever since the elf in the stocks
had given her up. First to get away from the Demon's
Watch. Then hunting. Hunting for this whitecoat.

Trying not to think about what the cat had said.

I've already dealt with the mongrel boy.

At first she'd demanded that they let her go.

'I'm afraid not,' the pale woman with the bald
head had replied. Something about her gave Tabitha
the creeps. No – *everything* about her. 'If your friends
come looking for us, we'll need a hostage.'

'So you're not going to kill me? Then what are
we doing?'

The cat had grabbed her jaw, squeezing tight and
making her flinch. 'You are a nosy little girl, aren't
you? Don't be so sure we'll let you live. Perhaps we'll
throw you to the sharks. Or perhaps we'll lock you in
a lobster pot and ship you off across the ocean. Does
that sound familiar?'

She'd kept quiet after that.

Until now.

'Who is he?' she whispered.

The hand on her collar tightened, and another
came round to clamp over her mouth. It was hot

and sweaty and stank of horses. She wrinkled her nose, uselessly.

The cat turned to the others, his face half lit by the glow from the tavern. 'With me.' He stepped out into the street. The others followed, Tabitha dangling like a marionette from the big man's grip, stumbling, her feet only just touching the ground.

The drunk man might have been a whitecoat, but in truth his jacket was mostly brown and yellow now, stained with spilt grog and worse. He was large, soft and podgy with sandy-coloured hair – but even through the haze of grog, something about him suggested a fighter. And it wasn't just the hefty curved sword that swung from his belt.

As the shapeshifters padded towards him, the man turned, red-rimmed eyes struggling to focus, and Tabitha drew in a sharp breath at the sight of a horrible scar on his forehead.

'Whatareyer . . . Whassgoin . . . ?' he said, the words slurring into each other.

'You know what we want, my friend,' said the pale woman.

'Aye,' said the big man holding Tabitha. 'Where is he?'

The whitecoat lurched away. But the pale woman was beside him in an instant, and delivered a gentle push to the side of his head with one long white finger, as though tipping over a row of triominoes. The man overbalanced, sank to his knees and sprawled on the cobblestones, panting heavily. A slick of vomit bubbled down his chin. Tabitha's own stomach heaved, and she squirmed in the big man's grip.

There was some strange smell in the air, she realized, something beyond the stench of grog and sick. Something that she recognized.

The cat knelt and took the whitecoat's collar in both hands, bringing his face close. 'You disgust me, Hoake. What are you? You wear the League's brand on your head. You work for a filthy crook. And you drink yourself half to death every night.'

'Idonwanna . . . I duneven . . .' mumbled Hoake.

The cat motioned to the pale woman. She nodded, and suddenly was no longer there. Only her clothes remained, and they fell to the ground with a rustle. Something crawled out of the empty collar, midnight black, many-limbed. *A spider.* It scuttled across the cobblestones onto the butcher's jacket and began to move steadily closer to his face. Hoake's eyes grew even wider, and he began to cry.

Tabitha felt an unexpected surge of pity.

'Tell us,' said the cat. 'Tell us now, or you'll have taken your last swig of firewater.'

At the mention of firewater the whitecoat groaned, rolled over and threw up noisily onto the cobbles, sending the spider scuttling away before he slumped face first into his own sick.

'Wake up,' snapped the cat. He stood and shoved the man's limp body with his shoe, but Hoake was utterly still.

'We'll get nothing from him till he comes round,' said the man with the horse's eyes. 'If he *does* come round.'

'That's not good enough,' said the cat irritably. 'It could take hours. The Snitch could have left Azurmouth by then.'

'Wait, what?' said Tabitha. She twisted hard, finally freeing herself. 'Did you say *the Snitch*? As in Jeb the Snitch? This whitecoat works for him?'

They all looked at her. The cat. The man with the horse's eyes. Even the spider paused, motionless.

'Indeed,' said cat. 'We handed your little friend over to him.'

Joseph. So he's still alive . . .

Tabitha sniffed the air again. That smell. So familiar. And at the mention of Jeb the Snitch, she realized what it was. She'd been right. She'd been right all along.

'Look at his boots,' she said. 'Look, there.'

Thick black gunk clung to the underside of the whitecoat's boots, like treacle. She knelt, and no one made any attempt to stop her. She sniffed once again. Yes – musty, sickly, somewhere between fresh vomit and rotten fish.

Griffin bile.

'You know what that is?' she asked.

The man with the horse's eyes shook his head. The cat watched her warily. The spider crept closer, stepping carefully around Hoake's unconscious body.

'Don't you know what Jeb does, when he's not lying and cheating and stabbing folk in the back?'

Silence again.

'I know,' said Tabitha. 'I can help you find him.'

'How?' said the cat.

'I'll tell you,' said Tabitha. 'On one condition.'

'We're not letting you go,' said the big man. 'So don't even ask.'

Tabitha licked her lips. Jeb the Snitch. *We handed your little friend over to him.*

'I don't want you to let me go,' she said. 'I want you to take me with you.'

INTERLUDE

*T*hey flinch as he enters the room, and he feels their gaze linger on his cheek. The bruise has turned a dark purple, swollen with blood, throbbing with pain.

No matter. The mongrel Captain Newton will pay for it.

He sits at the head of the table, as a servant pours hot velvetbean into a cup and sets it before him. The lords have barely touched their breakfast, plates of egg and toast gently cooling in front of them. They watch him, on edge. Light shines through the great windows of the state room in solid square beams. It is a beautiful morning. He picks up a knife and begins to spread butter, the only sound the rasping of the knife across the toast.

It is the Earl of Brindenheim who speaks first, of course.

'So, what of the contest? Corin's Day has passed, and we have no victor.'

The man has both fists on the table, tightly clenched, and his jaw wobbles with the effort of keeping his temper. Lucky Leo sits beside him, meek and silent as a mouse as his father speaks for him.

'The contest is of no importance.'

He savours the widening of eyes and the muttering that follows that.

'I disagree.'

'Of course you do.'

Brindenheim's face turns feral for a moment, but he holds himself in check.

'We cannot leave matters thus. Five fights are yet to be fought until a champion can be named. Think of the citizens of Azurmouth! They will not be content with this.'

'They will be, or my butchers will see to it.' The Duke sets his knife down beside his plate, and looks Brindenheim in the eye. He is pleased to see the old walrus blink, just like the weak younger lords. 'I have had quite enough of you and your son. Thieves, the pair of you.'

The table has fallen utterly silent. He spreads damson

jam onto his toast. A twinge of pain as he opens his mouth to eat. But nothing compared to what the mongrel captain will suffer.

Brindenheim stands. 'How dare you?' He speaks under his breath, quivering with fury. 'No man speaks to me like that.'

'You took my sword.'

'The sword was never yours. Our fleet won it at the Battle of Illon. Our men. Our guns. In an expedition which you had no right to lead in the first place!' He slams a fist on the table, making the cutlery rattle. 'For too long you have taken liberties. You should never have sailed against Port Fayt. You lost half our ships and returned with nothing to show for it but an ancient relic.' Brindenheim's eyes narrow, and a grim smile spreads across his face. 'And I know why you need that sword. You thought you could hide the truth from us, didn't you? But last night I had my men go through your magicians' quarters. It took them till dawn, but they found it. All your research. All your plans.'

'Very well. Perhaps you'd care to share this with our friends?'

'He already has,' Lucky Leo pipes up.

'Indeed,' growls Brindenheim. 'And we cannot allow you to proceed. Even if your magicians are correct, the ritual is far too dangerous. You have no idea *what forces you might unleash. We must bring this to an end.'*

The Duke sets the toast down on his plate, wipes his hands on a thick white napkin and examines the Earl of Brindenheim. 'What are you saying?'

Brindenheim draws himself up. 'I am saying that you are no longer fit to sit among us, and must be cast out from the League of the Light. We are all agreed. Who stands with me?'

Lucky Leo rises, his piggy eyes darting nervously around the room. The other lords look startled, uncomfortable.

'I said, who stands with me?' barks the Earl, a note of anger in his voice.

Cowards. They had hoped to keep their heads down and enjoy the show. But then Garvill clambers to his feet. Tallis follows soon enough, although neither will look at him. Next the Flatland lords, Juddmouth first. The least despicable, though that is no great achievement. Chairs scrape on the floor as the League rises.

Only the Duke remains seated, his breakfast barely touched.

'I'm sorry that you feel this way. All of you.' He catches the eye of Major Turnbull, stationed by the door. She nods and slips out of it.

'But I am not surprised. It is said that Corin the Bold once rode a hundred leagues in one week to the lair of the mountain dragon Sigrild. Then he fought the beast, two days straight, till he could barely lift his blade. Yet still Corin found strength to strangle the monster and set his head on a spike.'

'A story for children,' spits Brindenheim. He rests one hand on the hilt of his sword.

'And you . . . all of you . . .' The Duke stands suddenly, and the nearest lords cower away. There is doubt in their faces now, as they see the fury in his. 'The best of you can hardly ride as far as the nearest alehouse, and the most dread foe any one of you has ever faced is a roast suckling pig. You are weak. Pathetic. And you have forgotten our calling, to bring light into the darkness. To rid the world of demonspawn.'

'I'm the finest swordsman in Azurmouth,' says Lucky Leo, his voice little more than a squeak. Strange, how some men find courage at the worst possible moments.

'Indeed? Then it is to be hoped you are as handy with a butter knife.'

They realize now – something terrible is about to happen. The Earl of Brindenheim lets out a roar, draws his sword and lunges forward. But Major Turnbull has returned and trips him, sending the walrus crashing to the floor and dragging half the tablecloth with him. She *sets her boot on his back, pinning him down as his son looks on in horror.*

'I think we are ready now, Major,' says the Duke.

She turns, beckons, and the doors to the breakfast room are flung open wide.

He savours their faces, silent, twisted in horror. Can it really be? Oh yes. Yes it can.

'Count yourselves lucky,' he says. 'Corin fought a mountain dragon, big as a galleon. Next to that feat, this should be no challenge at all.'

They stalk into the room, moving slow, muscles tense. The morning sunlight makes their green scales glitter, and their bat-like wings unfurl like leather fans in the open space. The nearest opens its mouth to reveal teeth as long as fingers, and hisses.

'You cannot do this,' whimpers the Earl of Brindenheim. His face is as white as his whiskers.

The wyverns spread out, circling the lords and sniffing like dogs.

'But I can.'

The nearest flaps up, wings beating the air, alighting on the table and setting the crockery rattling. It whines hungrily, and a long red tongue darts from its mouth.

'You asked if they had hunted demonspawn before,' the Duke says quietly. 'They have indeed. The elves last the longest, in general. Daemonium Pulchrum.

They run faster than the others. The dwarves, on the other hand, are always the first to go. They are slow and heavy, and they lack the cunning of an imp or a goblin. Of course, that is in the forests. Here, there is nowhere to run. Nowhere to hide.'

'Please,' begs Brindenheim, all trace of defiance gone, as the wyverns close in. 'Let us talk like men. Perhaps we could—'

'No.' The Duke clicks his fingers, and the air fills with the rustle of wyvern wings.

As the first screams tear through the room, he closes his eyes and smiles.

PART THREE
Elijah

Chapter Twenty

Morning – and Joseph hadn't slept a wink.

It had taken him most of the night to find what he needed for his plan. After that the boarding houses had all been closed, so he'd slid under a broken-down cart and snatched a couple of hours of rest, until he was woken by a rat snuffling at his face. Breakfast had been a half-eaten loaf of bread dropped by a clumsy seagull.

He was more tired and hungry than he'd ever been before. But it didn't matter. All that mattered was the plan.

He forced his feet to keep walking.

The sky was a strip of grey above the

rickety rooftops, and the streets of Azurmouth were as quiet as they ever seemed to get. Just a few early morning fishermen making their way to the quayside, a delivery boy whistling and hefting a massive sack on his back, and rats – more rats – fighting over a broken crab carcass. Joseph went quickly, with his head down, but thankfully there were no butchers to be seen.

Left here, then right.

At last his nostrils picked up the scent of the griffin bile, even more pungent in the morning air. Improbably, it made his belly rumble.

He turned the corner and saw the tavern they'd stopped at the night before. It was just as grimy as he'd imagined. The tavern sign was painted with an image of an empty treasure chest, though it was faded and peeling. The place looked ramshackle, like it might collapse at any moment.

The scent of the bile was stronger here. Joseph followed his nose down the road to a dead end – a high white wall, with a large archway and heavy wooden gates set into it. He backed up, standing on tiptoes to get a look at the buildings beyond it, white with blackened beams and thatched roofs, just like the other houses on the street.

There was no sign above the gates, but the smell

was overpowering, and Joseph's heart skipped a beat as he saw two more black slicks on the road, smeared by cartwheel tracks that led from the archway.

This was it. This had to be it.

Joseph patted his waistcoat pocket, checking for his father's silver pocket watch. He checked his right-hand pocket for the wooden spoon, panicked for a moment when he found it empty, until he remembered: that was the whole point.

Last chance. He could turn back now. Or he could keep walking, straight into the dragon's jaws. He hadn't even brought his cutlass with him.

No. The plan was a good plan. Besides, it was too late for second thoughts.

I'm coming for you, Father. I'm going to find you.

He took a deep breath, stepped forward and knocked on the wooden doors.

It *was* a good plan, wasn't it?

There was a scraping and banging as someone unbarred the doors. They inched open a short way and a face peered suspiciously out.

Joseph froze in horror. The face belonged to a wiry, weather-beaten goblin, with a carved lump of wood for a nose.

'You!' yelped Wooden-nose. Then his face twisted into a snarl of pure rage. His grey hands shot out, clapped over Joseph's ears and tugged him inside, hurling him face first into a deep puddle of bile.

Joseph spluttered, desperately trying not to inhale. His eyes, nose and mouth were clogged with thick black gunk. As he tried to rise he felt a weight come down on him, then a hand clamped around the back of his head, forcing his face back into the glistening black puddle.

'Filthy little *thea thlug*!' snarled Wooden-nose. 'Got me kicked in the fathe by a *horth*, didn't you? Do you have any idea how much that hurt? It thmathed my nothe to thplinterth, you maggot!'

Joseph bucked and writhed, but it was hopeless. He was out of breath. He choked in a mouthful of griffin bile, and it burned as it slid down his throat. How many more mouthfuls would it take to kill him? *Drowned in bile*. It wasn't part of the plan.

'Oi!' said another voice. 'That's him! That's the boy!' And the next moment he was pulled out of the puddle, coughing and retching and trying to rub the bile out of his eyes.

When he cleared them, he saw three goblin faces peering at him. One of them was Wooden-nose, who looked none too pleased at the interruption.

'Yeah, that's definitely him,' said one of his friends, and Joseph recognized the voice. It was the driver from the night before. 'Little privy roach gave us the slip.' He leaned in closer. 'What d'you think you're doing here, seaweed-brain? You soft in the head?'

'Letth find out,' snarled Wooden-nose. 'I'll get a rock.'

'Who cares why he's here?' said the third goblin. 'Let's take him to Jeb.'

Yes, take me to him. Take me to Jeb the Snitch.

Joseph was hauled to his feet, dripping bile. It spattered his shirt, cold and heavy, and he tried to wipe it away as his captors hustled him across a small, muddy courtyard strewn with feathers and enclosed by high, whitewashed buildings. The smell was different here – an animal stink of dung and sweat mingling with the stench of the bile.

The goblins were all wearing the same clothes, Joseph noticed. Boiled leather suits with metal plates attached like armour, and metal tools dangling from their belts.

There had been a griffin farmer in the Legless Mermaid once, back in Port Fayt, and after a few grogs he'd told Joseph how griffins usually fought against bile milking, and how sometimes the beasts got injured. Griffin blood was one of the deadliest poisons known to man or troll – hence the suits.

Joseph was beginning to wish he had one himself.

Wooden-nose strode ahead and swung open a door that led into a dark, cavernous interior. Immediately Joseph's nose was assailed by a stronger version of the griffin smell in the courtyard, and a strange cacophony of squawks and whines rose around him.

As his eyes adjusted to the darkness he saw cages on either side, packed one on top of the other and reaching all the way up to the rafters. There were movements inside – pawing of the ground and shifting of wings. Beady eyes glared out at him, glinting in the darkness, watching Joseph in a way that reminded him of Frank and Paddy with one of their ma's pies.

Before Joseph could look more closely there was a commotion up ahead, and a figure rounded the corner. It was a goblin, dressed in one of the leather-and-plate suits, and wearing a feathered tricorne hat that even the most grotesquely vain merchant would dismiss as too flashy.

Even without the hat, Joseph would have recognized him at once.

Those pale, cruel eyes.

The pointed teeth.

The sneer on his lips.

Jeb the Snitch.

Joseph's fists clenched. This was a goblin who had tricked him into betraying Port Fayt. A goblin who had shot his friend, the mermaid princess Pallione. The most treacherous, worthless, vicious goblin Joseph had ever met.

A goblin who knew where Joseph's father was.

He was so close now. So close to finding him.

Breathe. Slow and steady. Stick to the plan.

Another figure came hurrying after Jeb. A skinny human dressed in a long plain robe and a turban, leading a griffin by a halter. Joseph had always imagined griffins as majestic, powerful creatures, but this one limped like a beaten donkey. It had dull eyes, a chipped beak, and its wing feathers were ruffled and bent out of shape. Joseph could see ribs sticking out at the point where the griffin's feathered chest gave way to its furred hindquarters.

'Please,' said the man in the turban. 'Nell is all I have.'

Jeb the Snitch rounded on him. 'Call yerself a griffin-catcher? I seen starving seagulls wi' more life than this heap o' dung.'

'My family,' stammered the griffin's owner. 'I must feed them. I promise, you won't see better. At this time of year, griffins are impossible to find.'

'Two ducats. I'm being generous.'

'It has always been ten. Her bile will be thick, I swear. If not, you will have the ducats back.'

'You deaf? I said two.'

'Please. For the sake of our friendship.'

The Snitch just laughed.

'Jeb,' said Wooden-nose. 'Look what we found.'

Jeb spun around and saw Joseph. For a moment his face came alive with anger. Then his lips curled into a smile.

Joseph felt sick to his stomach. *I should be furious, shouldn't I? After everything he's done* . . . But instead, he was frightened. He knew what Jeb was capable of. And in the cold light of day, his plan didn't seem nearly as clever as it had the night before.

'Well, well,' said Jeb. 'Thought you were pretty smart running away from ol' Hoake, didn't yer? Thought you were the cat's pyjamas. I knew my boys'd catch yer.'

'Um,' said Wooden-nose. 'Acthually . . . he came here himthelf.'

Jeb scowled. 'Came here himthelf, did he?' he mimicked. 'That case he's even less smart than I thought.' He leaned forward, his long, hooked nose almost touching Joseph's own. 'Good thing you're here, mongrel. Them griffins are famished. I reckon it's breakfast time.'

'I don't think so,' said Joseph. 'I don't think you're going to feed me to the griffins.'

'Oh, yer don't? And why's that?'

'Because if you do, you'll never get the wooden spoon.'

'What did he say?' squawked one of the other goblins.

Jeb snarled. 'Never you mind.' His bony fingers dug into Joseph's jaw, and he dragged him across the floor to the nearest cage. Behind the metal bars, a dark shape shifted in the shadows and snorted, the breath condensing in the morning air. Its eyes caught the light, glinting. Joseph struggled, but was held in place, face pressed against the cold steel of the bars. His nostrils wrinkled at the stench.

'Looks hungry, don't he?' murmured Jeb, his breath hot on Joseph's ear. 'You'd be hungry too, I reckon, if you'd had nowt to eat all week but half a dozen mice.'

Somewhere behind him, the other goblins began to chuckle.

'Out with it,' hissed Jeb. 'Where's my wooden spoon?'

'I'm not telling.'

'Then I'll chop yer into bits and push 'em through the bars, one by one. Don't think I won't.'

Anger swelled inside Joseph at last, giving him courage. 'You didn't let me finish,' he said, his voice muffled by metal. 'I'm not *telling* you where it is. But I'll *show* you.'

He was tugged away from the bars and spun to face Jeb again. The goblin's pale eyes were staring into his own, probing, as though they might snatch the truth out of him.

'What are you saying?' snapped Jeb.

'I'm saying I'll take you to the wooden spoon.' Joseph licked his lips. 'But there's two conditions.'

'*Conditions*, eh?' said Jeb. 'Maybe you *are* a smart one after all. Let's hear 'em then.'

'The first is that you have to come alone. Just you.'

'Suits me.'

'And the second . . .' He reached into his pocket and closed his fingers around the silver watch. 'The second is that after you've got the spoon, you tell me how to find my father.'

A faint smile hovered on Jeb's lips. 'Thought yer might say that. You believe me, then? That he's still alive?'

Joseph had every reason in the world not to. After all the lies Jeb the Snitch had told, why should he be telling the truth about this one thing?

Except that he is. He's telling the truth.

Thalin knew how, but Joseph was sure of it. His father was alive.

'I believe you,' he said.

Jeb ran a long tongue over his pointed teeth. 'Seems I ain't got much choice then.' He turned to the other goblins and the man in the turban. 'Two ducats, Mr Mandak. We got a deal?' The man's shoulders slumped, and he nodded. 'Thought so. You boys iron out the details. Me and this mongrel are goin' to take a stroll.'

Chapter Twenty-one

They walked side-by-side through narrow alley-ways, Joseph's bile-soaked shirt drying and stiffening in the breeze. He'd wiped the worst of it off with a filthy rag given him by one of the goblins. Meanwhile Jeb had insisted on changing out of his griffin suit, and now he was got up like a drunkard's maypole – a vivid green velvet jacket over an eye-watering pink waistcoat, with a silver hat and breeches. The outfit made him look even less trust-worthy than before.

'Not going far, are we, mongrel?' said Jeb. 'These shoes ain't that comfortable.'

Joseph wasn't surprised to hear it. They were

absurdly long and pointed and made with strips of coloured leather so they looked like candy canes. What was the point of a shoe if it wasn't to make walking easier? 'Not far,' he said.

They crossed a bustling main road near the docks, and Jeb held onto Joseph's shoulder as they pushed through the crowds. 'Don't want you running off, mate,' he said with a wink.

Joseph didn't complain. He'd already noticed a pistol stuffed into Jeb's breeches. But then, he couldn't blame the goblin for not trusting him either.

It was a relief when they turned off onto quieter back streets again, where the houses overhung the cobbles, enclosing them so much it reminded Joseph of wading through the sewers to get to the House of Light.

At last they came to a tall, burned-out tavern, blackened with soot, its door gone completely. Joseph had found it the night before – the first of the two things he'd needed for his plan.

'This is it.'

This is where I find out the truth. The thought sent a little shiver down his spine.

'And how do I know this ain't a trap?'

'There's only one way to find out.'

Jeb narrowed his eyes. 'Get on with it then.'

Joseph did so.

Inside there was a bar, and space for lots of tables – though they were all gone now, of course. The layout reminded Joseph of the Legless Mermaid. He couldn't remember being handed over to his uncle after the death of his parents, but if he'd known then what the Mermaid would be like, he would have fought and kicked and cried his throat raw.

Behind him, he heard the click of a hammer pulled back, and he turned to see that Jeb had drawn the pistol and levelled it at him.

'One false move,' said Jeb. 'Just remember you ain't as smart as me, mongrel, so don't try nothing. Got it?'

Joseph nodded.

They climbed a spiralling stone staircase in the corner of the room. On the floor above there were several doorways, each leading out onto a corridor with rooms attached – probably bedrooms where customers could have stayed the night. That was one good thing about the Mermaid – Mr Lightly never had guests. For a man who ran a tavern, he didn't seem to like people very much. Particularly if they were goblins. *Shady characters*, Mr Lightly called them. *Don't know where you are with 'em. That's the problem. Can't trust 'em.*

They stopped at the top floor, a turret which was nothing but a large, empty room, where the floorboards were intact but singed and spattered with bird droppings. The roof was gone, leaving only a few wooden spars that stretched above. It was like standing inside a dragon's ribcage.

Joseph had considered spending the night here, but it offered no shelter at all. And in any case he hadn't felt like staying in this spooky mirror image of the Legless Mermaid. It brought back too many memories.

The open sky was still grey above them, and a breeze swept through the glassless windows, chilling him to the bone. He stepped into the room, positioning himself carefully, according to the plan, next to a loose floorboard. A very particular loose floorboard.

Jeb looked around, unimpressed. 'If this is a joke . . .'

'It's not a joke. Look, over on the windowsill.'

A small, homely object lay there.

A wooden spoon.

The goblin's eyes lit up with greed, and he started towards it. At the same instant Joseph knelt, lifted the floorboard at his feet and pulled out something from beneath it.

'Wait.' Jeb turned back. 'How do I know that's the real—'

'It's not. *This* is.' Joseph stood, brandishing the

wooden spoon. The one he'd brought with him across the Ebony Ocean. Every bit as small and homely as the one on the windowsill.

'You stinking little—'

'I was afraid you might try to cheat me. Then I remembered how the shapeshifter tricked you back in Port Fayt, giving you an ordinary spoon instead of the magical one. So I did the same.' Joseph nodded at the one on the windowsill. 'I took that one from a soup stall last night, after I got away from your whitecoat.' *The second thing I needed for the plan.* 'And you fell for it, just like last time.'

The goblin's face twisted into a mask of fury, but Joseph stood his ground, gripping the wand tightly and fighting the urge to run. His cutlass lay at his feet, underneath the loose floorboard, but he made no move to take it.

Finally Jeb managed a sneering smile. 'Well, congratulations. But it don't make no difference. If yer don't hand over that wand right now, I'll blow yer brains out.' He raised the pistol again. 'No one's goin' to miss you. Most likely no one'll even find yer, 'less you count the gulls. They'll have a feast, I reckon.'

It wasn't the first time Joseph had been on the wrong side of a loaded gun, but that didn't make it any less frightening. He swallowed his fear and pointed the wooden spoon at Jeb, just like the goblin was pointing the pistol at him. *Don't be afraid*, he told himself. *You used it before. You can use it again.*

'Why don't you just tell me the truth?' His voice trembled. 'Tell me where my father is. It can't hurt you, can it?'

A strange expression came over Jeb's face. But the next moment it was gone, like a passing storm cloud, replaced by his familiar smirk.

'You don't want to know, mongrel. Now gimme the real spoon or I'll shoot you dead and take it anyway.'

Joseph locked eyes with Jeb. He concentrated hard, harder than he ever had before, trying to remember how it had felt in the carriage with Hoake. *Just think the right thoughts.*

I'm Jeb. I'd do anything for more ducats. Betray anyone.

'I'll count to three,' snarled Jeb. 'Then it's goodbye, mongrel.'

Joseph's head began to throb. It felt heavy, potent with magic.

'One.'

The magic spread, a tingling warmth, suffusing his body like hot velvetbean swallowed on a winter night. It was happening faster this time. As though it was easier to inhabit Jeb's thoughts than it had been with Hoake. Or was it just the practice? *It doesn't matter. Focus.*

'Two.'

I'm a bile trader. A snitch. A thief. A liar.

Into his chest, his arms, his hands. And now the spoon itself was vibrating. From the corner of his eye Joseph saw that the air around it was swirling, distorting with magic. But he kept staring at Jeb, climbing out of himself, forcing his way into the goblin's mind.

'Three!'

Jeb's finger tightened round the trigger, and at the same instant the world jolted, and Joseph wasn't Joseph any more.

Chapter Twenty-two

He was Jeb.

Jeb the Snitch, who knew Port Fayt better than anyone, made more ducats in a day than most sailors made in a week, whose clothes were the finest, the smartest, the best. Who had the Grey Brotherhood in his pocket, and had built a griffin bile farm from scratch. Who had set up trading links throughout the Old World, using nothing but his wits.

Who was never good enough, no matter what he did.

Why, in all his life, had no one ever respected him?

*

Joseph was there, inside the goblin's head. Soaring through his mind like the fairies that darted and swooped in the skies of Port Fayt. He scoured the deepest recesses, scavenging for the information he needed. *Elijah Grubb. Elijah Grubb. Elijah Grubb. Where are you?* They had to be there – thoughts of Joseph's father, lurking somewhere in the goblin's mind. And he was going to find them.

A boyhood memory. A cold day. Jeb had got up early and snuck out with his fishing rod, shivering on the pier for hours to catch one fat flounder. Afterwards he had taken a short cut home, through an alley-way where he was ambushed by two trolls from the roughest part of the quarter – not much older than him, but three times as big, fists the size of his head. They wanted his catch.

As he was about to hand it over, another goblin boy appeared in the alleyway, shouted at the trolls, ran at them, swinging his fists. He wasn't much bigger than Jeb, but his anger frightened the bullies enough to make them slink off, muttering empty threats as they went.

Saved. It was such a relief that Jeb actually cried, and the goblin boy put an arm around him. Jeb hated that, almost as much as the bullies.

'It's all right,' Elijah told him. 'I'm here now.'

Elijah.

Somewhere far away, Joseph reeled in shock. So Jeb *had* known his father. Known him from when they were boys. Known him all their lives. What did it mean?

He delved deeper, drawn like a moth to a flame.

Another memory, years later. Jeb sat at a table with Elijah. It was a tavern – they were both older now – but young enough that the smells, the sights, the atmosphere of the place were thrilling. Jeb took a sip of grog from a giant pewter tankard, and it tasted sweet and foul, and above all *dangerous*. They were goblins fully grown – or near enough.

He leaned over the table, his eyes darting left and right. Over there, a human whispering something to a dwarf woman. And there, money changing hands between two tall, proud elves.

Secrets. Knowledge. Power. It was the lifeblood of Port Fayt. He knew that now, and he knew that it was the only strength he'd ever have. He was no troll, with a chest like a barrel and a jaw like a jutting cliff face. He was a goblin, and goblins had to use cunning to make ends meet.

Now he was telling Elijah of his own secret. Of his

girl, and what had happened between them. How she was going to have a baby. Jeb's baby.

Elijah's face lit up. *This is wonderful news. We must celebrate.* He was bigger and stronger than Jeb, his arms already taut and muscled from long days at the docks, working as a stevedore, carting barrels of dragon grease from the Northern Wastes, crates of wyrm scales from the Flatland Duchies, bottles of blackwine from Garran. His skin was darkened from the sunshine, his hands worn and his face a little wrinkled, but his eyes were bright and full of life, and when he smiled it was like looking through a window to a better place – a place where you could be honest and truthful and good.

Jeb hated Elijah and wanted him all to himself, both at the same time.

It's not like that, Jeb had explained. *It's complicated.*

You don't love her? asked Elijah.

Maybe he did. But Jeb was a coward. He couldn't let his parents find out about the child. His father would beat him, or worse. *I'm going to end it with her,* he said. *I'm going to forget it ever happened.*

The way Elijah looked at him then, his eyes so cold, his mouth a thin line. It burned in his memory. *She can't forget,* Elijah told him.

The words twisted Jeb's gut. He'd thought Elijah would understand. Elijah, of all people.

Elijah, his brother.

No. No, it can't be true.

And yet Joseph knew that it was. He could feel Jeb resisting him, but it was no good. Here, now, his mind belonged to Joseph.

My uncle's mind. Jeb the Snitch is my uncle.

Joseph felt sick. He didn't want to know any more. He could sense, somehow, that there was something worse coming – something terrible. He wanted to turn away. But now a third memory surged up like a tidal wave, and engulfed him.

A few months later. Jeb had hardly spoken to his brother since the day he'd told him about the baby. He'd been so busy. The petty crooks on the docks had begun to call him 'The Snitch', but he knew so much now – a few secrets here, a few dark truths there – that no one dared touch him. Jeb the Snitch. He liked the sound of it. It was all going so well.

Until the day he walked past the house with the green front door, and heard laughter inside. He crept to the window and saw the girl sitting at the table, and opposite her Elijah, both of them smiling, practically shining with joy. Her belly was swollen. Inside it, he knew, was a child. *His* child.

He knocked at the door, and when Elijah opened it, he demanded to know what was happening.

They went back to the tavern. Their tavern, the one they always came to, though it was the first time in months. The last time too, though he didn't know it then.

Elijah explained. After Jeb had ended it with the girl Elijah had gone to see her, to give her money. Money from his own pocket, that he'd earned as a stevedore, to help her with the baby.

Idiot, Jeb thought. *For a goblin to make a living with his muscles.*

Elijah had begun to visit, at first just to make sure she was all right, that she would be able to look after the baby on her own. Then for more than that. They had fallen in love.

He told Jeb not to worry about it, that it didn't concern him. He was going to live with her, help look after the baby and do his best to make her happy.

You can't, Jeb hissed. *Think what Father would say. For Thalin's sake, you're a goblin and she's a human.*

That didn't stop you, said Elijah.

It's different. I would never have lived with her. What next – will you marry her?

Elijah's eyes went cold again, and his jaw set. He was sorry he hadn't told Jeb sooner, and even sorrier that Jeb didn't understand.

What about me? said Jeb. *You took her from me.*

You gave her up, Elijah told him. *You tossed her aside. You never loved her.*

Maybe it was true. Maybe he'd just wanted her, in the same way he wanted ducats, and power and respect. But still . . . His own brother. His perfect brother, whom everybody loved, who had just stolen her away.

He leaned forward across the table. He was angry, and he only had one card left to play. He told Elijah to stay away from her, or he would tell their mother and father.

Elijah shook his head. There was no coldness left in those eyes now, only sorrow, perhaps even pity. *Goodbye*, he said. *If you ever need me, I'll be with Eleanor.*

With Eleanor and Joseph.

Little Joseph.

Everything lurched, and Joseph dropped to his knees, choking. His head spun. The wooden spoon fell from his fingers and clattered on the floor.

No. Please, no.

The strangest thing – Jeb hadn't even lied to him.

His father was alive, had been all along. He just wasn't the person Joseph had thought he was.

His father stood two feet away, staggering, clutching his head. Jeb the Snitch. Who had once been just Jeb.

Jeb Grubb.

All Joseph's memories, everything he had locked away, every precious moment with the goblin he'd thought was his father – his uncle, Elijah Grubb – all of them rushed through his head in a torrent, redefined by the truth. The horrible, awful truth. The truth he'd fought so hard to uncover.

He barely looked up as Jeb stumbled forward, replaced the ordinary wooden spoon with the real one, his pistol still trained on Joseph. On his son.

'I didn't recognize yer at first,' muttered Jeb. 'Reckoned you'd died long ago, along wi' your ma. You got some o' yer old man's wits about yer, that's for sure. Using a wand, like you were some sort o' magician . . .' He tucked the wooden spoon in his pocket. 'Well, the fun's over now. Eli's gone. Eleanor too. Just you left.'

Joseph closed his eyes, squeezing them tight to stop the tears from falling. This was it. The end. Everything he'd thought he'd known was wrong, and the life he was about to lose seemed to belong to a stranger.

The son of the Snitch. Surely he deserved to die.

He would never see Elijah again. The goblin who had raised him, who cared for him even when he knew what Joseph was – the child of a monster. It racked his heart with love and pain. He would never again see Tabs. Or Newton. Or Frank, or Paddy.

So be it. They were better off without him anyway.

He was ready. Ready for the gunshot to pierce his body and for the life to leave it.

And the shot never came.

'Get up, for Thalin's sake,' snapped Jeb. 'I ain't goin' to kill yer.'

Joseph opened his eyes and saw the goblin stuff the pistol in his pocket.

'Not yet, anyhow. I've got plans for you, son.'

Chapter Twenty-three

The stench of griffin bile filled Tabitha's nostrils, making her head swim. She pulled her neckerchief up to cover her nose.

The shapeshifters were striding so fast she had to hurry to keep up. If their injuries were still bothering them, they weren't showing it. People scrambled to get out of the way, casting nervous glances at those strange eyes and torn white-coat uniforms, coat tails flapping like the wings of avenging seraphs.

The cat breathed in deep and nodded. 'The air smells foul. Just like Hoake's boots. Very good, little girl – let us hope your theory is correct.'

'For your sake,' added the spider, her voice a whisper.

'I'm right,' said Tabitha. 'Don't you worry about that.'

At the end of the road they came to a large white-washed wall with a set of heavy wooden gates, where the smell was so strong you could practically taste it. Tabitha drew a pair of knives from her bandolier, flicked them around her thumbs and caught them again. She was ready.

'Here it is,' said the big man. 'I'll knock.'

The double doors were made out of thick wood, but not thick enough. There was a scraping, sucking sound as the big man became a horse. It seemed so natural Tabitha almost forgot to be surprised. His clothing ripped apart and fell in pieces to the cobbles, and he spun, smashing at the doors with his back hooves.

BANG! BANG! BANG!

At the last blow, the doors gave way in a shower of splinters.

'Shall we?' said the cat.

But Tabitha was already leaping through. Three goblins looked up, startled, from a game of triomi-noes. They wore leather suits head to toe, covered in metal plates. As if that could protect them. Tabitha was on them in an instant, and her fury surged into her arms and legs. She landed a hefty kick on the nearest goblin's chest, sending him sprawling back in his chair. The next had a cutlass half-drawn, but she slammed her elbow hard into his chin, and his jaw clamped shut with a click of teeth as he fell too, scattering triominoes to the ground.

The spider had the third, her long pale fingers around the goblin's throat, lifting him off the ground. 'Where is Jeb the Snitch?' she hissed.

The goblin fought for breath. His nose was made out of wood and held on with a piece of twine. He was the ugliest of the three, which was no mean feat.

'He'th gone,' the goblin lisped. 'With a filthy mongrel boy.'

Joseph.

'Where did they go?'

'How in the bleeding blue thea thould I know?' snapped the goblin. He squirmed in the spider's grip. 'They went off into the thity.'

Tabitha felt panic surging up inside her. *Too late.* If they'd just got here a little sooner, maybe—

'Don't lie to me,' said the spider.

The goblin's eyes went wide as the fingers pressed harder into his throat. 'Gaaaaah! Not lying! I thwear!' The fingers released. 'Well, maybe a bit,' said the goblin. 'They did go off, but then . . . then they came back.'

*

Past the griffin cages, past beady eyes glinting. Up a flight of steps to a stone corridor lined with leather suits that hung from pegs. Joseph followed his father in a daze.

'Put this on.' A leather suit was thrust at him. He shook his head. 'Please yerself.' Jeb pulled on a suit of his own, swept off his silver tricorne and pulled up a leather hood in its place. For a moment, that face reminded Joseph of Arabella Wyrmwood, the shrivelled old witch who had tried to destroy Port Fayt. But no – Jeb was even worse than her. At least she'd believed in something, and died for it. Jeb believed in nothing but himself.

Six years. Six years he'd had to find Joseph, to tell him the truth and claim his son. And instead he'd left Eleanor to die, left Joseph to be adopted by Mr Lightly, who hated all goblins and Joseph most of all. Not even through malice – just because he didn't care.

Elijah's gentle voice came back to him. *There's a little bit of demon and a little bit of seraph in everyone, Joseph. Don't let anyone tell you different.*

Was it Joseph he'd been thinking of, when he'd spoken those words?

His mother, a seraph if ever there was one. And his

father, Jeb the Snitch. The most hateful creature in all the world. Joseph's chest tightened all over again at the thought of the goblin who had cared for him, when even his own father wouldn't.

'The men who killed my uncle . . .' he said. His voice sounded strange and distant, like someone else's.

'That weren't my fault,' snapped Jeb, hustling Joseph along the corridor towards a heavy, round iron door. 'Weren't nothing to do with him being a goblin, neither. I owed 'em money, that's all, and I couldn't pay. Those idiots reckoned they could hurt me by killing Elijah. They didn't know we hadn't spoken in years.'

So it *was* Jeb's fault. Everything was his fault.

Jeb set a key in the lock, turned it and pushed the door open. Then he grabbed Joseph by the collar and shoved him through.

If the stench was bad before, here it was a hundred times worse. It smelled not just of bile, and blood and dung. It smelled of death. Jeb locked the door, made a big show of breathing it in, and let out a sigh of satisfaction.

'Know what I smell?' he said. His pointed teeth flashed in a grin. 'Ducats.'

They were on a raised wooden walkway that ran all the way around an enormous room filled with gigantic metal vats. Jeb pushed Joseph forwards with the end of his pistol.

'Welcome to the dragon's lair,' said Jeb. 'Just a little joke o' mine. Dragons love treasure, see? And there's treasure here, I can tell yer.' He pointed to a set of metal doors below. 'The milking rooms are through there. That's our main trade, see. But it ain't just bile a griffin's good for. When they die, there's rich pickings to be had. Griffin feathers, for instance.' He pointed to a pile of greasy black feathers beside one of the vats, each over a foot long, being picked at and cleaned by a pair of suited goblins. 'Plenty of idiots'll pay good money for 'em. Griffin talons too.' He pointed at a goblin trundling a cart full of rattling ebony claws. 'And o' course, last but not least, griffin blood.'

They stopped above the largest of the vats, which was covered with a lid like a saucepan. Jeb pulled at a lever beside the walkway, and the lid lifted with a creak. Underneath it a red liquid shimmered like oil, coursing with magic.

'Deadly,' said Jeb. 'Most lethal poison known to man or troll. It'll strip the flesh from yer bones in seconds. Worth a pretty penny to the right folk, I can tell yer. And soon, I won't need any of it.' He turned to Joseph, holding up the spoon. His pale eyes shone with greed. 'Them Grey Brothers told me about your visit to the Whale, how you was waving this thing around like you knew what to do with it. Got me to thinkin'. The wand might be worth a fair few ducats if I sold it, but if I was to *keep* it, use it myself, see, I can have anything I want, whenever I want it. *Anything.* I can get shot o' this dunghole of a city. No more griffin bile. No more Grey Brothers scrounging off me, always asking for a hand-out. Just me and a giant heap o' ducats.' He leaned in close. 'And now I know you can work it. So yer goin' to teach me how. Right here, right now. Reckon if a pesky little mongrel like you can do it, anyone can.'

Joseph felt sick. He shook his head.

'This ain't a friendly request,' snapped Jeb. He grabbed Joseph's collar again, forced him out over the railing until his face hovered above the pool of blood. 'Get talking.'

Joseph could see himself reflected in it, a mongrel boy who had lost all hope. Still, this one last thing he could do. He would never tell his father how to use the wand.

Past the griffin cages, past beady eyes glinting. Up a flight of steps. Along a corridor. Tabitha raced ahead of the shapeshifters, knives drawn.

Come on. Faster. Whatever the Snitch wanted from Joseph, he wasn't going to get it.

Ahead was a round iron door. Tabitha skidded to a halt, stopping just short of it. 'Break it down,' she yelled. 'Quickly!'

The cat and the spider were hot on her heels. The horse came last, still in animal form, hooves clattering on the stairs. He whinnied, head bent to fit under the low ceiling, then turned and kicked.

CLANG!

The hooves just bounced off. Hopeless.

'Joseph!' Tabitha called. 'Joseph, are you in there?'

'Hush now,' said the cat. 'We are not beaten yet. My lady?'

The spider nodded, and the next moment she had disappeared, her black clothes rustling to a heap on the floor.

'Stand back.'

Tabitha did so, as a scuttling dark creature shot out from the empty clothes, crawled over the iron door and in through the keyhole. A moment later there was a heavy *clunk* and the door swung open.

Chapter Twenty-four

'You?' snarled Jeb.

Joseph twisted his head from the griffin blood. There, at the end of the walkway, was a girl his own age, with blue hair and blades in her hands. His heart leaped in spite of everything.

She came.

And then he was tugged away from the vat of blood as one of Tabitha's knives went whistling past, burying itself in a wooden rafter.

'You privy roach!' howled Jeb. 'Throwing stinking *knives* at me? Are you trying to *kill* me?'

'Don't tempt me,' said Tabitha.

The slim figure of the cat stepped through the

doorway, followed by the horse, hooves clopping, and the small dark shape of the spider, scuttling on the wooden walkway.

'Get out, all of yer,' spat Jeb. 'No animals allowed. And no kids neither.'

'So, the great Snitch is a bile trader,' sneered the cat. 'A repulsive industry. How fitting.' The shapeshifter prowled forward, tracking Jeb's every movement as though the goblin were a mouse. 'You tricked us, Jeb. You offered us the Sword of Corin in exchange for the boy and the spoon. But the sword wasn't there, and your drunkard Hoake locked us in and left us for dead.'

'Tricked yer, did I?' Jeb snarled. 'Look who's talking! You cheated me out o' my wooden spoon back in Port Fayt, didn't yer? Way I see it, we're square.'

'I don't think so,' said the cat. 'We've come for our revenge.'

'Well, you ain't getting nothing.'

Joseph was shoved face down on the walkway, and before he could wriggle free, Jeb's foot was on his back, pinning him.

'Let him go!' Tabitha yelled, but Jeb ignored her.

Joseph craned his neck to see the goblin looming above, aiming the wooden spoon like a pistol at the newcomers. 'You best scarper, you and your hairy friends, and that mouldy-headed little girl too, or else I'll use this wand on yer. I ain't a magician, but I know how to use it.'

Another lie.

The cat hesitated.

Tabitha was gaping at the spoon, open-mouthed. 'What the— How did—?'

'Oi!' Jeb shook the wand fiercely. 'Get lost, I said, before I magic you all inside a cage of angry griffins.'

Joseph looked deep into Tabitha's grey eyes, which were full of questions he couldn't bear to answer: *Surely you didn't take the spoon? Surely you didn't bring it here, to Azurmouth? Surely you didn't give it to Jeb the Snitch?*

He lowered his head.

Tabitha couldn't believe it.

The tavern boy who had taken on a witch to save her life – who had stolen the wooden spoon and crossed the Ebony Ocean in search of his father – he had given up.

It filled her with sadness, and with anger.

Where was the boy who'd tried to cheer her up with fried octopus when she'd been sad about her parents? The boy whose tongue stuck out in concentration when he practised cutlass strokes on the old wooden figurehead outside Bootles' – even though he was the worst swordsman she'd ever met? The boy who drove her mad with his stupid song about scrubbing dishes, but whose voice she'd missed the moment it was gone?

What had happened to him?

'Joseph,' she pleaded. 'Do something.'

Do something.

How many times had he asked himself the same question, since he'd joined the Watch?

What would Thalin do?

What would Newton do?

What would his father do?

That last one sent a jolt through his body. Every time he'd asked it, he'd been thinking of Elijah.

An image came to him – something he'd seen inside Jeb's mind. Elijah as a boy, running down the alley to scare off the trolls who were threatening his little brother. Standing up to the bullies, even though they were bigger than him. Now Jeb had become the bully himself.

For you, Uncle.

He twisted his body hard to one side. Jeb's foot lost its purchase, and the goblin stumbled as Joseph rolled and sprang up. He grabbed two fistfuls of Jeb's leather suit and shoved him back against the wall. His father must have seen the fury in his eyes because he crumpled at once, cringing, as though expecting to be hit at any moment. The wooden spoon went clattering onto the walkway.

Coward. My father is a coward.

And the rage burned out in an instant. Joseph didn't hit him. What good would that do? Instead he stepped back, let go of the suit.

'Go,' he said, his voice barely a whisper. 'Just go away. Please.'

'Joseph!' yelled Tabitha.

Tabitha started forward, but the cat caught her by the wrists, twisting them up behind her back. Her knife fell, thudding into the wood point first. And now it was her turn to be forced down on the walkway, until she felt its rough surface against her cheek.

'What are you doing?' she yelped. 'I thought we were helping each other!'

'We *were*, my dear,' purred the cat. 'And you've been most useful. But now that you've led us to the Snitch, I'm growing a little tired of you.'

A door banged open below, and out of the corner of her eye, Tabitha saw a goblin lead a griffin into the hall. A familiar griffin, half-starved, with thinning feathers and a blunted beak. *Could it really be her?*

'We've wasted enough time already,' hissed the voice of the spider. 'Let's take our revenge on the goblin.'

'What about the children?' asked the horse.

'An excellent question.' The cat stroked Tabitha's cheek with one finger. 'I believe a quick death will suffice.'

Tabitha squirmed in the shapeshifter's grip. 'Nell!' she shrieked. Her throat was raw, but she drew in breath and bellowed it again. 'Neeeell!'

On the floor below, Nell blinked and looked around, confused.

'Neeeeeeell!'

'Enough,' the cat murmured in her ear. 'Your game is lost.'

Tabitha barely heard him. The griffin had turned to look at her. Its beak twitched, and something shifted in those small black eyes.

'Fly for me!' Tabitha burst out. 'Like last time. *Neeeeeeell!*'

'Oi!' said the goblin, tugging at the halter. 'Stay still, you useless—'

Nell took a step forward. Then another. The griffin's wings spread like sails, and began to flap. The hapless goblin swung from the halter, then sprawled back onto the flagstones.

Across the floor, workers panicked and scurried to escape.

'Griffin loose!'

'Everybody out!'

There was a rush of air as the creature swooped up to the walkway, landed and began stalking towards them.

Tabitha felt a sudden thrill of fear, but there was no going back now. 'Help me!' she yelled.

'What in Corin's name—?' began the cat.

And then Nell let out a screech so loud it turned Tabitha's insides to water. The cat let go and Tabitha rolled aside, escaping the storm of flapping wings, raking talons and snapping beak. The cat was on one knee, the spider scuttling out through the iron door. The horse whinnied and reared up, but was beaten backwards by a flurry of attacks. All the while, Nell kept screeching over and over again. Hideous, unearthly noises that made Tabitha want to curl up into a ball and stuff her ears with seaweed.

Footsteps pounded on the walkway, and Tabitha saw that the cat had broken free and was charging full tilt towards Jeb the Snitch.

Joseph's father shoved him aside, sending him staggering to the edge of the walkway. He regained his balance just in time to see Jeb lunge for the wooden spoon again. *I don't think so.* Joseph leaped forward, bringing his foot down hard on the spoon.

The goblin turned on him. 'Let go, you stinking little rat!' he howled. 'Call yerself my son? Let go or I'll—'

'Joseph!' yelled Tabitha's voice. 'Look out!'

The cat was bearing down on them, his face twisted with feral fury. He fell on Jeb, kicking, punching and scratching, spittle flying from his lips.

Joseph ducked aside and snatched up the wooden spoon. Looking round, he saw that the griffin was prowling along the walkway, talons clicking on wood, wings arched like a prize-fighter's fists at the start of the big fight. It spread them wide.

'No!' yelled Joseph.

Too late. The griffin took off, thundering down the walkway and lifting into space with one great flap of its wings.

Jeb looked up from his struggle with the cat, and his pale eyes widened. He fought to escape, but the cat held him tight, oblivious to the danger.

'No,' said Joseph again.

The beast crashed into them in a blur of feathers, scrabbling with its talons, heaving them against the railings, up and over.

Jeb and the cat seemed to hang in the air, clutching each other in a tight embrace, and for an instant Joseph saw the terror on his father's face. Then they dropped like an anchor. The griffin blood surged up around them, sloshing out of the vat, splattering red droplets all around.

There was a fizzing and a hissing.

Then nothing.

Not even a scream.

Chapter Twenty-five

The griffin landed gracefully at the end of the walk-way, tucked in its wings and cocked its head to look at them. A spray of blood had caught its feathers, glistening red on gold.

In the vat the blood had settled, and nothing came to the surface.

A few seconds ago, Joseph's father had been here, next to him.

Now he was gone.

'Well, that's that,' said Tabitha. Joseph could tell she was trying to sound cheerful, but her voice trembled, giving her away. *It was griffin blood that killed her father,* he remembered suddenly. *And now it's griffin blood that's killed mine.*

Tabitha swallowed. 'I mean . . . I reckon they deserved it, didn't they?' She quailed, as though immediately regretting what she'd said.

Joseph realized that his fingers were still tightly curled round the handle of the wooden spoon. He couldn't bring himself to speak, so he just nodded.

They descended a set of steps to the ground floor. The goblins had all disappeared – run for their lives, Joseph guessed. The horse and the spider too. Tabitha found a set of keys hanging up on the wall, and they went from room to room, opening cages. Griffins emerged slowly, blinking in the light, stretching out their wings as though for the first time.

The griffin that had killed Joseph's father stood guard outside the round metal door – Tabitha seemed to know her, and called her Nell. The creature's homely name somehow made her seem even stranger and more frightening.

Joseph couldn't blame Nell for what she'd done. Those creatures all cooped up in their tiny cages, the bile milking equipment, the crates of griffin talons – all of it made him feel sick. All of it his father's work.

When they had set all the griffins free, and the building was full of them, pecking, scratching and preening, they threw open the great wooden gates and set out down the road, leaving the animals to fend for themselves. Joseph looked back just once, to see the first and bravest of them taking a step onto the cobblestones, as though onto ice that might break at any moment. Hardly daring to believe in its freedom.

It was Nell.

'So you took the wooden spoon,' Tabitha was saying. 'I should have guessed. Hal never told us. I s'pose he must have been embarrassed he lost it. It makes sense though, because he's been acting even more anxious than usual and—' She stopped in her tracks. 'All right,' she said, and this time her voice trembled. 'What have I done? Why aren't you speaking to me?'

Joseph looked at her – really looked at her – for the first time. Her hair seemed uneven, as though someone had cut a lock from it. Her grey eyes were moist, full of pain, and Joseph felt a lump form in his throat.

'He was my father,' he said, his voice barely a whisper.

'What do you mean?'

'Jeb the Snitch. Elijah was my uncle, and Jeb was my father. All along. It was him . . .'

Tabitha opened her mouth and shut it again.

After all, there isn't anything to say. Only the truth.

His father was the lowest creature in all the Ebony Ocean. And Joseph – Joseph was nothing. His ears drooped with misery.

'Come with me,' said Tabitha.

She led him down an alleyway, to a set of rickety steps that ran up the side of an old boarding house. When they reached the top, she gave him a leg-up to the roof, then told him to wait for her. Joseph did as he was told without questioning it. Why not? It was all over. He'd come to Azurmouth looking for his father. It was to be a new beginning. Instead it was the end.

He sat on the roof, dangling his legs over the side and kicking aimlessly into space. His hands were thrust in his pockets, holding onto the silver pocket watch and the wooden spoon, just like he had on board the *Dread Unicorn*. Back then they were his whole world – his hope for the future. Now they were just objects. A lump of metal and a lump of wood.

After a few minutes Tabitha returned with a greasy bag. She hauled herself up beside him, took his hand and led him up the slope of the roof, until they were perched right on the top of the building. She made him steady himself on a dragon-shaped weathervane as they sat.

Azurmouth sprawled out all around them. Joseph could barely remember the way he used to picture it. The white marble colonnades, the fountains and the palm trees. Perfect. But nothing in all the Ebony Ocean was perfect. Azurmouth was crowded, filthy and cruel. Even the seagulls were scrawny and savage, picking fights with one another and screeching like banshees. The sun had gone behind a cloud, casting the jagged rooftops into shade, robbing the city of colour. Only the House of Light seemed to shine, pure white, the foul heart of a foul city.

'Octopus,' said Tabitha.

'What?'

'Have some octopus.' She offered him the bag. 'It's fried.'

Joseph shook his head.

'Don't you remember?' she pressed on. 'Your father used to bring it to you once a week, as a treat.'

'You mean my uncle,' snapped Joseph. Immediately he felt guilty. It wasn't her fault.

Tabitha shrugged and took some herself. She munched as they sat in silence.

'Why are we here?' said Joseph at last.

'Don't you remember? Back in Port Fayt, at the Festival of the Sea – we sat up on a roof looking over the town. I was feeling sad about my parents. And you tried to cheer me up.'

'I remember.'

Tabitha's parents had been good people – they'd tried to rid Port Fayt of the League of the Light.

Joseph's father had been a thief, a swindler and a murderer.

'But don't you see?' said Tabitha, and there was a note of anger in her voice. 'That's the point. You're still the same person you were before. You're not like Jeb – you never were. When that witch Arabella Wyrmwood captured me, you tried to rescue me. You threw yourself into the ocean and you faced a sea demon just because it was the right thing to do. Would Jeb the Snitch have done that? Of course he wouldn't.'

'What about Pallione? She was our friend and I betrayed her. She almost died because of me. Because I was selfish, like Jeb.'

'You made a mistake. Everyone makes mistakes. But you tried to fix it. You fought for Port Fayt, and for the merfolk. You almost died for them. And then you came here, all the way to Azurmouth, risking everything for your father.'

'For the Snitch.'

'I didn't mean him. I meant Elijah Grubb. He was the one who raised you. The one who loved you. And you loved him back.'

'I—'

'What was it he used to say, about seraphs and demons?'

Joseph swallowed hard. *'There's a little bit of demon and a little bit of seraph in everyone.'*

'I reckon that's true. But there's something else too. There's love. That's what it is, to be a father, to be a mother, to be a son or a daughter. It's love. It doesn't matter who they are, really. So long as they love you, and you love them.'

Joseph looked at her, and saw her eyes filmed with tears. And he knew then that she wasn't talking about him – not just him. Newton had raised her since she was a baby. He was never her father – never her real father – but he loved her all the same.

Just like that, his heart didn't feel so heavy any more. He reached across, placing his mottled grey hand over her soft pink hand, as he thought of his father and his mother. Of how Elijah used to take Eleanor in his arms and hug her as she laughed and squirmed, and hugged him back. Of how he used to sit and listen as his father told him stories, his mother leaning in at the doorway, beaming at them both.

Of how they used to tell him every day: *We love you.*

'You remember what Pallione told us?' he said

softly. *'Always do the right thing.* Maybe that's all we can do. Make the best of it.'

Tabitha smiled at him, and he smiled back.

It felt good.

She sniffed, and wiped her nose on her sleeve. 'Aye,' she said. 'And we've still got a family, remember? Well, sort of.'

Joseph nodded. 'We do.'

Not a normal family. Not a perfect family. But a real family, all the same.

'Let's go,' he said. 'Back to the Demon's Watch.'

Chapter Twenty-six

There was no light in the cell, and no sound except for the occasional stifled whimper from Cyrus Derringer as he nursed his injured hand.

Newton had tried to sleep, but it was no good. Every time he'd been drifting off, disappointed faces had come whirling into his head. Frank, Paddy and Hal. Tabitha. Joseph, lost somewhere in the city. And most of all Jon, his oldest friend, frowning gently. All the people he'd let down.

He was almost glad that Jon wasn't here to see him now. To see the terrible mistakes he'd made that had landed him and Cyrus here, in the dungeons of the House of Light.

At least things can't get any worse. But even as he thought it, he knew it wasn't true. The Duke of Garran wouldn't just leave them to rot. He would be devising some far more terrible punishment.

He closed his eyes and flexed his cramped limps, pulling himself to a sitting position and resting his head against the dank stones of the cell wall. There was nothing to do but wait.

'Captain Newton.'

'Aye?'

A rustle of clothing, as the elf shifted position. 'I don't know what's going to happen to us. But I . . . I wanted to thank you.'

Newton's eyes flicked open. 'For what?'

'You tried to save me.' A pause. 'You shouldn't have bothered. I'm not worth it.' The elf's voice was a hoarse croak, as though every word was an effort.

Newton could scarcely believe what he was hearing. He thought for a moment before he replied. 'That story you told about Governor Skelmerdale . . . It's not true, is it? He didn't send you to fetch us back.'

Another pause.

'At the Battle of Illon,' said the elf at last. 'When the merfolk came and saved us all, I told the governor it was because of me. That I persuaded them to fight.

He thought – he thought I was a hero. That is . . . until he found out the truth.'

'Aye,' said Newton. There wasn't much else to say. Derringer had been in charge of the fleet all right, but when the battle started he'd hesitated, then left Newton to lead the attack. He certainly hadn't had anything to do with the merfolk. That had been Tabitha and Joseph.

'It was stupid,' said Derringer. 'I should have known it wouldn't last. And of course, some impish captains went to him. Told him the truth.' He was talking faster now, as though desperate to get it all out. 'The governor was furious, so I fled. Came here in disguise. I thought if I brought you back to Fayt, maybe he'd forgive me.'

'Maybe he will.'

'Then you wanted me to fight in the contest, and I thought even that could be a chance to prove something. But I was beaten. That League woman with the blonde hair. She was better than me.'

'It wasn't a fair fight,' said Newton. He bit his lip. He was no good at this kind of thing, but he had to say something. 'You're not so bad, Cyrus. Least you admitted what you've done. Fact is, you've always tried to do the right thing. You just . . . made a few mistakes.'

Thalin knows, we've all made mistakes. Newton was losing count of his own.

Derringer let out a ragged sigh. 'You mean that?'

'Aye. I don't blame you. Sounds like you blame yourself enough for both of us.'

'I . . . You don't know what that—'

Footsteps. A key, scraping in a lock. Then the door opened and lantern light flooded in, followed by white-coated butchers.

'On your feet!'

They didn't wait to see if the prisoners would obey. Newton was grabbed under his arms and dragged, stumbling, from the cell. *It's time*, he thought, as they marched him up a winding flight of stairs and through a heavy triple-locked door. *Time for the Duke's punishment.*

Fear turned his stomach. But he was scuppered if he was going to show it. Long ago, Tori the hobgoblin had taught him never to show weakness. In their training Tori had beaten him black and blue on more than one occasion, and each time Newton had gritted his teeth and taken it, and sworn that the next day he'd fight better. *Never despair*, Tori always said. *There is no faster road to defeat.*

The mantra hadn't failed him before. But the words felt a little empty here, in the House of Light.

They were in a wide, high-ceilinged passageway now, with vast windows on one side letting in dazzling midday sunshine, so much that Newton had to screw up his eyes as they passed through. At the end of the corridor stood a large set of oak double doors engraved with a series of interlocking sun emblems. A delegation of trading officials in velvet jackets and wigs were waiting outside, and they flinched when they saw the two prisoners. The leading whitecoat ignored them, pushing open the doors and leading Newton and Derringer into the room.

More sunshine, though Newton's eyes were getting used to it now. The windows opposite stretched from floor to ceiling. The walls were hung with brightly coloured tapestries, and a large mahogany dining table dominated the centre of the room.

Sitting at its head, spreading jam on toast, a single figure, seated. The beams of sunshine from behind threw him into a silhouette, so that his expression couldn't be seen. A pot of velvetbean sat at his side, and the steam that rose from it was incongruously beautiful as the sunshine caught it.

'Sit,' said the Duke of Garran.

The butchers walked Newton and Derringer to chairs on the near side of the table and shoved them roughly down into them, before melting away to the edges of the room.

For the first time since they'd been captured, Newton got a proper look at his companion. Derringer's elven skin was paler than ever, white as a sail, and there were bags under his eyes. His hands were clamped together to staunch the bleeding, and blood was crusted over most of his wrist and fingers.

That was going to be the least of his worries soon enough.

'It is rather late for breakfast,' said the Duke. 'But I've had a busy morning.' He was dressed finely, a red coat over his spotless white shirt and waistcoat. The bruise on his face had flowered, dark purple and spreading across his cheek, out of place in the civilized surroundings. *Or not so civilized*. If the stories were true, that coat had been dyed with the blood of trolls. 'How did you enjoy your cell?'

Newton said nothing. Derringer stayed silent too, and Newton was pleased to see his lip curl in a familiar sneer. In spite of everything, the elf wasn't beaten.

'Very well,' said the Duke. 'If that's how it is to be.' He polished off the last crust of toast, wincing as he bit, then dabbed at his mouth with a thick white napkin. 'Damson jam. My favourite. I had hoped my fellow lords of the League might join us, but I'm afraid they are a little indisposed at present.'

Newton's eyes flicked to the other dining chairs. Some were out of place, as though they'd been recently rearranged. He spotted some marks on the carpet close by. *Are those . . . blood?*

A smile hovered on the Duke's lips, as though he had guessed what Newton was thinking. 'You hit me,' he said quietly. 'Why do you think you are alive?'

Because you want to hurt me back. Because killing me wouldn't be enough. 'You tell us,' said Newton.

The Duke clicked his fingers, and his ogre stepped out of a shadowy corner of the room, holding a long black leather sheath. He bowed his huge head as he offered it to the Duke. 'The Sword of Corin,' said the Duke, standing, drawing the weapon from its sheath and holding it up to catch the sunshine. 'Ironically, this blade is your salvation. A blade that has spilled enough demonspawn blood to fill the Ebony Ocean.'

'That fat young nobleman know you've got it? I don't reckon he'll be too happy if he finds out.'

The Duke blinked and smiled without a trace of anger. 'Oh, I shouldn't think he'll mind, Captain Newton. Not any more.'

He spun the blade in a circle, watching its point like a child might watch a dancing firefly. 'You Fayters believe that you won the Battle of Illon. I'm afraid you could not be more wrong. *I* won the battle. The ships that sank . . . the men and demonspawn that died . . . all that was irrelevant. This weapon – *this* was the true prize.'

Newton's gut twisted. It was exactly as he'd suspected. The Duke had been after the sword all along. *And I gave it to him. I insisted on bringing it into the battle. I fought with it, and I lost it.*

'A sword is a sword,' he said. But he wasn't sure he believed it. 'What's it to you?'

'It is everything, Captain Newton.' The Duke raised the sword, pointing it at a huge tapestry that covered the wall next to the windows. 'Behold, the Scouring.'

The tapestry showed a landscape on fire, forests burning, belching out black smoke, farms and towns all ablaze and people fleeing. Newton recognized the image at once. It was just like the one in the children's book, back in the Academy: misshapen people with red eyes, even horns and pointed tails; their tormentors, winged and dressed in white, with weapons of gold. Seraphs, raining down fire on the demonspawn. Newton saw one black creature pierced by ten or more golden arrows, another whose head had just been lopped off by a golden scythe. A third speared by a golden lance and lifted off its feet by the impact.

'The Scouring,' said Newton, trying to keep his voice calm. 'Aye, I've heard of it.'

Beside him, Derringer let out a splutter of laughter. 'Nonsense,' said the elf. 'The Scouring is just a nursery rhyme.'

'Believe that, if it comforts you,' said the Duke. 'Nevertheless, after the Battle of the Three Forests, and the foundation of Azurmouth, Corin the Bold made a bargain with the seraphs. That in our hour of need they would return, to purge the Old World of every last taint of demonspawn. To scour it utterly, striking down all false, foul creatures, and leaving the land to its rightful owners. "Winged vengeance shall fall." That was their promise to humankind.'

'What does this have to do with the sword?'

The Duke gave another crooked smile, distorted by his bruise. He laid the sword on the table and settled back into his chair. 'Ah yes. I have been waiting, planning this moment for so long, Captain Newton. Like you, I once believed the Scouring to be no more than a foolish story. But my magicians tell me otherwise. They found ancient lore, texts that spoke of deep magic wound into Corin's sword. It was enchanted by the seraphs not merely as a weapon, but as something more. Much more. It will call them back again.'

'A spell,' said Newton. 'With the sword you can cast a spell to call the seraphs.'

'Not just the seraphs,' said the Duke. 'They say . . .' He paused, savouring it. 'They say that Corin shall lead them.'

The words of the children's book ran through Newton's head, chilling him to the bone:

At the call of the sword, twelve stones shall sing,
Twelve seraphs rise, in a golden ring.
At the river's birth where the hero was lain,
Corin the Bold shall walk again.

In the Dark Age it was said that demons and seraphs walked amongst the people of the Old World. Newton wanted to doubt it, with every fibre of his being. But he'd seen the Maw – the terrible sea demon that had slain Thalin the Navigator, founder of Port Fayt – and that had been real enough. If demons could rise again, why not seraphs too? Why not a dead hero?

'I had believed the sword was lost for good,' the Duke went on. 'That is, until I spoke with one Arabella, the mother of Eugene Wyrmwood, late governor of Port Fayt. Perhaps you know her?'

'Aye.' *Arabella Wyrmwood*. Newton remembered the last time he'd seen her, howling as the Maw tugged her beneath the waves. She'd wanted to destroy Port Fayt. *She still might.*

'Arabella came to Azurmouth to conduct some research of her own. But in passing she mentioned that the Sword of Corin was preserved in the library at Wyrmwood Manor, in Port Fayt. Clearly she knew nothing of its true power. As you know, I made plans to obtain it for myself. My magicians have now examined the blade, and they believe the ancient writings are correct. This sword is *soaked* in magic. But the spell requires a little more than just the weapon itself. It requires sacrifice. It requires blood to be spilt. Only then will the seraphs return.'

'Why are you telling us this?' spat Derringer. He lifted his head to glare at the Duke, like some beaten dog about to snap at its master. 'Just kill us and be done with it.'

The Duke cocked his head, examining Cyrus. 'Some say the elves are beautiful,' he said thoughtfully. 'I myself have never seen it. To me, your pale skin and silken hair makes you all the more grotesque. All the more dangerous.' He waved a hand dismissively. 'You will die, elf, have no fear of that. But not yet.'

'You need us,' said Newton. *Though Thalin knows*

why. He felt a grin tug at his mouth. It was ridiculous, but there was nothing else he could do. 'And you reckon we're going to help you.'

The Duke smiled too – a cold, joyless smile. 'Indeed.' He clicked his fingers.

The ogre in League livery shambled forwards and clamped Cyrus Derringer's throat tight in his two enormous fists. He began to squeeze.

Newton leaped from his chair, but was instantly caught and held down by a pair of butchers.

Cyrus went red, then purple. His face distorted horribly, and he let out a strange hissing sound. The ogre squeezed tighter, and tighter, his face expression-less, as though he were doing nothing more remarkable than ringing out a tea towel.

'Stop!' roared Newton. 'What's wrong with you? Stop, for Thalin's sake!'

Out of the corner of his eye he saw that the Duke was watching him, ignoring the elf entirely. At last, he clicked his fingers a second time, and the ogre let go and stepped away. Cyrus Derringer slumped in his chair, half-conscious, his eyes almost popping out of his head.

'Unfortunately,' said the Duke, 'I only need you, Captain Newton. You are uniquely suited to my purposes – so you will help me. Unless you want to see this elf die before your very eyes.'

Derringer fell forward, rattling the cutlery as his head hit the tablecloth.

The Duke chuckled. 'Oh dear. I don't believe he enjoyed that. Still, he will live. For now.'

He'll live. Maybe it wasn't much of a life, but Newton wasn't going to have the elf lose it on his account. 'Very well,' he said. 'What now?'

The Duke smiled. 'Such weakness. It is the demon in you, Captain Newton, which stops you from doing what needs to be done.' He slid the Sword of Corin back into its black sheath. 'There is just one last matter to attend to before we leave. Morgan?' He clicked his fingers a third time, and the ogre's massive fist slammed into Newton's face, knocking him sideways off his chair.

Newton's jaw hummed with the shock of it, as the ogre bent down and picked him up again. Agony, pulsing, throbbing. There was blood in his mouth, and he spat it out.

'I cannot kill you, Captain Newton,' said the Duke. 'Not yet. But that is in return for my face.' He stood. 'Now, we must make ready for our trip.'

'What trip?' said Cyrus Derringer, his voice no more than a croak.

'Why, our trip down the River Azur,' said the Duke. 'To the hero's tomb.'

Chapter Twenty-seven

The Azurmouth Academy gleamed in the afternoon sunshine, as Joseph and Tabitha crunched across the gravel driveway towards it.

Joseph had never been more exhausted. They'd had to take a long, roundabout route through the city to avoid the main roads, and Tabitha had insisted they stop at the burned-out tavern to pick up Joseph's cutlass – it had been a gift from Newton, after all. But in the end she'd had to go in on her own while Joseph waited outside.

He didn't want to see that place, ever again.

Even here at the Academy, he couldn't make himself relax. The white towers that loomed overhead, the curving white walls and the great wooden drawbridge over an ornamental moat – they all reminded him of the House of Light. *These magicians are different,* he had to remind himself. *They don't belong to the League. Hal was one of them, for Thalin's sake.*

The gatekeeper let them pass with no more than a raised eyebrow, and soon Tabitha was leading Joseph around a large neat square of grass in a silent courtyard. A robed figure swished past, throwing them a curious glance. A bespectacled man peered at them through a window, quickly disappearing when Joseph spotted him.

They've never seen a mongrel before.

'Jaster's staircase,' muttered Tabitha. 'Room forty-two.'

She took him up a curving flight of steps and through a small oak door, without knocking. 'Guess who's back?' she was saying, as Joseph followed.

The room was small, and cramped by overflowing shelves and towering heaps of books lying all around. Frank, Paddy and Hal were sitting on chairs around a wooden table, and Joseph felt a rush of relief at seeing them again. Standing by their side was a tall, birdlike man with chaotic white hair and a wispy beard, wearing a black gown and eyeglasses and looking anxious. It had to be Master Gurney.

Last of all Joseph spotted Ty, sitting on the table on top of another little pile of leather-bound books. Newton's fairy looked dejected, with his head in his hands.

'Thank Thalin you're here,' said Frank.

That was it. No grin, no hug, no bad joke. The troll looked pleased at least, but exhausted, as though he hadn't slept at all.

'Sit down,' said Paddy.

'Is that all the welcome we get?' asked Tabitha. 'I'll have you know we—'

'Where's Newton?' said Joseph.

Master Gurney pulled out two more chairs for them. 'I think it's best you both have a seat.'

They sat, dread building in Joseph's gut. Tabitha didn't even breathe a word of complaint. She could sense it too – something was wrong.

'Like I was saying, he's been arrested,' said Ty, when they were settled. 'Him and Cyrus Derringer. Master Gurney here arranged for them to enter the Contest of Blades, but they never came back. So this morning I flew over to the House of Light, listened in on some gossiping whitecoats. Seems Cyrus beat Lucky Leo, took his sword off him, then the Duke of Garran stepped in and took Newt and the elf prisoner.'

Joseph slumped in his chair. After all they'd been

through, it wasn't over. *Newton captured. By the Duke of Garran.* It was too horrible to think of. He cast a glance at Tabitha and saw that her lip was trembling. He stopped himself just before reaching out to her. *She wouldn't like that.*

'What in the name of the Maw was Newt playing at?' said Frank, rubbing his great green brow. 'Why did he enter Derringer in the contest in the first place?'

'That's what I've been—' started Tabitha. Then she cut herself short, hesitating. 'I s'pose there must have been a reason,' she said at last. 'He must have known what he was doing, even if he didn't explain.'

'Well said, Tabs,' murmured Frank.

'Wait,' said Joseph suddenly. They all turned to look at him. 'Did you say Cyrus took Lucky Leo's sword – and that was when the Duke of Garran stepped in?'

'That's right, mister,' said Ty.

'This sword – what did it look like?'

Ty shrugged.

'I'll bet it was silver, with star-stones in the hilt.'

Tabitha gasped and thumped the table with her fist. 'The Sword of Corin! Newt was reading about it in the library. He wanted to know everything about it.'

'The Duke locked it up in the House of Light,' said Joseph. It was all falling into place now. 'He must have taken it and brought it back after the Battle of Illon. And they were trying to steal it from him – the cat and his gang of shapeshifters – only someone else had got there first. Whoever it was, they must have given it to Lucky Leo.'

The cat's frantic voice came back to him. *Where is it? Where is the Sword of Corin?* Now they knew the answer.

Paddy shook his head. 'I still don't get it. Why would Newt risk everything just for a sword?'

'Perhaps it is rather more than *just a sword.*'

They all turned to the speaker – Master Gurney. His eyes were bulging, magnified by his glasses. He raised a finger, his other hand held behind his back, as though he were about to deliver a lecture to a hall of eager students.

'There are some, you see, who theorize that the Sword of Corin is in fact a form of vessel, or a conduit, if you will. In fact C. R. Willis uses the term "conductor". I cannot say I subscribe to it myself. Rather far-fetched. But if you refer to his 1638 work *Arcane Objects and Magical Phenomena*, yes, which I expect you'll have studied in—'

'What's it do?' said Frank.

'Ah yes, of course. To the point. Fear not, my friends, I shall be—'

'Brief,' said Paddy, who looked as close to losing his temper as Joseph had ever seen him. 'Please? What's it do, in ten words or less.'

Master Gurney knitted his brow, and his eyes swivelled upwards as he thought. After a few moments, he beamed. '*If* the theories are correct, and that is a rather big if . . . then the sword of Corin summons seraphs, thereby inducing the Scouring, in which all so-called demonspawn will be wiped off the face of the Old World.'

There was a long, stunned pause.

'That ain't ten words, mister,' said Ty, at last.

'Close enough,' muttered Frank.

'Right then,' said Tabitha. She stood, readjusting her bandolier of throwing knives, her eyes glinting with purpose. 'This Scouring – where does it start?'

'Allegedly, at Corin's Tomb,' said Master Gurney. 'But it's pure speculation. I really don't believe it can—'

'The Duke believes it,' Tabitha interrupted. 'So we have to get going.'

'No.' Paddy stood, stooping slightly to fit under the low ceiling. 'You two've got yourselves into enough trouble as it is. We'll handle this – me and Frank and Hal.'

Joseph searched his face for any sign that he was joking – but for once, the troll was deadly serious.

'My brother's right,' said Frank. 'You're back now, safe and sound, and Newt would never forgive us if anything else happened to you. Us – we're more disposable.' He smiled a tired smile.

'Fear not, little ones,' said Master Gurney. *Little ones*. Joseph could practically hear Tabitha grinding her teeth at that. 'I shall look after you here at the Academy. Master Harrow is delivering a rather fascinating talk this afternoon – *Thaumaturgically Accelerated Herbology: Ars Magica and the Growing of Grass*. It's only three hours, but afterwards we could—'

'Joseph,' said Hal. It was the first thing he'd said since they'd entered the room, but he spoke in such a serious tone that it silenced everyone. 'Do you have it?'

'Have what?' said Frank.

Joseph knew exactly what the magician was talking about. He drew the wooden spoon from his pocket.

Hal sank back in his chair, letting out a sigh that seemed to deflate him entirely. 'Thank Thalin.'

'Wait – you mean Joseph's had that all along?' said Paddy. He shot a glance at Hal. 'So Newt's not the only one who's been keeping secrets.'

'Pardon me,' said Master Gurney, 'but is that the wooden spoon you mentioned when you arrived?'

'Aye, that's the one,' said Frank. ''Cept it's not just

a wooden spoon. It's a special type of wand. It's a . . . what do you call it? A leash.'

Master Gurney's eyes almost popped out behind his spectacles. He fished in his robes for a handkerchief, and mopped his brow. 'A *leash*? Goodness, I— But how in all the Old World did such an extraordinary item fall into the hands of a common tavern boy?'

'It was my fault,' said Hal, his voice trembling. 'The night after the Battle of Illon, it disappeared from under my pillow. I thought Joseph might have taken it, but I wasn't certain. I was ashamed, and I didn't— I mean, I knew he wouldn't be able to use it, so—'

'I used it,' said Joseph. 'Twice.'

Hal went as white as a sail.

'And he's been brandishing that wand all over Azurmouth!' spluttered Master Gurney. 'Why didn't you mention this before, dear Hal?'

'I'm so sorry, I—'

Master Gurney turned to Joseph. 'Young man, you have been extremely fortunate. Had the spell gone wrong, the consequences could have been disastrous.'

The cat's warning flashed through Joseph's mind once again, giving him an involuntary shudder. *So it really is as dangerous as he said.*

'Let me get this straight,' said Paddy, raising an eyebrow at Master Gurney. 'You're not bothered about a magical legendary sword, but when it comes to a battered old wooden spoon—'

'You should have told us, Hal,' said Frank gravely.

'I know.' Hal looked distraught now. 'Please forgive me, Joseph. I truly didn't believe that you would be capable of—'

The door slammed open, and a spotty youth in a black robe burst through it. He was sweating and panting heavily. 'Master Gurney!' he gasped. 'You won't believe what's just landed in first quad. Follow me!'

'We'll continue this conversation later, Hal,' said Master Gurney gravely. 'A leash! Dear me.'

The youth led the way as the watchmen all rose and clattered down the spiral staircase, out onto the gravel of the courtyard. Black-robed figures clustered in doorways and leaned out of windows, all staring at the square of grass in the centre of the courtyard.

Joseph caught his breath.

Ty whistled, and Tabitha whooped. 'Nell!'

The griffin strutted on the lawn. Out in the open her feathers shone more brightly, and her eyes seemed to glisten with life. *With freedom.* She opened his beak and let out a gentle squawk, stretched her wings and flapped once, sending a gust of wind that flattened the grass. She clawed at the ground with her talons, ripping up a chunk of turf.

'Keep off the grass, you brute!' squeaked an outraged old magician.

Nell ignored him.

'What in Thalin's name is she doing here?' said Tabitha.

Joseph shook his head.

'You know this beast?' asked Master Gurney, stroking his beard nervously.

Tabitha nodded. 'We saved her from a bile farm.'

'Ah, well then!' said Master Gurney. 'Griffins are rather intelligent creatures, you see, with a surprisingly refined sense of justice. At least, according to Dr Matlock's *Griffins: A Study*. I've never actually encountered one in the flesh before. In any case, if you helped it, I can only assume that it wishes to return the favour.'

Tabitha jabbed Joseph in the ribs. 'Follow me,' she whispered. Then she took off, running across the grass.

'Tabs,' said Frank, in a warning voice.

Joseph lurched after her, clutching the wooden spoon tightly. He could see what Tabitha was planning, and he couldn't let her do it alone.

'Joseph!' shouted Paddy.

'The leash!' yelped Master Gurney.

But Tabitha was already scrambling up onto Nell's

back. The griffin ruffled her feathers and tossed her beak, but made no attempt to throw her off.

'Here,' said Tabitha. 'Take my hand.'

Joseph did so, clambering up onto the griffin. Its feathers were soft, but beneath them Joseph could feel a taut, muscled body. He tensed his legs, squeezing them into the creature's sides, and wrapped his arms around Tabitha's middle. Already he felt dangerously far from the ground.

'Put that wand down at once!' Master Gurney cried. 'Please, you can't possibly think of using it. Even if you've succeeded before, without the proper training it's not safe. Not safe at all. The spell will only back-fire, and then you'll be letting Corin-knows-who into your own mind. Do you have any idea how dangerous that is?'

'You should listen to Master Gurney,' said Hal. But he didn't move. None of them moved. They just stood watching, faces unreadable.

'I'm sorry,' called Joseph. 'We have to get there fast, before—'

Nell spread her wings with a sound like unfolding parchment, smothering Joseph's last few words.

Oh, Thalin. Is she going to . . . ?

She was.

Nell began to trot, jolting her riders up and down.

Then the trot became a run. A leap. Her wings flapped like sails in a storm.

'No!' shouted Master Gurney.

A huge rush of air hit Joseph, buffeting his face, bringing tears to his eyes and forcing them half closed. The Academy tilted crazily as they swerved in a spiral, up and away from the receding green square of grass.

His stomach flipped.

He leaned out as far as he dared, looking down at the three watchmen and the panicking magician below. Frank had his hands cupped round his mouth, shouting something up at them. The roar of the wind was deafening, but Joseph heard it all the same.

Good luck.

PART FOUR
The Hero's Tomb

Chapter Twenty-eight

A squad of white-coated butchers escorted the prisoners to the top deck.

Newton's chains clanked as he climbed the steps, metal rubbing at the red marks on his wrists – the marks he'd earned in the zephyrum mines, all those years ago.

Back then he'd worn manacles of cheap iron, every day, until he'd finally stolen a wire cutter from a sleeping guard, broken the metal and escaped into the darkness. It was the day his mother had died. His family had all gone the same way, one by one beneath the ground, and she had been the last.

It was his grief that had driven Newton to action.

And more than that, his anger. Anger at the injustice. Anger at the cruelty.

The same anger that had landed him in chains all over again.

Cyrus Derringer stumbled at his side, haggard and pale, but still scowling. As long as the elf kept scowling, Newton knew he was all right. *Never despair.* He'd learned that lesson in the mines first, even before he'd met Tori the hobgoblin.

Raindrops spattered his face as they reached the deck. Scattered rain from a grey sky, that promised more to come. A storm, perhaps. His muscles ached and his face throbbed from Morgan's fist. After hours in the hold his boots were waterlogged, and the damp had crawled up his breeches and coat tails, along with a few cockroaches trying to escape the bilge sloshing below. He was tired – so tired.

Still. *Never despair.*

He took in his surroundings. The vessel was a shallow-hulled river cruiser with triangular sails. There were two more on the river, one on either side. Absurdly, Newton thought of the three ships of Thalin the Navigator – the *Cockatrice*, the *Redoubtable* and the *Morning Star* – the ships that had crossed the Ebony Ocean so that Thalin could found Port Fayt as a home for all people.

For trolls, elves and goblins as well as humans.

Three new ships to undo everything that Thalin ever achieved.

The river stretched ahead and behind them, a curving green ribbon, broad and slow-moving. To their left, woodland. To their right . . .

Newton caught his breath as he took it in. The grass rose up into a hill that was so high it was almost a mountain. It dominated the surrounding countryside. On its lower, gentler slopes, white-coated magicians were setting up rings of wooden torches that stretched around the hill like necklaces. Newton could just pick out the red fireballs emblazoned on the magicians' arms, the mark of the League's Magical Infantry. Calculations were being made. Wind direction measured.

'Move,' said a woman's voice, and he turned to see Major Turnbull glaring at him, her heavy broadsword sheathed on her back, a long white overcoat covering her white uniform. Her blonde hair hung loose, and it twisted in the breeze.

'Aye,' said Newton. It hurt to talk.

They were led down a gangplank into the marshy shallows, where Newton's boots squelched into the soft river bed. They waded through the reeds and clambered onto the bank, feet heavy with the clodded mud. Newton felt an involuntary shudder at the cold. Here, out of Azurmouth, the wind swept across the countryside, whipping at their faces. His eyes watered.

They began to climb the hill, Newton and Derringer side-by-side with Turnbull following. Newton considered making a break for it, but there was nowhere to go. And besides, if he ran, there was no way he could stop this madness.

Instead, he took it all in, making some calculations of his own. There were at least twenty magicians he could see, but there were probably more around the other side of the hill. They had butchers with them, at least twice as many. Looking back he saw even more on board the riverboats, which were starting to look like toys, bobbing in a bath.

Not good odds.

'Look,' croaked Derringer.

Newton followed his pointing finger up the slopes. Near the top of the hill, craggy grey rocks broke through the green. It was misty up there with the light rain, but he could still make out a ring of standing stones on the summit, black as pitch.

The hero's tomb.

Another cluster of the Magical Infantry stood there, taking measurements, arguing with each other. And waiting beside the stones were two familiar figures:

the small, rounded shape of the Duke of Garran, and the hulking ogre that served him.

'Who is he?' said Newton.

Turnbull ignored him.

'That ogre, Morgan. From the mines, is he?'

She shrugged.

'So what's he doing here?'

'The Duke,' she said finally, stiffly, as if that explained everything.

'Go on.'

'He keeps him. I don't know why. He likes to study demonspawn.'

'Demonspawn,' repeated Newton. 'Ugly word, if you ask me. Seems to me there's plenty of your kind act like demons.'

Turnbull's face came alive at last. 'My mother was killed by elves,' she spat. 'In the Miners' Rising. So don't talk to me about demons.'

'It was whitecoats did for *my* ma,' said Newton. 'My pa too. My grandpa and my grandma. All of them died deep underground at Wyborough. Your father ran those mines, didn't he?'

Turnbull went white.

'I don't blame you, by the way. You had nowt to do with it – you were just a child. And I'm sorry about your ma.'

A happy child with blue eyes and blonde hair, who didn't deserve to be the daughter of a League man. Who didn't deserve to have her mother murdered. Turnbull opened her mouth as if to say something, then thought better of it.

No one said anything after that.

The ground became steeper, and Newton's breath grew short as they climbed on towards the summit. The wind was fiercer here, and his coat was damp from the hold, and the rain. He shivered. He could practically hear Derringer's teeth chattering beside him.

Ahead, the Duke of Garran was dressed in League white, still as a statue, impervious to the elements. His bruise was a deep purple, matching Newton's own.

'How good of you to join us,' he said in his soft voice. 'Welcome to Corin's Tomb.'

Newton bent over, panting, taking in the scene at the top of the hill. There were twelve stones in all, each one a towering slab of smooth black marble that loomed over them, stark against the grey sky. Silent, faceless giants. Within the ring was a flat grassy circle, and in the very centre was a boulder the size of a crouching man, jagged and irregular, with a roughly flattened top. It looked out of place next to its more impressive marble neighbours.

'Corin is buried beneath the stone,' said the Duke.

'When night falls, we will light the fires. They will burn despite the rain – the wood has been enchanted – and the smoke will act as a beacon to guide our guests. Corin's sword will shed blood on his tomb. Mongrel blood. That is what the spell requires, Captain Newton, and you are the man to provide it. Then they will come.'

They will come. He made them sound like friends invited to a dinner party.

The Duke let out a long, happy sigh and turned away from the tomb. He threw out an arm. 'The Old World. Beautiful, isn't it?'

It was. Even with the rain hazing grey above the horizon, Newton could see for miles – lush green grass spreading out in every direction in gentle slopes, like waves frozen in time. Wooden fences crisscrossed here and there. Sheep dotted one hillside, and a farmhouse stood on another, smoke curling from its chimney. In the distance, the sunshine had found a chink in the clouds and lit up a solitary tree on a hilltop, shining golden like a lighthouse.

Yes, it was beautiful. But all that Newton could think of was what lay below. The dark underworld of the mines. The glint of zephyrum. The pale faces of the miners.

'East, Captain Newton,' said the Duke. 'Do you see it?'

Newton knew what lay in that direction. He didn't want to look, but he couldn't help himself.

'Wyborough,' breathed the Duke. 'I'm sure it brings back memories. For you – and for Major Turnbull.'

The League officer tucked a stray curl of blonde hair behind her ear, and said nothing.

The town was closer than Newton had imagined. The nearest settlement by far – but still some distance away. It lay in a valley, and he could just make out carts winding along the dirt roads in and out of town. Carts full to the brim with ore, torn from the earth. Mostly tin. But zephyrum too.

'They say the Sword of Corin was forged with zephyrum as well as steel,' said the Duke. 'Perhaps it was one of your ancestors who mined it from the earth, Captain Newton. Even in the Dark Age, ogres toiled beneath the ground, at the bidding of dark magicians. It would be strangely fitting, wouldn't you say?'

Newton said nothing.

'Your servant,' said Derringer suddenly. He nodded at the still, looming figure at the Duke's side. 'He's an ogre.'

The Duke raised an eyebrow. 'And they say elves are clever creatures.'

'But why?'

'An excellent question. I found Morgan many years ago. He was a child then, curled in the ruins of a town in Garvill, in the south. The townsfolk had resisted our soldiers for nearly a week, but no darkness can resist the Light.'

Newton's anger flared briefly back into life. 'You mean innocent folk with nought but pitchforks can't resist an army with guns and cannons. Aye, I'll give you that.'

Derringer caught his eye and smiled weakly.

'Very good, Mr Newton,' the Duke went on, unbothered. 'Nevertheless, the town had fallen. It was all ablaze as I rode through the streets, so hot I was sweating and choking on the smoke. At times I could see no further than my horse's neck. And I came across him, lying in the rubble of a house. His parents had abandoned him, left him for dead.

'He was grotesque, of course. No ordinary baby, but hideously overgrown and malformed, his jaw stretched, his eyes small, like a pig's. An ogre, beyond doubt. But he was crying, and I pitied him.'

The Duke turned to examine the ogre.

'I *pitied* him. Demonspawn. And before I could realize my mistake, a whitecoat stepped out of the smoke, sabre drawn, and spied the child. He raised his blade . . . and I rode him down. Without thinking.

His blood spattered onto the baby's cheek. It was too young to understand, of course.'

He paused for a moment, and Newton saw that he was considering whether to continue.

'I saved the child. The demonspawn. And I killed a human to do it. I understood then, truly, how dangerous these creatures are. How deceptive. And I knew that I must never forget who we are – we, the children of seraphs. And who they are – the spawn of demons.

'So, Mr Derringer, to answer your question . . . I keep him as a reminder of the weakness inside every one of us. He has been my burden. A symbol of how much the League has yet to achieve. But tonight, at last, we achieve it. The world will be scoured of demonspawn for ever, and the seraphs' promise to their children will be fulfilled.

'*Winged vengeance shall fall.*'

Chapter Twenty-nine

Wind battered Joseph's face. His eyes streamed and his thighs ached as he squeezed them tight into the griffin's flanks. His arms were clamped round Tabitha's waist.

The sky was darkening, and only a glimmer of orange lingered in the west. Far below, the first lanterns had been lit, like scattered stars among the crowded sprawl of buildings that was Azurmouth.

'Don't look,' Tabitha shouted over her shoulder. 'Just hang on. I'm not having you falling off, all right?'

Joseph couldn't tear his eyes away. The city looked tiny and insignificant from above, no more important than a cluster of barnacles on a rock. At the edge of it he could see the docks and the black ocean stretching out into the distance, a few white caps breaking the glassy surface, lit by a single streak of crimson from the dying sun.

His problems seemed so far away. What did they matter up here, among the clouds? Here, now, he was free. He felt the muscles of the griffin moving below him, its wings beating slowly, like oars on a row boat, feathers glinting gold.

A fat raindrop spattered on his hand, sending a shiver through him as he realized suddenly how cold it was.

His own worries might be done with, but somewhere on the land below was Newton. The Captain of the Watch. The man who had taken him in, who'd come over the ocean to look for him, and who'd put himself in deadly danger to save them all.

Somewhere.

'Which way do we go?' he shouted above the roar of the wind. The rain was really falling now, plastering his shirt sleeves to his arms and trickling from the corners of his hat. Even the wooden spoon was damp in his pocket. *Will I have to use it again?* And could he really risk it, after what Master Gurney had told him? *You can't possibly think of using it. It's not safe. Not safe at all.*

'*The river's birth,*' Tabitha called back. Her blue ponytail was sodden against the back of her waistcoat. 'If I'm right, Corin the Bold is buried at the source of the Azur. So that's where the Duke will be, and Newton too. I just know it.' She patted Nell's neck, pointing down at the ribbon of black water that snaked north of the city, leading east into the countryside. 'Follow the river, Nell!'

Somehow, the beast seemed to understand. It banked, causing Joseph to cling on even tighter, then swooped lower, following the water's course. Meadows lay on either side, their long grasses flattened by the wind and the rain. Beyond, forests of tall trees swayed.

Joseph felt suddenly very exposed. Just him, Tabitha and Nell. Further from the ocean than he'd ever been. *The Old World*. His ancestors had all come from this land, centuries before. But he felt like a stranger here.

'Are you ready?' said Tabitha.

She was a stranger here too. He was a mongrel boy, the son of Jeb the Snitch, and she'd come to save him. They'd all come. Tabitha, Newton, Frank and Paddy. Hal. Even Ty.

'I'm ready,' he said.

'Good. Because – look!'

Through the rain, silhouetted against the darkening horizon, rose a black hill. It was higher than anything else for miles around. At its summit stood a collection of huge stones, and the whole hill crawled with movement. As Joseph watched, he saw a green fire burst out on the lower slopes. Another sprang up beside it, blood red. The third was vivid purple. In moments the whole hillside was lit with coloured fire.

'Corin's Tomb,' said Tabitha. 'I knew it!'

Joseph nodded. *Let's just hope the Duke brought Newton with him.* But before he could reply, a blue flash lit up the sky and distant thunder rolled.

'Thalin save us,' he muttered.

'That's no ordinary lightning,' said Tabitha. 'It's a tormenta. A magical storm.'

A distant memory stirred. The night before Joseph had found the black velvet package dropped on the floor of the Legless Mermaid – the package that had contained the wooden spoon. The night before his life changed for ever. Before he was taken in by the Demon's Watch. There'd been a tormenta that night too.

A bad omen. That's what Mr Lightly had always called them.

Perhaps he was right.

The rain had begun to fall when the first flames licked up, an unearthly green colour, on the lower slopes of

302

the hillside. More fires were set – purple, blue, red – until the whole hillside was a mad riot of colour.

The League magicians around the stones had exchanged their coats for long white cloaks, each with the blazing symbol of the Golden Sun embroidered on the back, each hood drawn up against the rain. Newton wished he had a hood. The rain battered his shaved head and soaked him to the bone, as whitecoats removed the prisoners' chains and dropped them to the ground.

'Take off your coat please, and unbutton your collar,' said the Duke of Garran pleasantly. Half of him glowed in the light from the fires. Now red, now orange, now blue. The other half lay in shadow, unreadable.

Derringer suddenly darted forward, reaching for the Duke's neck. Morgan caught him, wrestling his arms behind his back and forcing him down in the mud with a soft squelching sound. The elf looked even more haggard than before, but furious.

Newton felt an unexpected rush of warmth for Derringer. *At least he's trying to do something. And what are you doing? Waiting for the end?*

No. He wouldn't go down without a fight.

He took his coat off slowly, deliberately. It was only at the last moment that he moved, flinging it hard into Major Turnbull's face. She flinched, unsure for an instant what had happened. And in that instant Newton went for her belt, for the pistol thrust through it. *Loaded and primed.* He'd seen her do it. Turnbull might be a better swordsman than him, but Newton was far, far stronger. He shoved her stumbling through the mud and swivelled, one eye already closed, pistol aimed at the Duke of Garran.

Close range. He couldn't miss. He squeezed the trigger.

There was a deafening crack, a puff of smoke, and for a moment Newton's heart sang. For a moment.

Things happened so fast he could barely tell what order they came in. The Duke's face was blank, unfrightened. The air quaked between them, and Newton saw the pistol ball frozen in mid-air, then slowly, comically slowly, drop to the ground. A wave of ice seemed to engulf his arm, from his pistol up to his shoulder.

He caught a glimpse of a magician reaching out, and then others, all pointing at him, and he fell to the mud as though pushed by some giant, invisible hand.

That was when the pain began.

Searing. Excruciating. It was as though his body was burning all over, inside and out. Blood pounded in his ears. He let out a sound he didn't even know he could make. Raw, animal panic. He twisted, mud smearing his clothes, but he didn't care. There was nothing but the pain, staggeringly intense, like nothing he had felt before.

This is what it's like to die, some part of his brain told him. *No – this is worse.*

And all at once it was gone, utterly. No lingering aches, no trace of the agony he had just been suffering. Gingerly he flexed his fingers, uncurled from the ball he'd ended up in. Panted.

A figure loomed against the night sky above him. 'Paincraft,' explained the Duke placidly. 'An unusual field of magic, but my magicians are veritable experts in it. I have found it useful in my dealings with demon-spawn. If you try to shoot me again – or stab me, or strangle me, or even touch me – I shall set them on you once more. And this time I will not call them off. Do you understand?'

Newton's stomach roiled. He couldn't speak.

'Excellent,' said the Duke, beaming. He turned to Morgan. 'Take him.'

He was bundled to his feet, half shoved, half dragged into the stone circle. His strength was gone, and his limbs felt useless, dead weights slowing him down.

'Newton!' called Derringer, struggling to rise, but Major Turnbull held the elf down on his knees in the mud.

The rain was drumming on the great black stones on every side, and the hero's tomb was shining, slick with water. Morgan hoisted Newton on top of it and pinned his arms to his sides. He lay still, his face spotted with rain, as the Duke stepped up on the tomb beside him. He had the Sword of Corin in his hand, and Newton could have sworn that it was glowing – actually glowing – like a slice of the moon. The point of it came to rest on his throat, and at the same instant the sky flashed with unnatural blue light, and roared with thunder.

A tormenta. Just like the night the old woman had arrived in Port Fayt, so long ago.

That was the night it all began.

He closed his eyes.

And this is the night it all ends.

'Look at me,' said the Duke. Newton looked, saw that the blade had been lifted now, and the Duke's gaze was fixed on the point of it. A tiny bead of blood was crawling down towards the hilt. Newton hadn't even felt the steel nick his throat.

'That's all?' he said. His voice was no more than a croak.

The Duke smiled at him, and the flickering of the fires danced in his eyes.

'Of course, Captain Newton. A drop of mongrel blood will quite suffice. When it begins, Morgan shall be the first to die. A meagre honour, but he has earned it in my service. For you, I have something different in mind. When the seraphs come, I want you to witness it. I want you to understand how utterly you have been defeated.'

Cracks of musket fire sounded from below, and Tabitha felt a rush of air as a crossbow bolt whirred past, horribly close to her face. Nell let out a panicked squawk and swerved higher, away from the whitecoats on the hillside.

'No!' she yelled. 'Lower, Nell! To the hilltop!'

She felt Joseph's hands grip onto her waist, steadying himself. 'I don't think she understands,' he shouted.

But Nell swooped lower all the same. Lashed by rain, they could hear the shouts of the butchers now, and feel the heat of the fires.

'Shoot them down,' someone shouted. 'Don't let it get to the tomb!'

Tabitha drew a knife, sent it slicing through the darkness towards the pale faces below. But it was impossible to aim. No way to defend themselves. All they could do was keep going. 'Faster, Nell!' she howled.

The griffin screeched in reply, and flapped its wings harder.

'We're going to make it!' yelled Joseph, his voice high with excitement.

Tabitha nodded. Up ahead the hilltop loomed closer and closer. Something was happening there. The air was hazed with magic; white-robed magicians stood among the black standing stones, and the stones were – yes – they were actually *shaking*. Solid rock, quivering with power.

Her mouth went dry.

The ogre tugged Newton into a seated position, still gripping his arms as firmly as the chains he'd worn on the boat. They watched as the Duke of Garran stepped down from the tomb and strode to the outer circle.

The magicians had taken up position, each one in between two standing stones. They laid their hands flat on the stone to either side of them, creating an unbroken ring of flesh and rock. Their eyes were closed, their cloaks drenched with rain, their bodies tensed.

As the Duke reached the first stone, he murmured three words: 'In Corin's name.'

There was a *clang* as he struck the stone with the bloody blade – a surprisingly musical sound. A sound which lingered unnaturally, turning to a gentle, low hum. Newton peered closer, hardly trusting his eyes. The air around the rock had begun to smudge with magic. But stranger still, the rock itself seemed to be moving. As though shivering with cold.

As though something was inside it, and trying to escape.

The Duke moved to the next stone, spoke the same words, and struck it in the same way. Once again came the strange sound that stretched on, harmonizing with the music of the first stone.

Singing, Newton realized. *The stones are singing.*

At the call of the sword, twelve stones shall sing.

Soon the Duke had struck every stone, and the music filled the air, at once beautiful and frightening, almost painful to experience. It seemed to pass straight through Newton's ears and make his whole head vibrate. The stones were shaking, *squirming*, like eggs on the point of hatching. Out of nowhere, Newton felt a laugh bubble up inside him. He was delirious. This was absurd. Ridiculous. But it was happening. Derringer looked at him in utter bewilderment as the laugh spilled from his lips.

A voice cut through the music. Major Turnbull's voice. 'Your grace. There's a griffin approaching.'

Could Newton have heard her right? *A griffin?* But it was hardly the least surprising thing that had happened tonight. And now, he knew, the night was only just beginning.

The Duke turned from the last of the standing stones. For an instant his face was an animal snarl, cast in shadow and coloured light from the fires. He hesitated, considering. 'How inconvenient,' he said finally. 'Have my wyverns bring it down.'

Three dark shapes rose from the summit of the hill, winged like bats.

Joseph couldn't tell what they were, but they set his heart racing. Fear turned his body icy cold. 'Look out!' he yelped.

He felt Tabitha freeze up, as though unsure what to do. But Nell kept flying, oblivious to the danger.

The three shapes circled the hill and then, as one, came streaking towards them.

Too late, Nell let out a panicked squawk and veered away, almost throwing them off her back. The next moment the flapping creatures were on them.

Wyverns, Joseph realized. They were as big as

hunting dogs, scaled and taloned, eyes glittering with hunger. Their open mouths were cluttered with teeth. Teeth like the jagged rocks that wrecked ships on the eastern coast of Arla. Teeth like splinters of bone, lethally sharp.

He barely had time to be terrified before the first one came smacking into him, wings outstretched. Sharp claws tore at his clothes, and the beast's cold, reptilian snout lunged forward, snapping so fiercely he could hear the click of its jaws.

Joseph raised an arm to bat it away, but it was too strong. Ahead, he heard Tabitha snarling as she fought the second wyvern. The third was harrying Nell, spooking the griffin into a wild spiral.

As Nell banked again Joseph let go, and at once he slid off the griffin's back, plummeting through the night sky. The wyvern followed, screeching in triumph. Joseph's vision blurred with coloured light from the fires, whitecoats racing across the hillside towards them, and then suddenly everything was green, and he thumped heavily into something that broke his fall and sent up a shower of sparks. It was a stack of branches.

A stack of branches that was on fire.

The heat hit him in a wave and he threw himself to the side, rolling into the grass beside the fire. Tongues of green flame licked in his wake, but he rubbed his body on the ground as hard as he could, covering himself in mud and damp grass to extinguish them. Above, he saw the wyvern screech again.

No. Please, no . . .

Whitecoats were approaching like ghosts in the night, but as they saw the wyvern they backed off, giving it space. It swooped, hissing like a snake, and its jaws hinged open. Its teeth glinted ghoulish green in the light from the flames as it descended on him.

The ringing of the stones had merged to become a single note, a low, insistent thrum that made Newton feel nauseous. The magicians were shaking as much as the stones themselves, and it felt as though the ring might split apart at any moment.

Through the distortion of the magic and the rain, Newton saw the Duke approaching again, holding the sword in the crook of his arm like a sceptre. The ogre tugged Newton backwards, off the stone and into the mud, leaving him slumped beside Cyrus Derringer, like two children waiting to hear their bedtime story.

The Duke leaped lightly onto the tomb. His smile seemed full of emotion for the first time – a cruel sneer of triumph.

This was what he was planning all along. When he

sailed to Illon. When he killed Old Jon. When he locked us up and brought us here. His moment, at last. This was the real Duke. The man behind the mask. It was an ugly sight.

The Duke swung the Sword of Corin downwards, the blade's point hovering above the tomb, then raised it again. Holding the hilt with both gloved hands, he closed his eyes. 'In Corin's name,' he said reverently, and for the first time he was answered by the magicians around him.

As one, they spoke: 'In Corin's name.'

The blade fell.

At first there was nothing but a cold, short click as it touched the stone. And then the click became a chime that surpassed all the others, searingly high in pitch and getting louder all the time, at once uniting and outstripping the sounds of the other stones.

The tomb itself began to quiver, then to shake. Major Turnbull backed away, but the Duke stood firm. He was still holding the sword in contact with the stone. The smile that spread across his face was tinged with something else now. Madness. Ecstasy.

Newton could actually *feel* the magic. It seemed to tug at his body like gusts of wind, pushing every which way but most of all from the stone in the centre. He tried to draw in breath, but the air was suddenly thin.

Derringer grunted a single word. 'Look.'

Something was coming out of the standing stones. Shreds of white mist, coalescing into figures that dragged themselves from the rock as though escaping from quicksand. Each one was twice the height of a human man, long-limbed and fine-featured, their backs sprouting wings of pure light. Their eyes were golden points in the mist, so bright it hurt to look at.

Newton felt as though he was frozen in time, unable to do anything but watch.

Twelve seraphs rise, in a golden ring.

Chapter Thirty

Tabitha fell, with the wyvern clawing at her face. She tugged a knife from her belt, but the creature bit her forearm, small sharp teeth digging in viciously. She cried out and dropped her weapon, desperately shoving the wyvern away from her as they hurtled down. Her arm throbbed, slick with blood.

They streaked downwards, faster and faster, through the rain and the darkness, and any moment now they would hit the hillside and then it would be over . . .

Except the wyvern had grabbed hold of her clothing now. Its talons pierced her waistcoat and tangled with her knife belt. Its wings stretched like sails above and beat, slowing their fall, turning the fall into a swoop before climbing again.

Tabitha was paralysed. She wanted to fight the creature with every instinct in her body, but if she did – if it let go – she was dead.

The wyvern's head darted down suddenly and tore away her bandolier. It tumbled into the night, and Tabitha felt a wash of cold fear. *Defenceless*. The beast let out a shriek and raised its head, a long red tongue flickering across those sharp white teeth. It watched her, sizing up the meal to come.

It wouldn't be quick. Every bite would hurt.

She closed her eyes.

The wyvern shrieked a second time. But there was a different note to it – one that made Tabitha open her eyes again. A note of panic.

A rush of wind, and a sound like beating wings.

Nell?

Yes – no. A new griffin cannoned out of the darkness ahead. It bore two passengers, and their faces filled Tabitha with joy in spite of her fear. A pale, bespectacled young magician, and an enormous green troll.

'Oi, lizard-face!' roared Paddy. 'Drop it!'

Tabitha saw Hal reach out with his hands, each one shimmering with magic. They seemed to draw in light, then mould it, forming a cannonball of blue energy. With a thrust of his arms, he sent it streaking towards the wyvern.

The lizard shrieked a third time, and suddenly there was nothing holding Tabitha up. Her captor soared upwards, fleeing the magic, a demonic shape against the black sky. And after an eternal moment of stillness, Tabitha began to fall.

THUMP!

She landed hard on the griffin's back as it swooped below. Strong green hands gripped her, holding her tight as she scrambled upright.

Tears pricked in her eyes. *Safe. I'm safe.* She checked her arm and saw that the blood was drying. The bite marks were savage, but she'd heal.

Paddy ruffled her hair, and for once, she didn't mind. 'Can't leave you alone for two minutes,' said the troll. 'Found these two feathery fellas pecking around near the Academy, so we thought we'd join the fun. Apparently some madman let them loose from a local bile farm.' He gave her a wink.

'Thank you,' Tabitha croaked. 'And thank you, Hal.'

'Reckon his magic came in handy for once.'

Hal shook his head. 'It was nothing. Nothing compared to *him*.'

Tabitha followed his pointing finger and saw another griffin flying below them. Frank was hanging onto the beast's neck, and the pinprick glow of Ty darted alongside. Behind Frank sat Master Gurney, long black robes streaming in the wind. With a flick of his wrist, the magician unleashed a torrent of red flame that scorched the hillside, lighting up fleeing whitecoats and sending the second wyvern flapping desperately for safety.

'Said he wanted to come with us,' said Paddy. 'It was that wooden spoon that did it.'

Tabitha felt her jaw drop at the sight. The eccentric old academic didn't seem quite so useless any more.

The griffin dived low to the ground, and Frank grappled a small, wiry figure onto its back.

Joseph. Thank Thalin.

Tabitha looked up, hunting the skies for Nell. At last she saw their friend, a distant dot disappearing over the horizon, well clear of the third wyvern. Then her gaze snagged on something else. Something she couldn't look away from.

The summit of the hill was glowing, but not from the fires. Twelve figures hovered in the sky above the tomb, tall and slender, each one twice the height of a man, winged and robed in light. They seemed to be watching the centre of the circle, as though waiting for . . . something.

The griffin carrying Frank, Joseph and Master Gurney drew up alongside, and together they flew on towards the stones. Ty frowned as he joined them, his wings blurring. Master Gurney was sweating, his eyes wide in disbelief. Joseph looked frozen with fear, and even Frank and Paddy seemed uneasy.

No one said it. No one needed to.

Seraphs.

A burst of light came from the centre of the circle, painfully bright. And somehow Tabitha knew that, whatever the seraphs were waiting for, this was it.

The light of the seraphs shone down, illuminating the stone circle as brightly as if it were day. The magicians threw themselves flat in terror, or worship, or both.

If the rain was still falling, Newton didn't notice it. But it wasn't the twelve ghostly figures floating above that held his attention. It was the Duke.

He was still standing on top of the tomb, his eyes closed, a faint smile on his face. But his body was shaking violently. For a moment Newton thought he was having some kind of fit.

Until he saw the sword.

Something was coursing up from the rock, through

the blade and into the Duke. Something that couldn't be seen – but it came in waves of energy, which racked the man's body like a scrap of broken driftwood in a storm.

'What's wrong with him?' yelled Derringer over the noise. The hum of the stones still lingered, setting their clothes vibrating, so loud their voices could barely be heard.

Newton had a terrible feeling he knew the answer, but he couldn't bring himself to say it out loud.

Corin the Bold shall walk again.

There was a sudden, dazzling flash of light. The Duke gave one last violent shudder, and was still. Then slowly, like a man waking from slumber, he opened his eyes.

Different eyes.

Blue eyes like shards of ice, both beautiful and terrible to behold. The eyes of a warrior.

He smiled, and it wasn't the Duke smiling – Newton saw that at once. It was a savage grin, full of fierce joy. The smile of a man who had died long ago, and now, at last, lived again.

'Ohhh,' said the Duke – a sigh of pleasure. His voice was doubled, as though two people were speaking with the same mouth. One voice was the Duke's. The other voice . . .

'Corin,' said Newton. He felt as though his heart might explode from his chest, it was beating so hard. 'Corin the Bold.'

'No,' said the man with the Duke's face, and the warrior's eyes. 'And . . . yes.' He laughed – a twofold laugh – then hefted the sword, brought it slashing through the air in an elaborate pattern, quicker than thought. 'How I have missed this land! And how it needs me now. Centuries, I have slept. Yet my name still rings through the ages.' He stepped off the tomb, staring at someone at the edge of the circle.

The ogre in white.

Morgan shall be the first to die.

Whatever Morgan had done, he didn't deserve that. Newton scrambled to his feet, fighting every instinct in his body, and placing himself in the path of the man with the sword.

'Stand aside,' the man commanded. The blade danced in his hand.

Newton shook his head.

'Very well then. Count it an honour. My sword has drunk demon blood a thousand times. But now I am returned, yours will be the first it tastes.'

Newton dodged away, slipping in the mud, but there was no escape. He could sense the magic in the air, binding him within the stone circle.

Above, the seraphs watched.

I need a weapon. Any weapon. If only he still had the Banshee – or a sword – or even a good solid branch . . . But the ground offered nothing except mud and grass.

The man laughed that strange double laugh, his voices mocking Newton in chorus, as he swung the blade. The Sword of Corin sang through the air, forcing Newton to veer away. His boot slipped again, and he had to reach down to steady himself. He wiped his hand on his breeches, stepping carefully as he backed off, as the man came forward.

Morgan and Major Turnbull stood motionless at the very edge of the circle, allowing their master as much space as he needed. Their faces shone white with the seraphs' light. Derringer had scrambled to one knee, his body tense. His eyes were locked on Newton's, meaningful, trying to tell him something. '*The sword,*' mouthed the elf.

Thanks, Cyrus. I think I know about the sword. Newton spun to the side as it came slashing again, keeping well clear this time. The man didn't care, just laughed again. *He's a few centuries out of practice. But he'll get me soon enough.*

Derringer was still glaring at him, mouthing, '*The sword!*'

Wait. Newton had been so busy focusing on the attack, he hadn't seen what was right in front of him.

A second sword – the Duke's sword – hanging from the man's belt. If he could get to it somehow . . .

. . . or if Derringer could get to it.

He caught the elf's eye and nodded. Derringer nodded back.

The man tossed his blade in a spiral and caught it again, so fast Newton wasn't entirely sure it had happened. He wasn't rusty after all; he just hadn't been trying. Carelessly he stepped forward again, brought his sword in a long, curving backhand swing.

Newton kicked him. It was a move he'd learned from Tori. A last-ditch defence, to be used only when disarmed. There was no recovery from it, so if you missed, you were finished. But what did he have to lose? He kicked hard, and he kicked high, aiming for the man's chest.

He felt his foot make contact, felt the man go sprawling backwards, and at the same moment the Sword of Corin bit deep into his shoulder.

Pain. Nothing but pain.

He sank to his knees.

Derringer was on his feet, kicking up mud, diving at the man from behind.

Pain.

Newton bit hard, felt his teeth crack, screwed his eyes shut. When he looked again Derringer had rolled clear, and a length of steel was gleaming in his hand.

Newton smiled, still gritting his teeth. He felt blood seep through them, brimming in his mouth and dripping down his chin.

Pain.

So much pain.

Chapter Thirty-one

An explosion of light. It seemed to free the seraphs, as though they had only just woken up. They turned as one, their golden eyes watching the approaching griffins.

Joseph felt his skin prickle with fear. The gaze of the seraphs pierced his soul. Their faces were smooth and shining, formed out of solid white mist, and featureless apart from those terrible, beautiful eyes. He dug his fingers deeper into the griffin's feathers as they flew on, lashed by rain, towards the tomb and its guardians.

'Seraphs,' breathed Master Gurney, his voice taut with excitement. Joseph had imagined Hal's old teacher as a doddery old genius, and . . . well, he was.

But he also seemed to be utterly fearless. It made Joseph feel a little braver himself.

'I can hardly believe it. To think I am finally seeing one for myself! And not one indeed, yes, but twelve. *Twelve!* That ought to silence that oaf Perkins. All that nonsense about *The Ovine Anatomy of the Seraph*. He'll get the shock of his life when—'

'If you've quite finished,' roared Frank, over the howling of the wind. 'How do we get past them?'

Master Gurney cleared his throat. 'Ah yes, well, to be honest . . . I have absolutely no idea.'

'Right,' said Frank.

'At least they're not armed,' said Joseph.

The seraphs held out hands shrouded in mist, and golden objects took shape in them, appearing out of nothingness. In each left hand, a curving sword, and in each right, a long, pointed spear.

Ty let out a whimper and dived into Frank's pocket. Joseph swallowed, hard.

'Can you make this thing dodge?' said Frank.

Master Gurney didn't reply. Turning, Joseph saw that he'd gone a little pale.

The griffin squawked in panic, and Joseph's attention snapped back to the white figures above the stones, whose golden spears were arcing towards them like comets.

They banked hard, the world tipping as a golden shaft shot past, so close it ruffled the griffin's feathers.

'Faster!' yelled Frank. He had a pistol in his hand and let fly, sending out a sharp crack and a puff of smoke. As if that could possibly harm those creatures of mist.

The tomb was looming closer and closer. Joseph tugged his cutlass from his belt. His heart was pounding. He laid one finger on the blade, feeling the engraving of the shark – the mark of the Demon's Watch. A tiny moment of reassurance.

For the Watch. For Captain Newton. For Elijah Grubb.

The next moment, they were in among the seraphs.

Newton swayed, clutching his shoulder. He felt faint. His wound was screaming at him to look down, but he didn't want to. Didn't want to see his jacket stained with blood, and still more of it trickling through his fingers. Instead he watched the fight.

Cyrus Derringer was hefting the Duke's sword, testing its weight. Back in Port Fayt, the elf had worn a smug little smile that never seemed to leave his face. But tonight he was scowling as his blade flickered in an arc, dazzling as it reflected the light from the seraphs. His uniform, normally so clean, so impeccable, was torn and streaked with mud. His blue eyes tracked every movement of the man in white.

If it *was* a man.

The Duke's body moved like a puppet, strong and quick and light on its feet. He sprang in to attack, viciously fast, sword blurring. Every blow was neat and precise, but savage. Derringer met each one with his own blade. He caught the last on his crosspiece, and shoved the man away. Then he spat contemptuously on the ground and smoothed his damp hair back.

A flicker of rage sparked in his opponent's face, so intense that it made Newton shudder.

'Major Turnbull.' Once again the deep growl of Corin mingled with the calmer, softer voice of the Duke. 'Kill the elf.'

At the edge of the circle, Major Turnbull's hand reached for the long broadsword strapped to her back . . .

And paused.

She turned from Derringer to the man who had been her master. Finally her gaze settled on Newton. She was frozen in time, her eyes wide, the eyes of a lost little girl.

That's what she was, once. An innocent little girl playing catch, hopscotch and hide and seek with her friends. Little Alice Turnbull.

Slowly, she lowered her hand.

The man's face twisted horribly, and he began to laugh. 'You child,' he said, when his laughter had died away. 'What a moment to turn traitor. When the Light has triumphed at last.' He raised the sword, pointing it straight at her. 'You will die for it soon enough. But first, the elf.'

Then his blade darted like a serpent at Cyrus Derringer.

A golden sword came curving out of nowhere. Joseph flung his cutlass up and felt the impact jar his arm, so hard he cried out in pain. The face of another seraph appeared in front of them, and their griffin climbed in panic, throwing all its riders back so that Joseph had to hold on tight with both hands.

Ty popped his head out of Frank's pocket, and ducked straight back down again.

To his left, Joseph caught a glimpse of yet another ghostly white figure, this one swooping towards the second griffin. Paddy was slashing wildly with his cutlass – blows that would be deadly to a normal creature, but simply passed through the seraph as if it were air. The seraph raised its golden sword, and it was only at the last moment that the griffin swerved clear.

Hal wasn't fighting. In fact, he was clinging onto

the griffin with both hands, his eyes closed. Turning, Joseph saw that Master Gurney was the same, murmuring to himself as though he was asleep. Joseph had seen enough magic to understand what was happening. *They're casting a spell* . . . He just hoped it was a good one.

The next moment the two magicians threw out their arms, and all sound was muffled.

Joseph blinked. They were underwater. Or at least, that was what it felt like. Everything wobbled, refracted as though by fast-moving ocean currents. Joseph saw that it was the same with Hal's griffin – the tremor of the spell swirled around them in a protective sphere of magic. *That must be what we look like too*, he realized.

'A shield spell,' said Master Gurney. 'The best we could do. But I fear it won't last long.' Joseph could hear the tension in his voice, as though he was straining every muscle in his body to keep the magic in place.

A golden lance shimmered towards them, striking the bubble and bouncing off it with a sound like a clashing cymbal.

'Not bad,' said Frank.

Joseph leaned over the side of the griffin, peering into the stone circle as they flew low above it. Through the haze of magic he saw white-cloaked men lying prostrate between the stones. Inside, four more figures. No, five – one was collapsed, wounded on the ground. Two more engaged in a sword fight. Joseph gasped as he saw that one of the fighters seemed to be glowing – actually glowing – with light.

'*Corin the Bold shall walk again.*' It was Master Gurney who spoke. 'Or his spirit, at least. It appears he's using the Duke as a vessel, from which to command the seraphs.'

Something clicked in Joseph's mind. 'So if we could drive out Corin, he'd lose the seraphs?'

'Perhaps.'

For the Watch. For Captain Newton. For Elijah Grubb.

For everyone who's ever helped me, in spite of who I am.

'I don't like that look in your eye, Joseph,' said Frank.

'Wait!' yelped Master Gurney. 'Don't let him—'

Joseph's fingers closed on the wooden spoon, as he threw himself into space.

Tabitha watched in horror as a scrawny little figure dived off the other griffin. He tumbled out of the magical shield and dropped ten feet, landing unsteadily on top of the nearest stone, stumbling, arms windmilling, before he flung himself off again to collapse in a sprawl of limbs inside the circle.

'Joseph!'

How many times did she have to rescue him? *Once more, at least.*

'Don't let him . . . use the . . . wand . . .' gasped Hal, sweating with the effort of keeping up the shield spell.

Their griffin was soaring out of the circle now. If Tabitha jumped, she'd land outside it – and hard.

'Throw me,' she said.

Paddy looked at her as though she'd lost it. Coming from Paddy, that felt particularly insulting.

'You have to throw me! Joseph is down there. Please, Paddy.'

The troll wavered for a moment, then his jaw set in determination. Just as Tabitha began to regret it, his two great hands took hold of her waist and he launched her from the griffin's back.

At first the magic tugged at her, but then she was through the shield and falling fast towards one of the standing stones, fingers reaching for the rock. They found purchase half a second before she slammed against the side of it, clinging on for all she was worth, pain bursting across her body. She hauled herself up and pushed off as Joseph had done, dropping and landing in a crouch, skidding, splattering mud.

The first thing she saw was the fight. Two figures, one in white and one in black, swords swinging so fast they could barely be seen. She almost didn't recognize Cyrus Derringer – the elf was smeared in mud, hollow-eyed and pale. He held one hand behind his back, bandaged and crusted with blood. But he still fought like a demon.

The other man . . .

Tabitha swallowed hard at the sight of him. He looked ordinary enough – small and plump – but the way he moved was unnatural, fast and deadly, and each motion seemed to trail white light. There was something utterly *wrong* about him, though she couldn't say what it was.

The Duke of Garran. It had to be.

There were others at the edge of the circle, she realized. Magicians lying prostrate, as though entirely drained by some enormous magical effort. A hulking ogre and a blonde-haired woman, both in League white. On the far side, she caught sight of Newton, and her heart leaped at the sight. *He's here!* But the Captain of the Watch was on his knees, one hand clamped over his shoulder, his blue coat soaked black with blood.

Tabitha ran to Joseph and grabbed hold of the

tavern boy's jacket, pulling him to his feet. He let out a yelp of pain and clutched at his ankle.

'Come on!' yelled Tabitha. 'It's not safe here. We've got to get Newt and—'

She was distracted by a horrible gurgling sound from the centre of the circle. Spinning round, she saw that the man in white had twisted the sword from Derringer's hand and grabbed the elf by the throat. Slowly, but without even a tremble in his arm, the man lifted Derringer until his boots left the mud.

'You fight prettily, elf,' said the man, and there was something strange about his voice. It sounded almost like two people speaking at the same time. 'But you are still scum.' He hurled Derringer hard, and there was a hideous cracking sound as the elf's head struck the tombstone in the centre of the circle, before he slumped to the mud, completely motionless.

'No!' shouted Tabitha.

But it was too late. The man in white sneered and turned away, prowling towards the edge of the circle, his eyes fixed on the ogre in League livery. He cut the air in a practice stroke. 'Now, at last,' he said, 'it is your turn.'

The ogre stood watching, rooted to the spot. His brow creased in confusion, as though he didn't understand what was happening.

Why isn't he moving? Any moment now, the ogre would meet the same fate as Cyrus Derringer. But the ogre didn't do a thing. His small eyes darted in every direction, utterly lost. *He's a slave*, Tabitha realized. *He doesn't dare lift a finger against his master.*

The man swung, the blade whistling through the air, and the ogre stumbled backwards.

'Do something!' shouted Tabitha. 'He's going to *kill* you!'

The blade swung again and caught the ogre's arm, sending dark blood spattering onto the grass. The ogre let out a whimper like that of a wounded animal, and the man in white laughed.

'You cowardly creature,' he hissed. 'Worthless demonspawn scum. Face me.'

'Please,' cried Tabitha.

'Listen to her, Morgan.' It was Newton who spoke, still kneeling in the mud and clutching his shoulder. 'That's not the Duke. That's Corin the Bold. You've got to fight back.'

'Yes, fight!' said the man in white. 'Fight me, you cockroach. You snivelling wretch.' He twisted his sword, slapping the flat of it against Morgan's back and sending him staggering again.

Finally, something shifted in the ogre's face. He let out a low sound – a warning – and when the man danced in closer, he swung a fist. Tabitha could see at once that he'd never really fought before. The blow was too slow, too clumsy. The man dodged aside and slammed his sword hilt into the ogre's stomach, sending him reeling for a third time. He slashed again, then again, driving Morgan backwards.

The ogre tripped and fell back against one of the standing stones. He cowered away, curling into a ball and hugging his knees like a child.

'Pathetic,' spat his master. He raised the sword, double-handed. 'It is not easy to take off an ogre's head with a single blow. But I have done it many times before.'

Tabitha sprang forward, sliding to a halt in between the two of them. The ogre blinked at her, frowning in confusion.

'Leave him alone,' she said. She'd meant it to sound tough, but it came out petulant, like a child's complaint. If only she had her knives . . .

Up close, Tabitha could see the man's eyes properly for the first time. Cold, blue eyes that didn't belong in the face that wore them.

'I don't want to hurt you, little girl.' It really *was* two voices, speaking as one. 'But you leave me no choice.' Tabitha tensed, ready to dodge. But instead of swinging his sword, the man kicked at her feet, sweeping her legs away so that she fell in the mud with a thump. He loomed above, his blade glinting.

'Don't touch her!' Joseph's voice.

Tabitha rolled over and saw that he had stepped forward, limping slightly. His eyes were wide, as though even he couldn't believe what he was doing. He drew the wooden spoon from his pocket and aimed it at the man in white.

The man laughed. 'A goblin with a spoon. What next? A fairy with a feather duster? Well, I've had enough.' He strode towards the tavern boy, with the ogre's piggy eyes tracking his every movement.

Tabitha could see Joseph's chest heaving as he took deep breaths, fighting to control his fear. Hal's words flashed through her mind. *Don't let him use the wand.*

'Joseph!' she yelled. 'Put the spoon away. Please! It's too dangerous . . .'

But he didn't seem to hear her.

The man in white was coming closer and closer.

Focus, Joseph. You can do this.

Fear gripped him suddenly, and he almost flung the wand away in a panic. Tabitha was lying in the mud, yelling at him, telling him not to use it, but he had to block that out. He couldn't let anything break his concentration.

Think the right thoughts. But what were they? What was it like to be the Duke of Garran – or whatever creature was inside him? With Jeb it had been so easy, but with this man he couldn't imagine. He felt like he was stumbling in the dark, with nothing to hold on.

Please. It has to work. It has to.

His head ached as though a hundred fairies were trying to smash their way out of it, and still there was no warmth, no tingling in his body. The spell wasn't happening.

The man's fingers closed around Joseph's throat. And at the same moment Joseph looked deep into those ice-blue eyes, and he knew. The thoughts came surging up inside him, flooding his mind.

I am justice. I am fury. I am hatred . . .

I am the Light.

The magic arrived all at once, a heat which exploded out of him, racking his body more fiercely than ever. He almost dropped the spoon, but he clung on, as though to a broken spar in a shipwreck.

The air thrummed, the man's blue eyes went wide with shock, and the next instant Joseph was . . .

Chapter Thirty-two

... **S**omewhere else.

Bright light streamed in through high, arched windows. The walls were of white stone and hung with white banners. Even the floor was polished white marble. Everything seemed to glow. It was a hall, big enough to fit a galleon inside.

Joseph looked down at the battered wooden spoon in his hand, at his skin and his clothes, still the same dull greys and browns.

He didn't belong here.

The hall was empty but for two figures in the very centre of it. Sitting on a white wooden throne was the Duke of Garran, dressed in the same mud-spattered uniform he'd been wearing half a second ago, on a distant hilltop. He was smiling, but his pale eyes stared blankly straight ahead.

Standing behind the throne, one hand resting on the back of it, was a slim, ordinary-looking man with long brown hair and a hooked nose. He wore chain-mail under a long white tunic, and a winged sword was stitched in silver on his chest.

At the sight of Joseph the stranger tensed, his hand tightening on the wooden throne. 'What are you doing here?' he said.

Joseph stumbled forward. What was this? It hadn't been like this with Jeb. He had stepped straight into the goblin's mind. He *was* Jeb.

'Answer me, mongrel. Who are you?'

'I-I don't— Where is this?'

The man's eyes narrowed. Icy-blue eyes. The eyes Joseph had seen in the Duke's face, moments ago. 'You are in the Duke's mind,' said the man. 'The furthest reaches of it. The space which lies beyond the limit of his perception. And all of it belongs to me.' He rested his chain-mailed hands on the Duke's head. 'Leave now, while you still draw breath.'

'Why don't *you* leave?' said Joseph, trying to ignore his rising fear. 'Whoever you are. You're not real.'

The man laughed scornfully. 'I am not real? Each

day they tell new tales of me, raise new statues to me, write new songs of me. I am the hero that never died. I have lived centuries longer than you ever shall.'

And suddenly, Joseph understood. *He looks nothing like in the paintings, back in the House of Light.* But there couldn't be any doubt. 'You're—'

'I am the son of Leth. The child of the storm. Corin, sometimes called the Bold. Yes, indeed. Perhaps you were expecting a taller, stronger man? But my power never lay in my body. It lies in my heart.'

Breathe. Slow and steady.

Somehow he had to go deeper into the Duke's mind, to a place where he could drive out Corin and take control.

'Please, I need—'

'Leave, half-and-half.' Corin's voice was growing harder and colder, and his hands clenched tight around the Duke's head. 'Unless you intend to slay me with that wooden spoon. I will not tell you again – this mind is taken, and you should not be here.'

'My name's Joseph.'

The hero sneered. 'I have no use for the names of demonspawn.'

Joseph's cheeks flushed with anger. *Mongrel. Half-and-half.* He'd heard it all before. He thought of his uncle, red-faced and podgy, who never called him

Joseph. They were just the same, his stupid uncle and this stupid warrior. Just as petty. Just as cruel as each other.

And now he wasn't so afraid.

You goblins are all alike, Mr Lightly had told him. *Thieving, sneaking, crafty . . .*

Well, then. He'd show them how crafty he could be.

Joseph tucked the wooden spoon away in his pocket and brought out the silver pocket watch instead. He held it up, letting it swing gently on its chain, as he stepped forward. *I have to get past him. I have to get deep inside the Duke's mind.*

Corin frowned. 'What is that?'

He's never seen one before. Back in the Dark Age, they never had watches.

Joseph smiled. 'Magic,' he said. 'Goblin magic.'

'You're lying,' snarled Corin. 'A filthy little greyskin like you . . . you stole it, didn't you?'

Joseph took a step towards the throne, and there was a soft clink of chain-mail as Corin moved in response. *Was that a flinch?* The great hero – Corin the Bold – could he be frightened?

'How do you think I got here?' said Joseph. 'Goblin magic.' The words came out unbidden, and his mind raced to keep up with the lies. *What would Jeb do?* 'My father gave this to me. He was Jebedee the Sorcerer. A great magical craftsman.'

The hero drew his sword in a flash. The famous sword. It glittered in the dazzling light from the windows. 'Keep away from me, magician.'

'I *am* a magician,' said Joseph. His voice sounded strangely detached, as though it was coming from someone else. He held the watch higher, as Corin took a step back, edging away from the Duke's throne. 'And this,' said Joseph, 'is my . . . my soul stealer!' He laid one finger on the watch face. 'All I need do is break the glass, and you will be sucked into it, held captive for ever with all the other souls I've stolen. You see? I am a thief, just like you said. Just like my father!'

Corin hesitated, and something changed in his face. 'You're no thief,' said the hero. 'You're a liar.'

Joseph lurched forward, hands reaching for the Duke of Garran.

Corin the Bold darted round the side of the throne, but he was too late. Joseph dropped the watch, leaving it to clatter on the marble floor as his fingers closed around the Duke's head.

'No!' howled Corin.

The Duke's pale eyes went wide, drawing Joseph into them until he was rushing towards the mind within.

Or was the Duke rushing towards Joseph?

The two of them speeding into each other, fast, then faster.

Faster than light.

So fast that Joseph lost control. So fast he could no longer tell where he was.

Who he was.

What he was.

A single thought surged up from nowhere, consuming him, before their minds came together and everything spun away into nothingness. The warning of a kindly old magician.

The spell will only backfire, and then you'll be letting Corin-knows-who into your own mind. Do you have any idea how dangerous that is?

*J*oseph, did I ever tell you the story of how the world
began?'

Whose voice is that?

*The Duke turns, looks into the face of a goblin sitting
beside him. He glances down and sees with a shock
that his hands are someone else's hands. Long, slender
fingers, mottled grey and pink.*

The hands of a mongrel boy.

Where is he? What is happening to him?

*Just a moment before he was standing on a hilltop,
filled with the power of Corin. Now Corin is gone, and
the hilltop too. Now he is in a memory – someone else's
memory. The memory of a mongrel boy.*

They are sitting on a pier, just him and the goblin, swinging their bare feet to and fro above the waves – his, grey-pink; the goblin's just grey. In the distance, the sun is setting, staining the ocean crimson.

'Long, long ago,' says the goblin, 'before humans or goblins or elves, the land was crafted by demons and seraphs. They made everything – the Old World, the New World and the Middle Islands, the mountains and seas and the creatures that walked the earth. The world is soaked in their magic, and it's that same magic that magicians use in their spells, even today.'

The Duke tries to stand, but he can't. Strange feelings are welling up inside him. The feelings of a mongrel boy. Love for his father, and the warmth of his father's love for him.

How can it be? These creatures are not capable of such emotions. And yet they are there, filling him up, making him feel safe, making his heart overflow so much it nearly chokes him.

Who dares do this to him? Who dares make him feel like this?

'Now, many years later, war broke out between the creatures of the Old World. That was the Dark Age. And in those days, the humans used to say that the seraphs had made them in their own image, and that it was only the other creatures – the imps,

trolls, ogres and so on – that were shaped by the demons.'

'What do you think, Father?' The words are his – and not his.

Elijah smiles and puts an arm around the Duke's shoulders. 'I think they worked together. There's a little bit of demon and a little bit of seraph in everyone, Joseph. Don't let anyone tell you different.'

Chapter Thirty-three

Tabitha felt the tremor of magic. She saw Joseph's eyes glaze over, the air refracting all around him. The man in white had jerked rigid, his blade frozen in mid-air, his hand still clamped round the tavern boy's throat.

The world seemed to hesitate. Then light exploded from the man's body, blindingly bright. The hum of the seraphs rose to a piercing scream, and they were sucked away as though by whirlpools, tugged back into the great standing stones.

At the same time, a strange image forced its way into Tabitha's mind – a blue-eyed man in armour, his mouth open in a silent howl as he faded into thin air

– and then the ghostly figure was gone, and there was only Joseph and the Duke of Garran, both staggering, dazed and blinking.

It was night once more. Dark but for the soft, coloured firelight from the hillside. Silent but for the gentle sounds of the wind and the rain.

Tabitha dragged herself to Joseph's side, half crawling, half slithering. *I told you not to use the wand. Master Gurney said it was too dangerous.* He had fallen unconscious in the mud, his fingers clamped tightly round the wooden spoon. But he was smiling.

Looking up, Tabitha saw that the Duke had opened his eyes, and they were his own again.

'I . . .' said the Duke. He blinked fiercely, as though trying to shake something from his mind. 'Who was I . . . ?'

His gaze fell on Joseph and fury twisted his features, more terrible even than the ice-cold glare of the warrior who had been inside him just moments ago. 'You demonspawn filth!' He took the sword in both hands, raised it high one last time. 'What trickery was that? What have you done to me?'

Tabitha flung herself in front of Joseph's body, and the Duke's snarl turned more savage still. 'You think that will stop me? I'll kill you, both of you, I'll—'

A bestial roar split the air.

The Duke half turned. Morgan had surged upwards, wide-eyed with fear, and with anger. He charged, smashing into his master, bearing him backwards with all the force of a cart of rocks rumbling downhill.

They fell together, squirming in the mud, the Duke crushed in Morgan's tight embrace. Every muscle in the ogre's arms was bulging. He was growling like a dog, while the Duke let out a soft, strangled whine.

Tabitha clamped her hands tight over her ears and buried her face in Joseph's waistcoat.

It seemed to go on for ever.

When she looked again, she saw the pair of them lying there, smeared with mud, smeared with blood, and silent.

The Sword of Corin had fallen point first in the ground beside them. It stood upright, quivering, and at last was still.

Major Turnbull took Morgan gently by the shoulders and helped him up. The ogre's fingers were still curled, rigid as rock, as he left the Duke's body slumped into the mud.

Newton felt fainter than ever. There was a pool of blood around him, staining his knees. He looked down at his hands – both gripping his shoulder – and saw that they were utterly white.

He fought to raise his head again. Even that was an effort. Butchers had appeared around the circle, stepping over the prostrate magicians and levelling muskets at the watchmen. Tabitha lay curled protectively round Joseph. There was a soft flapping from the sky, and the two griffins landed on standing stones opposite each other, their riders watching, anxious and uncertain. Cyrus Derringer's body was propped up against Corin's Tomb.

The rain fell, and the only sound that rose above it was Morgan's breathing, hard and fast. Major Turnbull guided him to the tomb and he sat on it, fingers still stuck in that same position, eyes staring madly through the mud drying on his face. Gradually, the panting slowed. He blinked. Flexed his fingers. His hands fell limp at his sides, and his head rested on his chest.

Major Turnbull stepped up onto the hero's tomb, and everyone turned to her. She hesitated. Newton could tell she wasn't used to this. To being important. Her gaze met his, and for an instant her lip trembled. He watched her expression settle as she made a decision.

'Whitecoats,' she called, her voice low and commanding. Feet shuffled, and muskets were raised. 'Fall back.'

Newton felt his lips twitch into a smile, as his mind

seemed to drift out of his body. His gaze lingered on the griffins perched on the stones above.

Winged vengeance.

The last thing he saw was the mud looming towards him, as he fell into it.

PART FIVE
The House with the Green Front Door

Chapter Thirty-four

'**G**oodbye,' said Tabitha.

She laid her hand on Nell's head, smoothing the feathers. The griffin gave a gentle click of her beak, and half stretched her wings. They caught the morning sunlight, and Tabitha thought once again how beautiful she was. She turned away.

The stable boy hustled the three griffins back inside and swung the wooden stable doors shut. Master Gurney pressed a coin into his hand.

'Now you mustn't worry yourselves,' said the magician, turning to Tabitha and Joseph. He was still wearing his dusty black gown, but Tabitha could have sworn there was a little extra colour in his cheeks now. Ever since the adventure at Corin's Tomb. 'The Academy will take excellent care of your feathered friends. They'll be far better off here than they were in that ghastly bile farm.'

Tabitha nodded. She knew they couldn't take Nell back to Port Fayt with them, but she was still sorry to see her go. 'Just promise me one thing,' she said.

'Yes, my dear?'

'That you won't try and turn her into an egg?'

The magician laid a solemn hand on her shoulder. 'I swear it by Corin's Sword.' He winced as he realized what he'd just said. 'Or, I mean . . . perhaps I should say, *by Thalin's breeches*. That's the expression, isn't it?'

Just that morning, the sword had been melted down in the Academy's smithy. Master Gurney had hated every second of it – losing such a precious historical artefact – but he knew they had no choice. The Sword of Corin was gone – and the Old World was safer for it.

'Thank you, Master Gurney,' said Joseph. He was dressed in a clean blue coat, white shirt and breeches – the smartest Tabitha had ever seen him. He was still a little pale after the fight at the tomb, and he seemed even skinnier than before. But the biggest change was in his face. There was a strange kind of peace there. A look she hadn't seen since . . . well, ever.

'You are most welcome, young man,' said Master Gurney. 'I must admit, I found it all rather . . . exhilarating. I would never have dreamed of meddling in League affairs, but I couldn't allow that wooden spoon to fall into the hands of the Duke of Garran. Now, do you have it with you?'

Joseph reached into his pocket and drew it out. Master Gurney took the spoon at once, sweeping it inside his gown as though it might catch fire if it was in the open for too long. 'You have my word that I will take proper care of it.' He beamed. 'Well. Your friends will be waiting for you.'

They walked together, footsteps crunching in the gravel as they made their way past the neat green squares of grass, through the courtyards of the Academy.

Master Gurney led them, his cloak billowing behind him like a raven's wings. *He's even standing a little taller now*, thought Tabitha. She noticed other magicians steal quick glances at the master and the two children following him, readjusting spectacles and peering over piles of books to get a better look.

Word's got around.

The carriage was waiting for them on the gravel driveway beyond the drawbridge. It was a smart, shining black Academy vehicle, with its motto inscribed on the lacquer in letters of gold: *To LEARN is to DO.*

It had never made much sense to Tabitha. *To DO is to LEARN* seemed more like it.

'Have you said your goodbyes, Tabs?'

It was Hal who spoke. The magician was standing by the open door of the carriage, rubbing at his spectacles with a handkerchief. He looked a thousand times better now that the burden of his secret had been lifted.

'Aye, just about.'

Paddy heaved the last bag of provisions up onto the roof of the carriage and lashed it down. The trolls had spent most of the morning in the kitchens, sniffing around for some loaves of black bread, joints of ham, and some enormous multi-coloured cheeses from the Duchy of Henge that Frank had become fond of.

'Where's Newt?' asked Tabitha.

'Beats me,' said Frank, rounding the carriage. 'We'll miss the tide if he's not here soon.'

'I could go and find them?' Joseph suggested.

Paddy chuckled as he clambered down and dusted off his hands. 'I reckon you've done quite enough. I'm not letting you out of my sight again, you little rascal.' He made to deliver one of his friendly punches, then stopped himself as Joseph flinched.

'Ah,' said Master Gurney. 'Here they are.'

Everyone turned.

Three figures were making their way across the drawbridge. Two of them walked side by side – a tall, thin elf and a large, strong human. Cyrus Derringer wore a bandage around his head, and his clean black uniform hung a little loose on his shoulders – but he was clearly on the road to recovery. Newton wore his blue watchman's coat over one shoulder, the other exposed and covered in bandaging. Ty rode in his front pocket.

At the rear came a hulking, shambling creature, his footsteps clumping heavily on the wooden planks of the drawbridge. Morgan had become even quieter since the fight at the tomb, if that was possible. Tabitha didn't blame him. The Duke of Garran might have been a cruel man, and likely a worse master – but he was still a person, and Morgan had killed him. That wasn't something he was going to forget.

The ogre came to a halt a little way behind his two companions, waiting like a faithful hound. He was dressed in shirtsleeves and an Academy gown to replace the white League livery he'd worn before. It was far too small for him and the material was strained in several places, but it covered his back at least.

'Thank you, Morgan,' Tabitha called out. *Thank you for saving our lives*. She smiled at him, and the ogre gave her a confused, wary look. As though he'd never seen a smile before.

'The wounded veterans return, eh?' said Frank. Tabitha thought he was making a joke for a moment, but he looked grave. Everyone did. There was a strange atmosphere, as though something was going on. She turned to Joseph, and saw that he felt it too.

'Captain Newton, I—' began Hal. He was staring at his feet, looking anxious all over again. 'I don't know if anyone told you . . . About the wooden spoon, I—'

'I heard,' said Newton. 'And I understand. I can't blame you, Hal. Especially after all I've done.'

'All the same . . . I'm sorry.'

There was another long, awkward pause.

'Are we going then?' said Tabitha briskly.

Newton nodded. 'Aye,' he said, and his deep voice trembled a little. 'Aye, you should.'

'What do you mean?' said Tabitha. She felt dizzy.

'You're not coming?' said Joseph.

Newton laid his hands on their shoulders, one on Tabitha's and one on Joseph's. The bruise on his face was a pale purple now. He smiled at them – a sad smile, but more than that, a weary one.

'Listen to me closely. Cyrus and I, we've been talking, and we've decided that he'll come with you. He'll captain the Watch from now on – he's proved himself,

I reckon.' The elf looked solemn, and Tabitha remembered how he used to smile all the time – or smirk, at least – and how she hadn't seen that in a long while.

'What about you?' she asked.

'Me and Ty, we're staying here in the Old World.'

'But—'

'I've thought about this a lot, Tabs. I've made some mistakes lately. Big ones. And I reckon . . . well, I reckon I'm tired.' He paused a moment, eyes glazing over, and at once Tabitha thought of Old Jon. His friend. Now dead and gone. 'Someone should be here,' he added finally. 'For now, at least. Alice Turnbull's at the House of Light, and she's doing what she can. The lords of the League are all dead now, and it's a chance to turn things around. Maybe destroy the League for good. Who knows? But I'm going to keep an eye on things. Besides . . .'

He turned and looked at Morgan. The ogre was standing still, fiddling with his hands and looking like a lost puppy.

'I reckon he needs me,' said Newton. 'What the Duke did to him . . . well . . .' He tailed off. 'Master Gurney here has offered us rooms in the Academy. It'll be a good life. And maybe one day soon I'll take a trip out into the countryside. To Wyborough. To the zephyrum mines.'

Tabitha took a deep breath, fighting down her tears. She was going to argue, but something in Newton's face stopped her. He looked so content, so sure that this was the right thing to do.

'I'll miss you,' she said at last, her voice wavering.

Newton nodded. 'Aye. I'll miss you too. But we'll see each other again very soon. I promise you that.'

Paddy clapped a big green hand on Cyrus Derringer's shoulder. 'Welcome to the Watch,' he said.

'Thank you,' said Cyrus. 'I . . .' He seemed a little embarrassed. 'I don't think I understood what the Watch really was, before. What it meant. But I won't let you down.'

Newton turned to Joseph. 'Goodbye, young 'un,' he said. 'You and Tabs look after each other, understand?'

The tavern boy nodded, and flashed a smile at her.

'I don't want to rush you,' said Frank. 'But the tide . . .'

'Aye,' said Newton. 'Best be on your way.'

He and Ty said goodbye to the other watchmen, one by one. At long last they clambered on board, and Joseph gave Tabitha the window seat. She stuck her head out and waved as the carriage jolted off, as it bounced along the gravel drive, faster and faster.

The wind tossed her blue hair across her face, breaking up her view of the figures waving back. The fairy hovering in the air, the tall, black-clad magician, the hulking ogre and the shaven-headed man in the blue coat. The man who wasn't her father, but who had looked after her like his daughter.

The tears came at last, blinding her, as they turned the corner and Newton disappeared from view. Ever since her parents died, he'd been the only family she'd known. And now he was gone.

Cyrus Derringer silently reached into a pocket of his uniform, drew out a handkerchief and passed it to her.

'We'll see him again, Tabs, don't you worry,' said Frank.

'Aye, and he'll write letters too,' said Paddy. 'Probably get Ty to deliver them.'

'They'll be misspelled with terrible grammar, if I know Newt,' said Hal.

'And we'll write letters back,' said Joseph. 'Let him know what's happening with the Watch. Remember what you said to me, on that rooftop? *We've still got a family.*'

Tabitha smiled through the tears. *The only family she'd known.* Maybe that wasn't quite true.

*

Joseph stood at the bow of the *Eternal Brilliance*, savouring the breeze and the salt spray that buffeted his face. The ship had been on the sea for almost an hour, and the Old World was just a thin blurred line on the horizon to stern. Ahead there was nothing but the sparkling ocean.

For the first time since the griffin farm, he was alone.

He reached into his pocket and drew out the wand. It looked just the same as ever – old, battered and chipped. A wooden spoon, just like the one he'd given Master Gurney. Tabitha had picked up the fake one from the burned-out tavern when she'd gone to fetch his cutlass. She'd had a hunch it might prove useful, and she'd been right.

Joseph hadn't wanted to give up the wand – not like that. It had started everything. That day back in the Legless Mermaid, when his broom had struck the black velvet package and he'd kept it in the hope of returning it to its owner and finding a better life.

The spoon was the beginning, and it made a funny sort of sense that it should be the end too.

There were footsteps on the deck behind him, and Cyrus Derringer joined him at the gunwale. The sea air seemed to have done wonders for the elf's complexion. The bandage was still wrapped around his head, but he'd mend – that's what Hal had said, anyway. He was fiddling with the hilt of his sword, gazing straight ahead.

'I wanted to ask you . . .' he began stiffly. He paused for a long while, and Joseph waited. 'I'm not sure I can do it. Lead the Watch. The way you are together it's like a . . . well. Like a family.'

Joseph nodded.

'How can I replace Captain Newton?'

'You can't.'

There was another long pause.

'But you know,' said Joseph finally, 'I never thought I could do it either. Be a watchman. If you'd told me, back when I was a tavern boy . . .' He smiled at the thought. 'They took me in, all the same. They acted like I wasn't just a mongrel boy. Like I was *someone*. Like I was . . . I don't know. Joseph Grubb.' He turned his smile on Derringer, and the elf smiled back. 'You'll be all right,' Joseph told him.

'I hope so,' said Cyrus. He pointed at Joseph's hand. 'What have you got there?'

'Oh, this . . .' Joseph held up the wooden spoon. 'This is just a spoon.'

Almost without thinking, he took it in both hands and snapped it over his knee. He felt a strange vibration through his palms, and the air shimmered, as though the magic was evaporating. He drew his arm back and hurled the two pieces out into the ocean.

'Why did you do that?' said Cyrus cautiously.

Joseph shrugged. 'I reckon I don't need it any more.'

They stood together in silence, as the *Eternal Brilliance* sailed on, towards Port Fayt.

Epilogue

It wasn't hard to find Bootles' Pie Shop – you just followed your nose.

Cyrus Derringer's belly rumbled as he turned into the alleyway and spotted the sign, squeaking as it swung in the breeze. The rich, mouth-watering scent was even stronger here.

Is that seagull pie? Or lobster . . . ?

'You sure about this, sir?' said Culpepper, as they reached the door. Derringer gave him a smile. The ex-sergeant had replaced his stripes with a colonel's silver on his shoulders and lapels. Culpepper was probably the most capable blackcoat in Port Fayt, which, he had to admit, wasn't saying much. Still, the new commander of the Dockside Militia was rising to the challenge admirably. He'd got his act together, and one or two taverns were going to go out of business as a result.

Derringer laid his hand on Colonel Culpepper's shoulder. 'You don't need to call me sir any more. And yes, I'm sure. Good luck with the militia, Colonel.'

'It's just . . . the Demon's Watch,' said Culpepper, squirming uncomfortably. 'You never liked them, sir – I mean, er . . . Mr Derringer.'

Cyrus shrugged. 'Maybe I was wrong. Maybe there is room for the blue coats as well as the black.' He smoothed down his new uniform. It was crisp and freshly laundered – just the way he liked it. He raised his hand to knock, and caught sight once again of the new shark tattoo inked on the back of it. The mark of the Watch.

The last time he'd been here, he'd ordered his men to attack the pie shop, tried to arrest Captain Newton and broken a good few windows. *I'll have to apologize to Mrs Bootle for those.*

Things were going to be very different from now on.

He couldn't wait.

The door opened, and a friendly green face peered out.

'Well, if it ain't that famous Captain Derringer of the Demon's Watch!' said Paddy, with a wink. 'Come on in. Joseph and Tabs aren't here yet, so that means more pies for us.'

Derringer smiled as he stepped inside, and the mongrel boy's words came back to him.

They took me in, all the same.

Yes. It felt like home.

Tabitha waited at the end of the road. Her blue hair stirred in the breeze, paler than usual. She'd told Joseph the night before – she'd decided to stop dying it and let the blonde colour return. She'd always hated being recognized as the Mandeville girl. *The girl whose parents were killed.* But she didn't feel like hiding any more. She was proud of her parents, and everything they'd done.

She smiled at Joseph and told him to take as long as he needed. She could tell this was something he needed to do on his own.

He remembered every cobblestone. Every battered doorway. And one more than all the others.

Of course, it wasn't really green any more. The paint had flaked and chipped away, leaving a few scraps of colour, some of it red – as though the door had been painted and repainted. Joseph couldn't even tell if the red had come before or after his parents had lived there.

He laid his hand on the rough wood, remembering. He'd been sure the house would be abandoned, but when he tried the door it wouldn't budge. He edged to the nearest window, and saw that it had a broken pane, but that someone had attached a scrap of sackcloth over it.

He peered inside. The room beyond hadn't changed a bit. The same old table and chairs, the same bare wooden planks on the floor. Even the same cracked mirror and a couple of bad paintings of fish tacked to the walls. Joseph felt a lump in his throat.

He started as someone entered the room. An elf woman, young and beautiful, dressed in tattered old clothes. She was humming as she went to the stove, took the lid off a pot and stirred the contents. A fine aroma filled Joseph's nostrils. As she turned, he saw that she was carrying a baby, swaddled in a thick blanket. An elf child, gently slumbering.

Joseph's gaze returned to its mother. She was looking straight at him, eyes wide with alarm, her mouth hanging slightly open.

A pause.

He raised a hand in greeting.

She looked confused, then angry. Then her mouth

twitched up at the corners and she raised her own hand.

Joseph stepped away from the window, turned back up the street towards Tabitha.

He'd imagined returning so many times, to the house with the green front door. In his dreams it had been just the same, and his parents were there to welcome him. It was his home.

Now he knew that dream wouldn't haunt him any more. It was still a home – it just wasn't his.

As he walked back towards his friend, his hand slipped into his pocket and closed over his parents' silver pocket watch.

He ran his fingertips over the engraving – *To my dearest Elijah, with all my love, Eleanor* – and he smiled.

Acknowledgements

Thanks once again to the good people of Lutyens & Rubinstein and particularly to Jane Finigan, the best agent in town. To my friends, fellow writers and colleagues, and to the extremely brilliant team at DFB – Simon, David, Anthony, Rosie, Phil, Bron, Linda and Sue. To Alison and David, whose artwork has shaped my characters and stories. And finally to my wonderful and extraordinarily patient family, not least Katrina, who has endured more nonsense about goblins than can possibly be healthy, and Sandy, who mostly just slept through the whole thing.